Praise for the *Brown Sugar* series

A *Los Angeles Times* Bestseller
Winner of the 2001 Gold Pen Award
for Best Short Story Collection

"Audaciously refreshing. . . . From Taylor's insightful and provocative
introduction to *Sugar's* last sentence, each story not only pushes
the envelope but also shatters taboos of African-American
love and sexuality."
Essence

"Particularly intelligent, varied and sexy. . . . A stylish anthology.
Many pieces weave serious questions of racial and sexual identity
into their racy scenarios."
Publishers Weekly

"*Brown Sugar* portrays sex as it is rather than how others
envision it to be."
The Boston Globe

"A sleekly edited collection. . . . It sets a noble standard
for collections that follow."
Black Issues Book Review (**starred review**)

Brown Sugar 4

Secret Desires

A Collection of Erotic Black Fiction

Edited by Carol Taylor

WASHINGTON SQUARE PRESS

New York   London   Toronto   Sydney

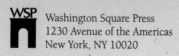
Washington Square Press
1230 Avenue of the Americas
New York, NY 10020

Library of Congress Cataloging-in-Publication Data
Brown sugar 4 : secret desires : a collection of erotic Black fiction / edited by Carol Taylor.— 1st Washington Square Press trade pbk. ed.
   p. cm.
  ISBN 0-7434-6687-X (trade paper)
    1. Erotic stories, American. 2. American fiction—African American authors. 3. African Americans—Fiction. I. Title: Brown sugar four. II. Taylor, Carol.

PS648.E7B764 2005
813'.01083538'08996073—dc22   2004059559

First Washington Square Press trade paperback edition February 2005

10 9 8 7 6 5 4 3 2 1

Manufactured in the United States of America

For information regarding special discounts for bulk purchases, please contact Simon & Schuster Special Sales at 1-800-456-6798 or business@simonandschuster.com.

Brown Sugar 4 is dedicated to
lovers and lovers of fiction everywhere.

CONTENTS

ACKNOWLEDGMENTS

As always, many thanks to my agent, Tanya McKinnon, for her smarts, savvy, and good-humored guidance, and to my editor, Malaika Adero. Thanks to my family for making me who I am. Without you I am nothing. Thanks to everyone who's been there through thick and thin, and to Peter for keeping me going. Thanks to Steven and Lisa for sharing Fire Island with me. It's been a wonderful place to write. Much gratitude to all the cool writers who hooked me up with other cool writers. My deepest thanks to the writers who have so diligently and fearlessly created the original stories in *Brown Sugar 4*; you are on the cutting edge.

"Let's get it on."
—Marvin Gaye

INTRODUCTION

The Blacker the Berry, the Sweeter the Juice

I'd been in Amsterdam for two months and had decided I'd never leave. I'd fallen in love with the narrow rows of sharply dressed houses pressed up tightly against each other. I loved the strange combination of orderliness and casualness that pervaded the city, and the glittering canals and the cheery houseboats bobbing on the water, lit from within like fireflies in a jar. I even loved the screeching seagulls flying in packs over the canals, playing tag and bodysurfing on the sparkling water.

In the early morning with the mists shrouding the canals that ring the city it is easy to see why Amsterdam is known as the "Venice of the north." Although the streets change their name every block, the city is compact and easy to get around by foot, bike, tram, and even boat. Buildings are rarely higher than four stories, so there's always plenty of light and sky.

I'd fallen in love with a society that allowed for freedom of choice, late-night culture, and the right to simply be, no matter your race or background. I was in love with the Dutch people, who seemed to enjoy life the most and feel the least guilty about its pleasures. Actually, I'd fallen in love with one Dutch in particular.

I'd just finished breakfast and was sitting with my morning paper in Dimitri's Cafe on Prinsenstraat, when I saw the most beautiful man at the window. He was tall and thin, as many Dutch are, with a long face and narrow sloping nose. Stop there and he'd be just one of the many beautiful people I'd seen all over Amsterdam into Rotterdam and in parts of Belgium.

It was the potent mix of African and Dutch blood running through his veins that composed his features into an odd and wonderfully poetic juxtaposition. He had skin the color of rich cream with a sprinkling of nutmeg freckles across his nose. His eyes were the most astounding shade of blue I'd ever seen. His long nose was offset by full, thick lips and above his prominent forehead sat the biggest, most gloriously kinky, dirty-blond Afro I'd ever seen.

He was beautiful, like rain after a drought, the sun after a storm. He was a gift dropped at my feet and he was looking at me as though I was too.

I'd surprised myself. I wasn't usually attracted to mixed-race blacks, or I never let myself be. It was an unspoken oath, I guess, to not sell out my own deep blackness, which had been held against me for so long. So I signed on to the don't-mix-it-up-and-lighten-the-race program. It had been easy enough until now. Most light-skinned brothers weren't normally interested in me. They usually went for black girls my sister's complexion.

Of my three siblings I was the dark spot in every family photo. My sister's high yellow was at the opposite end of the color spectrum. We all had the same "Chinky" eyes but my sister got most of the Chinese in my Jamaican family. I got most of the

African. My two brothers fell somewhere between us. I was closest to my father in color, though two shades darker than he, and my sister was closest to my mother, who could have (and some say should have) passed for white.

Every time relatives put us side by side, fingered our hair, complimenting my sister on her wavy fall and café con leche skin, then turned to shake their heads at my nappy bush and espresso complexion, I put another brick in the foundation. Soon enough, I'd built a wall of ambivalence at best and hatred at worst for light-skinned blacks. They just seemed to have it easier: better hair, better job, lighter skin, lighter load. So it was always the darkest brothers for me. Why not? The darker the berry, the sweeter the juice, right? And I had no problems finding them since I was beautiful and they usually didn't have much luck with the light-skinned sisters.

So I was surprised when I felt an instant attraction to him. He was everything I was not, and everything I'd grown up wanting to be. Every secret desire I'd nurtured as a child and then discarded when I grew older of wanting to be popular, pretty, and light like the cream in my father's coffee and not the rich brew my mother drank black. He was every dream I left on my pillow, every wish on a starry night. Everything I wanted to be for as far back as I could remember was standing in front of me, smiling.

When I smiled back he walked in and sat down at my table. First he spoke to me in French, then German. When I told him I was from New York he switched to English. His name was Malcolm. He was Dutch, Belgian, and West African. He'd moved to Amsterdam three years ago from his hometown of Eindhoven in southwest Holland and was trying to make a living as a painter. His first words to me were "I love the color of your skin. It reminds me of the water in the canals at midnight. May I paint you? You are the most beautiful woman I've ever seen."

* * *

I'd come to Amsterdam to model. I'd had no luck in New York, where my "natural" look and "strong" features, which I knew meant my close-cropped hair, dark skin, and big lips, had fallen out of favor. I was in Amsterdam because of an apparent appreciation of dark-skinned black women in the Netherlands. They loved my looks here. This was a big change from New York.

Tar baby, coal black, darkie, the names had been endless and endlessly hurtful. That they'd come from friends and family had made it even more painful. "Keep out the sun now, you black enough as is" had started every summer as far back as I could remember. Though I'd grown up to be beautiful enough to make a living as a model, at castings the darkness of my skin always put me at a disadvantage. "Your color is too harsh for this season." "We don't have work for dark girls like you." "You're so beautiful. It's a shame you're so dark." The casting agent would then shake her head, close my book, and dismiss me.

Amsterdam was teaching me a thing or two about beauty. I was learning how to love myself without feeling I was too much this or not enough that. Here, as I walk along the canals, or cycle through the fields of windmills just outside the city center with the Dutch men smiling after me, I am learning how to love myself, how to feel beautiful and desirable.

*   *   *

So here I was at Odeon, the grooviest bar in Central Amsterdam, curled up on a comfy couch with D'Angelo's lyrics flowing out of the speakers, "*Brown Sugar Babe, I gets high off your love and don't know how to behave . . .*" and my fingers entwined with Malcolm's.

We'd drawn a crowd of stares on the dance floor, where we'd danced till we were drenched in sweat and funky. We'd pressed up tight against each other, bumping and grinding our way into the early morning. The humidity had frizzed my hair into a halo of kinky curls, my lipstick was smudged, the rest of my makeup was gone, my white T-shirt was transparent from sweat, and I didn't care. Laughing, Malcolm wrapped his big arms around me and fit my hips into his, matching his tempo to mine.

This was not a man I'd ever thought I would be attracted to, could not have anything in common with, but we connected in every sense. We had many of the same interests—we liked the same music and loved dance, art, and books. We'd even talked about our color, the prejudices we'd encountered because of it. I'd thought things were bad for me in New York, but some of Malcolm's stories of growing up an only child of mixed race in a small, all-white industrial town on the outskirts of Holland made me rethink my Brooklyn childhood. He certainly hadn't grown up privileged because of his color, nor did he feel that way. His father was often away on trips to Africa. His mother, though she loved him dearly, simply didn't know how to celebrate his blackness, or even understand the West African dialect his father had taught him. He told me of how he'd yearned to move to New York, where people looked like him and he could feel a kinship with other blacks, where he wouldn't stand out so much because of his looks or always feel as if he didn't belong.

As he spoke I tried to grasp what it would feel like to not understand your blackness. Not to feel a part of a community of people, to understand the language, the gestures, the unspoken things that connect us without us even knowing. And for once I felt as though I belonged, no matter my color. I felt like part of a culture, and a people.

*   *   *

When we stumble out the door the cold air makes me shiver as we walk to our bicycles locked up along the canal on the Prinsengracht. It's early enough for a faint rosy light to start to brighten the eastern sky.

Standing in his bedroom, the shower steaming up the bathroom, I watch Malcolm undress. He has broad shoulders and a strong back, and his oversized shirt had been hiding thick arms and a strong ass. His skin is so light I can see the intricate pathways of bluish green veins beneath it. His nipples, which are the color of melted caramel, are the darkest things on his body. He is lighter than any man I've ever been with.

He drops his shirt to the floor and steps out of his jeans. Naked, his legs are slim and sweetly bowed. His chest is wide, and curly blond hairs, barely discernible against his bronzed skin, taper down to his stomach. Malcolm watches me watch him. He smiles as he comes toward me, then whispers, "Your turn."

He pulls my T-shirt over my head. He grips my arms, pressing me into his chest. His hands move up to my hair. Tangling his fingers in my kinky curls, he pulls my head back and exposes my throat, kissing a moist, hot trail from my chin down to my neck. He bites me there, then his tongue explores my throat. He moves down to my collarbone and kisses his way to the center of my chest, breathes in my scent, then exhales deeply. I can feel his smile against my skin. He turns me around and pulls my skirt to my ankles, then slips my panties down to join it.

I hear him pull up a chair and sit behind me. I feel his hands on my hips tracing the geography of my flesh. Caressing the curve of my ass, he grips my hips in his palms and kneads them. He turns me slowly around and breathes a sigh into the dark hairs nearly invisible against my skin. He rests his head there. His hair prickles my flesh, caresses my breasts. He looks up at me and smiles. He loves my skin, he tells me. He loves my color. He holds his arm against mine, marveling at our differences. I am a queen, a cause for celebration, he tells me over and over again. He pulls me onto his lap and whispers in my ear that he loves me.

Why do I love Amsterdam? Because I am beautiful here. Why do I love Malcolm? Because he made me love myself.

Secret Desires

Ahhh, secret desires. We all have them, whether we admit it to ourselves or not. *Brown Sugar 4* focuses on secret desires because it is a bond that unites us. It doesn't matter who you are, where you live, or what you do. We've all secretly desired something, or often, some*one*. Our secret desires, those yearnings we hold closest to ourselves, are what most illuminates us, who we really are or who we really want to be.

The Disturbing Pull of Desire

We've all felt the disturbing pull of desire. It may have been brought on by a first glance, an unexpected encounter, the sensual curve of a shoulder, the look in someone's eyes or the smile they gave you, a lover's scent on your fingers or taste on your tongue. Desire is that magnetic pull of one body inexplicably, inextricably, to another. It is the need for something unexplainable, but unmistakable. Desire cannot be explained, because memory, attraction, our senses and needs—a subtle connection we could never imagine—shape it.

Secret desires are those things we deny ourselves, perhaps because we think it's not something we should do because it's wrong, because it's bad, or because it might just feel too good. Maybe you desire something outside of the everyday and you think it's wrong because it's not the norm. Or perhaps it's some*one* we don't think we should be with because of their background or lifestyle. Perhaps society has told us that person is wrong for us, or our parents made the decision for us years earlier. Maybe we abstain because we believe that once we go there we may never find our way back. Don't worry, you're not alone. We've all grappled for control over our needs; we've all buried something so deep down that we realize it's there only when we're facing it head-on.

The stories in *Brown Sugar 4* celebrate many different secret desires. Here you'll find stories of yearning with passionate and often surprising results. Whether you secretly desire the preacher's wife, your children's nanny, your best friend, your ex, your brother's wife, or your sister's husband, you'll find something to relate to, to give insight, or simply to turn you on.

These erotic encounters are told by bestselling authors, award-winning literary writers, and performance poets whom you already know and love, writing outside of their genre but in their own particular style about characters you'll recognize in places you'll know. What their stories give you are different glimpses into the many different worlds that make up black America, and truly represents what makes us tick sexually and emotionally.

Variations on a Theme

We know why we're here, what we're looking for. We read erotica for inspiration, sometimes to lose ourselves, though we often find parts of ourselves within the story. That is why, though I am straight, I can be stimulated by homoeroticism. Though I don't crave S&M sex, I can be turned on by it in well-written literature. Of course we all have our secret desires. How could we not? They are what make us who we are. They are why we are with the people we are with or not with the people we thought we'd be with forever. And sometimes it is why we are with people we never ever dreamt we'd end up with.

In the same way that every book I've read has changed me, every lover I've been with has taught me something—whether I wanted them to or not. I've learned something not only about them but about myself as well. These experiences have been invaluable. I'm old enough now to know and appreciate that. We should be inspired by the endless possibilities available to us, all the variations on a theme. But we limit ourselves to what we think we should or should not like.

Time Again to Come Correct

In *Brown Sugar 4* you will find secret desires portrayed in every color, shape, and form. Perhaps you yearn for someone like the enticingly young and beautiful Brazilian au pair in Trey Ellis's "Old Story," whose presence wreaks havoc on a couple's already rocky marriage. If you crave the feel of a warm, hard gun against your naked body, then go straight to Greg Tate's "A Ballistic Affair," a surreal and sexy story that crackles with energy and defies definition.

If it's your teacher you desire, the one you wanted in school but whose eyes you could barely meet, you'll be able to relate to Jervey Tervalon's "Always Running," a darkly sexy tale of love and loss. The unflinchingly told "Freda" is Edwidge Danticat's fable of social class and love that shows us how one can sometimes keep you from the other. If you're pulled to someone you never thought you'd be with, someone so different from you that it makes you question yourself, then read Angie Cruz's poignant and passionate "Until We Meet Again." You may never look at the Verizon man the same way again. If wanting the preacher's wife is giving you reason to repent, turn to "The Little Barton

Job," Mike Phillips's sensually unnerving story set in the English countryside about two people who are transported to a secret place outside of race and class. Sandra Jackson-Opoku's deft and wickedly funny "Iguana Stew" will make you smile and will touch you in places you'll wish it hadn't.

If you secretly desire someone you're already with, but in a way they would never guess, read "Where He's Getting It Now," Gar Anthony Haywood's tragic tale of death and desire, wherein a woman's husband proves to be more than he'd seemed but not what she'd suspected. Perhaps you burn with memories of a childhood tryst, a sexual exchange that left you reeling, changed forever. If so, read Lisa Teasley's transcendental "Voiceover," involving a character caught between the past and present, between the woman she is and the woman she wants to be. If you like it rough and ready, then read "Luzette." Darrell Dawsey's raunchy, hot, and riveting story will send you back to the beginning when you've turned the last page. Brandon Massey's "Ghostwriter" is a sly, otherworldly tale of seduction and writer's block that brings new meaning to the word "ghostwriter." If an office mate is driving you crazy with desire, go straight to "Blackout," Tyehimba Jess's raw and poetic tale of a lusty encounter between coworkers whose passions ignite during the blackout of 2003. It'll make you wish you'd been there.

If you're keeping it in the family then turn to asha bandele's "My Brother's Wife," the heartfelt story of a woman's yearning for her best friend, who later becomes her brother's wife. If your sister's husband is about to get you into trouble then read "The Day

After You," Preston L. Allen's climactic final story in his novella published in the *Brown Sugar* series. The end of Pam, Nadine, and Johnny's family drama about the obsession that comes with lost love perfectly illustrates what happens when family ties no longer bind. If it's your wife's friend you've been dreaming about, start with Kenji Jasper's "Little Get-Togethers," a cautionary tale of unfulfilled potential, desire, and regret. It might change your life.

If you're like me and it's your best friend, the one you promised yourself you'd never fall for but of course did, read jessica Care moore's "A New Tale of Two Cities" for insight. Her lyrical story of friendship and desire is a classic tale but with an urban twist. If you're caught between two men whom you desire equally, turn to "A Letter in April," Kalisha Buckhanon's beautifully depicted and quietly sexy story of a young woman who must choose between the love of her past and the man in her future. Reginald Harris's "Easy" is anything but. His surprisingly seductive tale of lust and fidelity, choices and regrets, will leave you with more questions than answers.

Powerful stories all, and you'll find them more familiar than not as they explore love, sex, and sexuality in a wide range of stimulating styles. These voices are diverse—wicked and wise, hot and cool, hard and soft—yet they converge and coalesce, are distinct and original. The writers in *Brown Sugar* are all part of the new black literary diaspora, and although divergent, they are bound by their common African heritage. Parts of the same whole, they represent the past, present, and future of black literature.

Editing and contributing to the *Brown Sugar* books has been a wildly fulfilling and exciting ride, and all those puns are intended. I think you'll agree that with *Brown Sugar 4*, the series goes out with a bang.

So come with me one last time, 'cause it's time again to come correct.

Brown Sugar 4

KALISHA BUCKHANON

A Letter in April

*I*t's April, that time of the year when winter and spring—the boldest and the shyest seasons—clash, fuse, then make love to each other coolly, like an old couple. Schoolteachers must now offer new incentives for children's attention because shelter from the cold no longer qualifies. The churches' expatriates will beg forgiveness around Easter, and for a little while, houses of worship will be full again. Everything depends on April. In the small town where we're from, where we grew up together, where we first met, April is testing time. I may call the big city my home but I'm a country girl at heart. Right now, the question weighs heavy on everybody's tongue but nobody will ask it out loud: *Will there be enough rain?* For the grass to rise, the gardens to bloom, the river to swell just so, the fields to succeed into profit, a certain number of inches must fall.

Of all the elements, people believe rain has the most spirit and utility; it operates as a cause rather than an effect. So people sit around on April nights and wait for it, talk it up, pray on it, pretend to squeeze it from their sweat and tears when heaven refuses to break. Everyone has a different relationship with the rain, which, unlike the wind or heat, can be tasted. Some be-

1

moan it when it finally comes, cry about it when their basements flood, curse it when it catches them unprepared; others collect it when the faucets rust, swallow it when the well seems too far, dance in it when God becomes too remote. They do not have to watch the news in order to know it's coming; they can predict it by smelling the air, assessing the stiffness of their knees, or observing which creatures emerge and which burrow. Then, depending on their mood and their need, they will celebrate or sigh. Either way, they will respect it.

But I am going off on tangents to avoid talking about the real reason I am writing you. Maybe the rain is why I couldn't say good-bye the way I am saying it now; there is something about a rainfall that seems to prohibit dishonesty. It was raining this morning when I left you, remember? Last night, you didn't even ask me if I had a lover in New York—the city of sin that had stolen me away from you and that stifling small town five years ago. The Emerald City of dreams where I arrived with a thousand dollars, just two contacts, and the crazy fantasy of becoming an actress.

Then again, why would you have reason to ask if I had a lover other than you, my first and, in your naïve ignorance, my only? I made love to you last night like a virgin, not calm with experience but excited into clumsiness, too frantic to keep the rhythm, my energy rising until steady pace became a thing of the past. I somehow missed your lips each time I kissed you, sloppy, like a virgin kissing for the first time. At one point you shuddered and mumbled Jesus, then cried God, your unbearable grip on my ass signaled your coming. We finished spent into loneliness—drowning slowly in hot sweat that clung to us like steam rising, our breaths hard and heavy as if we were breathing not just for ourselves but for all of mankind. We stared into the same lonely, dark blackness but we each claimed it solely as our own. Then we bathed.

You have never been a romantic man, so there were no bath bubbles. Only water hot as we could stand it cloaked our skin and melted us into each other. My sepia and your Cherokee red turned our water the muddy color of Kansas dirt. You rested your forehead on my kneecap, right against a scar still present from a fifth-grade fall out of the great oak that guarded my grandparents' yard. You knew the story of the scar because you knew the story of me: insecure and awkward junior-high days, a sudden blossom into popularity toward the end of high school, sheer determination in the form of three jobs to pay for theater school, the relentless drive that made me one day, out of the blue, pack a bag and announce to the world that I was moving to New York City to become an actress.

It has taken some time, but become an actress I did. Now, when I come back to our small Wisconsin town to see you and my mama, everybody calls me the "actress." I'm the one who made it out, the only brown skin to have keys to our city of 35,000 plus a dead-end street bearing her name. The little black girl who proved to all the rest of them that it was possible for our dreams to come true sometimes.

I soaped your back with the bar you bought especially for me—Dove fragrance free, for sensitive skin. You remembered. When my performance schedule started to become so much that

I could not visit as often anymore, I remember you told me you had nothing else to offer to get me here but your love. *I'll at least buy the soap she likes,* you must have thought. We were facing each other in the bath, so I had to lean in close to reach around your broad shoulders. Your embrace was smothering, and I moved my hands around and around your back until I was clutching you. My face was buried in your chest, and the water made the hair on your body feel like a baby's. You pulled my legs out from in front of me and wrapped them around your torso. You pulled me closer and I could feel your hardness rising out of water like an island. You wanted me again.

What the hell am I doing here? I thought as I looked around the tiny bathroom suffering inside the dilapidated house that you and your boys called home. Patches of paint peeled and hung from the ceiling like spirits trapped between worlds. The toilet had come loose from the floor, the medicine cabinet mirror was still cracked from the time you struck out at your reflection in frustration. I told you that dying house wasn't worth your father's $25,000-dollar life insurance policy, that the money to fix it up and pay it off would be too much for you. But grief has a way of making us blind. And you were young with a dream. We both were. But I believed in the possibility of the art gallery you wanted to create, though I wondered back then who in our small town had the money to buy art.

Over the years, you've imagined those three stories of warped flooring, ancient plumbing, peeling paint, and sad rooms to be a restaurant, a bed and breakfast, a juke joint, a gentleman's lounge, a recording studio, a ladies' fine clothing boutique. You never imagined it would be the last place we would make love, but it will be. Now, it has been declared condemned and the bank will soon foreclose on it because you haven't met the payments. This house full of dreamers and their dreams must be vacated by the end of the month—knockoff designer clothes hastily thrown into garbage bags, records packed into milk crates, Tupac, Biggie and Malcolm posters torn from these dingy walls, empty bottles of cheap champagne recycled. The last time I was here you told me you didn't even recall what you'd celebrated.

While I watched a spider building a web above our bodies making love in the bath, I thought of my small treasure in Manhattan—a renovated condominium loft I bought when I landed my first well-paying role. It's decorated with original artwork from some of America's hippest black painters and sits on the top story of a high-rise nestled on the Lower East Side. I just renovated, or *modernized,* as we say, my kitchen. I asked you when I first bought it to share this home with me. I told you, *Baby, if you're really serious about being a painter this is the place to be.* But you said it was small for two people. I knew then you were just too scared to leave the familiar behind and venture into the unknown.

The yellow lightbulb hanging from the ceiling began to swing as the wind picked up outside and flew in through the broken window. Chill pimpled my arms and you warmed me like firewood.

"I think I should move to New York with you," you whispered to my crotch and not my eyes as you tilted me up toward you, hands pressed into the small of my back to hold me up, your thumbs meeting around the tiny waist you always loved. You'd said this before, but this time I knew you might mean it; you would have nowhere else to go soon. The lips on your face met the lips between my legs, and water spilled over the side of the tub to join the water sliding down the floor from the leaky sink. The old refrigerator outside the bathroom door hummed momentarily, then became quiet. There was only the soft, steady splashing of water knowing and jealous as if it was standing outside lovemaking's door. I rocked with you as I was supposed to, in a rhythm familiar and stale, but this time it seemed brand-new because it was the last time— Did I tell you it was the last time?

"We'll see," I sighed, knowing that it was no longer possible. I thought of another's head buried between my legs, a head much smaller than yours because it is bald and you have dreads. I locked my legs around your neck to let you know I was coming even though I wasn't. Then, for the first time in the eight years after our simultaneously lost virginity, you quietly slipped a finger inside my anus. I cried out, since I was supposed to be both shocked and thrilled, and you smiled up at me with the pride of a lover who has introduced new tricks. But no, it had already been done to me; in a reefer-hazed ecstasy that had my hips spinning around and around so fast that I made myself and my lover dizzy. I'd reciprocated what he'd done with his finger by using my tongue. I thought of that moment, alone with him in a one-room, closet-sized Bronx studio when that was all I could afford, and then I came for real with you.

"Let me sit here awhile," I sighed as I leaned back and you rose from the water with a satisfied smile. I was breathless, and I felt tears gathering in my stomach, ready to collect as a lump in my throat and then push themselves out of my eyes. I didn't want you to see me crying because I didn't want to ask you to ask me what was wrong. I am an actress, but I can't lie to you. It hit me that I still loved you—a realization so stark and clear and finite that I couldn't stop thinking about your head bowed low as you soaked with me in the tub and I poured water over your dreads. *I still love this man,* I whispered, *despite* . . . But I could not finish the sentence. Despite the fact that he's here and I'm there? Despite the fact he has not lived up to my expectations? Despite the fact he probably hasn't lived up to his own expectations? But isn't the only love that matters the love that is given *despite*? I was scared and confused. I sucked in the cry that tried to escape me because I didn't want you to hear. I cried silently into my hands for as long as I could, then I coughed to disguise it.

"You want me to make you some tea for your throat?" I heard you say over Marvin Gaye.

"No," I shot back quickly. "I'm coming out."

I joined you in the bedroom. I was grateful to see a jasmine-scented candle lit because then you would not detect my red eyes. I burrowed into your body under the down comforter I had given you when I moved away. The small candlelight flickered and made the mural you'd painted on your walls come alive. Your bedroom was the only room you'd finished before you gave up on yourself. There was a black boy taller than possibility dunking a basketball over a sea of white faces, a man who looked like your father carrying tools, a portrait of you as a young man, a voluptuous woman busting out of a red dress and beckoning onlookers to come; I noticed she didn't look like me. It started to rain just as we began to slip into slumber.

It was still raining this morning as I prepared to catch my car service 150 miles to the nearest airport. We'd lain there for a while listening to raindrops, waiting for signs that the other was awake. I could tell you wanted to make love to me again before I left, like you always did. Your hand cupped my naked breast and you grew hard against my buttocks. Had I not known it would be the last time, I would have given you what you wanted. I would have turned toward you with my eyes crusted and my mouth still sour from sleep, and you would have received me just as I was.

I might have climbed atop you and let you enter me seemingly instantly, so fully that I would have been unable to remember the lifetime before you were inside of me. I would have gyrated atop you like our lives depended on it, like our fucking gave an energy to the world that only we could provide. I would have moaned and shrieked like no else was in the house, like the possibility that someone was in the kitchen next to your bedroom did not even exist. We would have caused the wooden slats that held the mattresses in the bed frame to slip out of place. Then the bed would slant and we'd tumble onto the hardwood floor, against the door where one of your housemates was masturbating to the rhythm of our bodies.

But this morning, I simply disentangled myself from you when the alarm sounded and gathered my bags that had pretty much stayed packed. I had thought it before, but never really meant it: *This is the last time we will see each other.* This morning, as I thought of my stifled cries the night before, I knew the guilt of dishonesty would kill me before you did once you found out my acting has not been limited to the stage. You once told me, after your father died and you burned several of your paintings in frustration, that I was the only good thing in your life. That was a lie, but it wasn't your fault.

"Do you want me to ride to the airport with you?" you asked through your sleepiness.

"How will you get back?" I wondered.

"I don't know. Greyhound, if you buy the ticket. I could pay you back when I get paid next week."

"That's okay," I said, and I pushed your dreads back to kiss your forehead for the last time. I mentioned it was the last time, didn't I? "You can sleep. I'll call you when I arrive."

My car was waiting for me outside. I told myself not to look back, because if I looked back I would forget everything I had worked for and die with you, in your arms, in that raggedy old house that could have been the most beautiful art gallery the world had ever seen. But as my Lincoln Town Car rounded the corner, my neck jerked around as if I had been slapped. I caught a quick glimpse of the house that wasn't even yours anymore. It was fringed with weeds and surrounded by a bald lawn. I saw your face staring out a window on the top floor.

I didn't call you when I arrived. Later that evening after about eight hours of traveling, when I opened the door to my New York apartment, my lover, a fellow actor, was waiting to carry my bags into the bedroom. He had the shower already running. He stripped me and brought me into the shower with him. He stood behind me and soaped me using the same brand I had soaped your back with. He forced my neck back so he could bite me salaciously and leave his mark behind. My love for you became a distant memory as my knees buckled under with passion for him. He grabbed the inside of my thigh and hoisted it onto the bathtub's ledge on his way to the soft space I had just given to you. He stuffed his fingers into my mouth so I could taste myself before he did.

He entered me from behind as I steadied myself against the slippery tiles. He grabbed at my breasts like they were flowers that needed to be pulled up from dirt. I screamed his name so I would forget yours. We stumbled out of the bathtub and somehow made it to the threaded rug in the center of my loft, and I took him in with the eagerness and energy with which I used to take you. Salsa music from the corner bar floated around us and kept our violent passion from arousing concern among neighbors.

There was a chill in the room when we finished, and I thought I smelled you. I thought I saw your face, right before my lover picked me up from the floor and carried me into bed. But I couldn't sleep. I harmonized my breathing with his while we spooned, because he can sleep only once he thinks I am dreaming. I gently pulled myself out from under him and began writing this letter in that journal I keep near the bed. You know the one with a single magnolia on the front, the one you sent me because you said the curves of the petals reminded you of my body? My lover has stirred once to ask me what I was writing.

"Just my lines for tomorrow's rehearsal," I told him. "I write them over and over again until I memorize them."

"Oh," he said. Then before he nodded and turned back around, "I really missed you, baby."

"I missed you too," I tell him, taking in the scent he has stirred with his movement. I've told the truth, but only partially. How can I tell him I'm not brave? How can he know, after the ferocity with which we've just made love, that I am really a coward? How can I tell him that I am writing my first love a letter to say good-bye because I was not woman enough to tell him to his face, while we bathed together during an April shower? When rain was the shedding of tears for both love and dreams lost.

The Day After You

*I*t is four A.M.

It's me, the darkness, the glowing green numbers on the clock, and Cassiopeia purring. She comes to me, and I pet the soft fur on the back of her head and neck as she climbs into my lap.

I've finally stopped crying for yesterday. For the dream that passed me by. The long-legged, sweet-faced dream. The dream that held my face and promised love. The phone rings. I see his number on the caller ID, but I know that it's Nadine.

"Hey, girl."

"Hey."

"Johnny's sleeping."

"Hmmm."

"I put him to sleep. I put it on him. I put it on him good. I put it on my man."

Cassiopeia purrs in my lap. I say to Nadine, "So what y'all gonna do?"

"Put this behind us." She sighs. "This shit is so whack. I musta been crazy. I musta been under some kinda spell."

I'm silent. Too much to say.

"You see what I got at home? You see my man? And I'ma leave him for Christopher?"

"Ol' waterhead Christopher." I smile.

"What was I thinking?"

"I don't know, Nadine."

"Ol' waterhead . . ." Her voice trails off. Then she says, "You think he ugly? You don't think he cute, just a little bit?"

"Not like Johnny."

"No." She is whispering. Her muffled voice tells me that she has cupped her hand over the phone and her mouth. I imagine them in bed together. I know that he is right up on her, the way he sleeps. He's a hugger. He likes to drape himself over his love. Big as he is, you'd think he'd be heavy. He's not. He likes to hold with his great big hands. To rub and soothe his love to sleep. He likes to suckle. He likes to have his lips on his lover's flesh as he falls asleep.

Nadine is a selfish sleeper. She sleeps like a ball, her arms in tight and her knees tucked up to her flat, boyish chest. When we were kids, I'd sneak into her bed and cling to her back until she'd push me off and tuck herself back into her selfish little ball.

She says, "But don't you think he has some good qualities?"

"Compared to Johnny? He's all right, I guess. He's got a nice complexion. That's about it."

"But he's sweet."

"Johnny's sweeter."

"Christopher's smart."

"He got big ears. He walks funny, and he talks like a white boy. Come on, Nadine. You musta been crazy."

"You really surprise me," she says. "I thought I was the shallow one."

"I'm not being shallow. All I'm saying is you already got a fine man at home."

"Johnny *is* fine." I can hear the smile in her voice. "And that sweet dick."

"I don't know about all that," I lie. "You keep your dick talk to yourself, you hear? That's between you and your man."

She's quiet. Is it something in the way I said it? The way she went after that white girl with the knife that time and all she did was look at Johnny. Nadine's a little bit paranoid, and she has a real fucked-up temper. I start to worry just a little.

She finally says, "It's crazy the way these men get to you. Crazy. I almost lost him, Pam. You think there's someone else?"

I'm the last person she needs to be asking this. I should hold back. I can't. "How could there not be someone else, Nadine? Johnny's a prize."

Another pause. Cassiopeia stretches as I rub her.

"Whachu mean by that?"

Nadine is like a switch, flipping on and off.

"Whachu mean?" Hissing loud through the phone. Forgetting she's trying not to wake him. Forgetting to keep her voice down so he can get his sleep after all he's been through. "Do you know who it is? Do you know who he's fucking?"

* * *

Oh, Johnny, I remember how easily you lifted me, chubby as I am, and carried me to bed. Your body, the perfect V—the broad shoulders and narrow waist. The sexy swells of your chest. The long, sleek lines and smooth bulges that define your legs and thighs. You are chiseled, firm, strong. Juicy. You called me juicy, but you're the juicy one.

I was jealous of Nadine for getting to you first, telling you the baby was yours when it wasn't, marrying you, and then dogging you. Throwing you away. For Christopher? She's the pretty one, so I guess she thinks she can just do whatever she likes to people and get away with it. Me? Some men say I'm even prettier than her, but I don't know about that. We have the same cinnamon complexion. She has the cute face. And that tight body. But don't let it fool you. She's all street. Before you, she dated nothing but thugs. And women. She's not the good one, Johnny.

I am.

My face, it looks a lot like hers, especially in the photos of us as children. Our hair in Afro-Sheen ponytails, our cheeks thick with bubble gum. We have the same high forehead, the same soft crescents around the mouth when we smile. But where her face is delicately angular, mine is roundish, with big eyes and lips. A cuter nose. I am taller than she is. I could stand to lose about twenty pounds, but men don't seem to be bothered by it because I have a good heart and I don't play mind games on people. You didn't seem to be bothered by it. Yesterday.

When I locked my legs around your waist.

Fuck me, I moaned. Fuck me. I sensed it. You were having doubts.

You leaned over me and smiled. I touched my hand to your face. I rubbed my pussy against your leg. Fuck me. Stay. It can work between us. I held your face in my hands. Your beautiful eyes looked down at me and made a promise.

You moved your dick around inside me. I was filled. You were fucking me. I sucked on your tongue. I remember spearmint. Unsweetened iced tea. I fucked you back. You pushed and pushed inside me, as the pillows and sheets bunched up around us. You pushed. Soon, we were hanging off the edge of the bed. You pushed me hard. Don't stop, oh shit, that's my spot, oh shit, harder, harder. I was licking your lips, your mouth, with my tongue. I was over the edge of the bed with nothing but your strength to keep me from falling. I threw my arms around your neck and hung on. My flesh was twitching, ready to give. I let go. I was coming. Coming. Over the edge. With nothing but your love to keep me from falling.

Promise me. Stay.

I licked your cheeks and tasted my perfume on your baby-smooth skin. Your cute nose, your eyelashes. I was licking your tightly closed eyes. I felt myself going over the edge of the bed, but you caught me. Your hands gripped my ass. So hard. Your mouth to my ear. Moaning love. What were you really trying to say? Gripping my cheeks so hard, pulling them slightly apart. It felt good. It got me to thinking dirty thoughts. Got me to think-ing about when you'd asked me to do anal and I'd said no. I was scared of that. You were soooo big, I couldn't imagine. You said my ass was so pretty, so thick. You couldn't stop thinking about it. But I had said no, and sent you away embarrassed for asking. Now, with your mouth moaning against my ear, your dick hit-ting my spot just right, and that finger teasing the crack on the sly with each thrust, I was asking why not? I've had your tongue there. Why not your dick? Do it to me any way you want.

I am yours.

I was hanging down off the bed almost to the floor. You opened your sparkling gray eyes. You smiled your smile. You kept right on fucking me, rocking the springs. Harder. I ground my hips into you. We were noisy as hell, with me screaming and you groaning and our flesh slapping loud like someone getting a beating. I was coming. My pussy slurped with each thrust. It was embarrassing good. We were so loud. Our love calls bouncing off the walls of my apartment. What will the neighbors think—! I was coming. I was screaming. I let it all go. Then I slipped out of your hands. I slid down, with you still on top. My head hit the floor.

You grabbed me quick around the waist. Suddenly your pretty face changed. You pushed your dick into me so hard and deep I gasped. Your shoulders hunched and your hips began their jerky moves. The strength of your orgasm rocked your body, rocked me down to the carpeted floor. You gushed into me. You did not rest. You flipped my legs off the bed and climbed the rest of the way down there with me.

I kissed your lips. I remember spearmint. The taste of sweat. Skin. Your smile. You rolled on top and started fucking me again. Oh, Johnny, you fucked me until you were dry and couldn't fuck anymore. Then you put me in the tub and washed me from head to toe with scented soap. You towel-dried my body and combed my hair. You heated up the soup and fed me. You took me back to bed. You told me you loved me as you strummed a soft lullaby on the guitar. Then you put me to sleep with your arms and legs draped around me, your face against my neck.

But that was yesterday, when you were mine.

*   *   *

I tell Nadine, "I'm just saying. Lots of women would want Johnny. You wanted him when you first met him at fifteen."

"And I got him—"

"Because you lied to him, Nadine, and you cheated on him."

"Stop judging me, Pam. You have since we were kids."

Nadine's not whispering anymore. I'm sure Johnny's awake now, trying to figure out what's going on. What's going on is, she cheated on him. She hurt him. Such a good, beautiful man. I've loved him for as long as I can remember.

"I'm not judging you."

"Yes you are. I told you stuff."

"That's not it."

"Pam, I'm human. Sometimes I fuck up. Johnny can't always give me what I want, what I need. I gotta go somewhere else sometimes. It don't mean I don't love him. I'll always love Johnny, but I'm gonna get what I need. I'll just have to be more careful in the future. Christopher did things to me Johnny never would. Things I needed him to do. But you wouldn't know about needs, would you, Pam? Not Pam the little church girl."

"Stop it, Nadine!" I'm not whispering anymore either. I hate it when she calls me that. Cassiopeia is twisting out of my hands. "What I'm saying is you didn't have to be the way you were. You could've been a good girl."

"I can't believe you're still talking that childish bullshit, Pam. I *am* a good girl."

There is silence.

"Nadine?"

"Oh, I see. It's like that." Flip on. Flip off.

"Nadine . . ."

"You church girl. Oh, I know you now. You're glad he found out. You're glad I got caught. You want him to leave me. But why?"

How can I answer her?

"You know the bad stuff about me, but you know the good stuff, too. You know, Pam. You know." She's blubbering. She's crying now. Nadine never cries. "I'm good. I'm very, very, very good," she says, almost hysterical. Then she bursts out laughing.

I laugh, too, like I always do when she gets like this. She scares me sometimes. It makes it real hard for me to love her.

She does not deserve him.

My neck is stiff from holding the phone. I'm tired. The machinery of the clock is whirring. Nothing is changing in this dark room. Not even the clock.

It's still four A.M.

"Nadine, what time is it?"

"Time?" After a pause, she comes back and says, "Six."

"Oh shit. My clock is broken. I'ma be late for work!"

Cassiopeia leaps out of my arms.

"You still going to work?" Nadine says.

"I gotta earn a living, you know?" I'm jumping out of bed, slipping my feet in my slippers, padding to the closet for my uniform and shoes. The phone in the crook of my neck.

"Uhm, Pam, what about . . . ? You think you should still go in after all what happened?"

"I still gotta earn a living, Nadine. The world don't revolve just around you."

Before I hang up, I hear Johnny in the background.

Even his voice is beautiful.

Good morning, my love. Good morning.

I grab my uniform from the hanger.

*   *   *

The day after you, I pull into the parking lot of Big House Eatery and Drinks.

By the time I clock in and get to my station, it is 6:55. I'm 55 minutes late. It's Saturday morning, and the place is packed. A bunch of truckers mostly, a few hospital workers, and other people who work the night shift. There are also a few younger people, who look like partiers coming down from their Friday night high.

Leroy's in the back with his sleeves rolled up, his head uncovered—a violation—and his stereo blasting Snoop Dogg, which is another violation because Christopher hates hip-hop and doesn't want it played in his restaurant. But Leroy is the best breakfast cook we got, so he gets chewed out once in a while, but never fired. This morning he's got the place smelling like bacon, eggs, and grease, and his spatulas are singing against the hot grill louder and badder than Snoop Dogg's bass.

Maria and Chanté have their hands full. They've got orders stuck in their waists and pencils in their mouths. They nod hello as they brush past. Chanté gives me the eye: Girl, we need to talk. I give it back to her: I know. Then I jump right into it.

"One Big House Special wid coffee, black, and a orange juice."

"Toast or bun?"

"Bun."

"How you like your eggs?"

"Scrambled. Well done, but not all dried out like y'all done last week." He's a rose-colored brother with a wide mouth and a round belly.

I stick my pencil behind my ear and flash my eyes in surprise. "I apologize for that, but you must not have come to me. I take good care of my customers."

Rose-colored, truck-driving boy says, "I'm sure you do, pretty lady."

"Well, thank you for that, sir. I'm gonna make sure and take good care of you this morning," I say, smiling and patting my 'fro.

"I'm sure you can, pretty lady. I wish you would take carea me. You sure is pretty, you know? I love them pretty eyes of yours." The words whistle through the fat cheeks and two missing teeth. But he is cute in his own way, and he always tips good.

"You're sweet. Lemme go get this started for you."

"Hurry back, pretty lady. Ha-ha."

I'm walking away, rolling my hips. "I will," I say. "I will. Ha-ha." Rollin' my hips for the tips.

By ten o'clock, when the breakfast rush has died down and the lunch crowd hasn't started to pour in, my feet are killing me. I drop a few quarters in the charity pot by the register, grab a pack of Juicy Fruit, and head out back where Chanté is sitting on the bench with her shoes off and her feet propped up, smoking. She's a long-legged girl with ebony skin, a pretty face, and a gravelly voice like Weezy Jefferson. Underneath the helmet of lustrous, intricately twisted cornrows is a brain that earns straight A's at the community college, where Chanté is enrolled in the nursing program. She hopes to make a better life for herself and her cutey-pie toddler, Sammy Jr. Sammy Senior took off years ago.

I plop down next to her and push off my shoes, stretch out my toes. Her cigarette smoke is tempting, but I'm seriously trying to quit, so I pull out a stick of my Juicy Fruit and slip it between my lips, start to chew.

Chanté puts an arm around me. "Girl, you need to give me the scoop. What went down with your crazy peeps yesterday? Hmmm. I got here for night shift, and there was cops and ambulances all over the place. Whuzzup with Johnny? Why he went off on Christopher like that?"

"I can't speak on it, girl," I say, chewing hard on my gum.

Her words tumble around the cigarette between her lips. "I heard Johnny went right up and swung on him and Christopher fell back and knocked over the register. Quarters and receipts was flying everywhere. Cops came and took Johnny away." Chanté leans in close. "It got something to do with Nadine, right? I seen the way Nadine and Christopher been sniffing around each other."

"I can't speak on it, girl. You know I would tell you if I could."

"Then it must be good." She slides her pocketbook off her shoulder and pops it open. "Did I show you the pictures I took of your li'l boyfriend in his new suit?" She pulls out an envelope from the Sears Photo Studio and presses it against her chest.

I laugh and reach for them. "Lemme see, lemme see," I plead, playfully. I can't pry her fingers open.

"Then tell me whuzzup with your peeps."

"Chanté, I really can't do that," I say. "Now show me the damned pictures, girl. You know you want to."

Laughing, she passes me the pictures. I flip them out onto my lap. Sammy Jr. does look sweet in the suit I bought him for his birthday. Chanté is chiding, "You know you doing me wrong. You know you is. I know it's something to do with Nadine and Christopher. Tell me I'm wrong. Or maybe it's something to do with . . . you?"

"Me?"

The door swings open. We both turn. Leroy's coming out, wiping his hands in his apron. He's beefy and brown-skinned with braids and a gold, gap-toothed smile. He's not smiling now. He points a beefy finger at Chanté.

"You need to get back inside and earn your dollar. Break is ovah."

Chanté gets up, taking a last drag on her cigarette before flicking it away. I get up, too, straightening my apron dress, following her inside. Leroy holds up a hand.

"Not you, Pam. I need to talk to you."

I shrug and hand Chanté Sammy's pictures. She takes them, giving me the eye again. Girls got to stick together. Leroy's a notorious flirt and fast with his hands. Sometimes he goes too far.

When Chanté disappears inside, Leroy lets out a long sigh. "I don't like doing this, Pam, I hope you understand. It ain't me. I'm just following orders." He looks down at his feet. "The thing is, you can't work here no more."

"What?" He must be kidding. Leroy is the biggest joker. Even when he's playing Mr. Big Time Assistant Manager. I put my hands on my hips. "Leroy, you're kidding, right?"

He mumbles, "Christopher said he don't want none-a y'all working here no more. I'm sorry. You're fired."

"Fired?"

He looks up at me sheepishly. "That's what he told me, Pam. You, Johnny, Nadine, he wants alla y'all gone. I'm just telling you what he told me."

"This is crazy." I have rent to pay. A cat to feed. I hide my face in my hands. I get choked up. "I didn't do anything. It's not my fault." I'm crying.

Leroy mumbles, "You can collect your tips from this morning, but then you gotta go. Pam, I'm really sorry about this. You know I think you're a fine girl, right? If it was upta me, this wouldn't be happening, you know that, right?"

I'm not answering. I'm not looking up. I'm crying. I'm thinking about you.

You cost me my job.

And you didn't stay.

The day after you, I leave the restaurant at 10:30 with my spare uniform and shoes in a paper bag. I'm walking fast. The restaurant's real quiet. The girls, the cooks, the kitchen, the cash register, even the customers seem quiet. Everybody's looking at me. I'm walking fast, but it's all in slow motion.

When I get outside, it starts to rain. By the time I reach my car, it's a downpour. I dump the paper bag full of my stuff in the backseat, then wrap my arms around myself and just sit there. The wipers are squeaking against the glass and the radio's murmuring on low. My eyes are burning with tears. I'm crying, and it's hard to see through the rain.

But there is a truck pulling in. My heart leaps.

Johnny's truck—

I jump out of my car, run through the streaking rain to the truck, pull open the door. It's you. You've come back to me.

*   *   *

I'm staring at Johnny with the tears pouring out of my eyes and none of it mattering because the rain is coming down. He is so beautiful with his big, sculpted body, his gray eyes, his curly hair, his heart-shaped lips. He's kinda biting his lip. His eyes seem sad.

I begin, "Johnny—"

He lifts a hand from the wheel and gestures. "Get in outta the rain, girl."

I get in. I'm soaked. He's shaking his curly head, and biting that bottom lip. He's wearing a white dress-shirt, opened at the collar, and the jeans I washed and ironed for him two days ago. His eyes are showing the strain. I reach for him. My hand is on his face at the side of his mouth against his cheek. He is freshly shaved. When he breathes, there is warmth as well as softness in my palm.

"Johnny—"

"No," he says, moving away from my touch. "We need to talk. I'm a married man. I love Nadine. You were like a sister to me."

But he's not looking at me. He's looking out the window at the rain. I don't know what the hell he's talking about. He's talking to the rain. Maybe the rain is talking back.

"—easier for both of us if we just end it and go on with our lives."

I lay my wet head against his big chest. He is warm and dry. He smells like soap, cologne, and Nadine. I slide my hand inside his shirt and rest it against his washboard tight stomach. He sighs in mid sentence, but he needs to shut up and love me. I am going to open the buttons on his shirt and kiss his nipples to shut him up.

"—I don't blame you. We were both caught up, is all it was. Can you believe what we did? I'm a man, and all, but she's your sister. She's your family."

The buttons are open. His broad, hairy chest. His flat stomach. The nipples swell before I even kiss them. I kiss them twice. Then I trace his chest with my lips back to the left one, the sensitive one, and take it in my mouth. He stretches back in the seat. Sighing. I bite his swollen nipple till I taste the blood. I am tearing off his shirt. His hand is on the back of my neck. He's groaning his pleasure. Mumbling something.

"We can't do this."

"She cheated on you."

He stiffens. His hand on my head grabs me by the hair and pulls me off. Then shoves me back roughly into my seat. I can't believe—. I am horny as hell, I am soaked with rain, I am brushed off by this man buttoning up his shirt. I glance down at his lap. His dick is not even hard.

"Pam, that was none of your business," he says, slowly and carefully, like trying to explain something to a slow child, "I'm serious about this. What goes down between man and wife is nobody's business. I shouldn't have gotten you involved. Me and Nadine got our problems, but that's between us. Hopping into bed with her sister is not the answer. I know better than that. I am better than that. You are, too. What I'm trying to tell you is this was a mistake. I love my wife. I really do."

I can scarcely breathe.

"You don't love me."

"No."

I'm trying not to, but I'm crying again. "You never loved me."

"No. No, I never loved you." Serious face. No hesitation.

I'm shivering in my apron dress, which smells like coffee grounds, oatmeal, and cigarette smoke. My butt is wet and cold against the leather seat. I plead, "Johnny . . ."

"I don't care a thing about you, Pam."

The rain is coming down in sheets outside. It is loud like a hurricane. I'm crying, and he's not putting his arm around me. He's not touching me. He's just sitting there in his ripped shirt, his arms crossed, letting me cry. I put my hand on the door handle, but I can't make myself open the door. I have nowhere to go. I feel like dirt. I feel like a big, fat blob, with my big, fat legs and my ugly Afro. I want to curl up into a ball. I want to go to sleep and never wake up. It is dark like night, and it just keeps raining.

Johnny's saying something to me. "That's the way it has to be."

I don't care a thing about you, Pam.

Yeah? You think so?

I whisper something back to him, my lips scarcely moving. I watch as it registers in his head what I'm saying. He begins to chew his bottom lip again.

In case he thought he heard me wrong the first time, I say the thing again, lower and sexier this time. I watch his face change. Mr. I Love Nadine. Mr. I Don't Care a Thing About You, Pam.

He's too ashamed to speak it. He says it by shifting eyes. He says it with the fat bulge pushing up in his pants at the mere mention of it.

I'm not playing this time. I'm serious about it this time. I'm already pulling up my dress. Johnny's got his fist against his mouth, trying hard not to look. I'm sliding my panties down my ankles. The panties are on the floor now and I am kneeling in the seat with my face against the glass and my juicy ass ready for him to do with as he pleases.

You like my ass so much you can have it, Johnny. But you have to do it right here. Right now.

For a second, there is silence. Just me with my face against the glass. Then I hear the jangle of his belt buckle. The *ziiippp* of his zipper. I feel a big, soft hand on each cheek. I rest my face against the cold glass. I feel the vibrations of a million droplets. I feel his tongue in there as he prepares me, prepares himself. He briefly touches the clit, but that is not where his true heart lies. He kneels up in the seat behind me, his cheek against mine. His lips to my ear. I groan as he enters me. It is thick. It is long. It's like inserting a watermelon. I want to scream. But I'm serious about it this time. He's holding me tight around the waist and kissing my ear. He's saying something over and over.

"Relax."

I relax. I relax. And gradually accept. I am widening. He is pumping slowly. I am widening like a mouth. He is sliding into me easier now. I feel him in me. He is in me. Pumping. I find his rhythm. His hand finds my clit. My face is warm and cold. My face is warm against his mouth and cold against the glass. We are pumping in rhythm and the pleasure is coming from a surprising place. My pussy is leaking.

His mouth is on my mouth, and his hand has moved from my clit to my Afro. We break our kiss and he grabs my hair. He is pulling my head back. He is fucking my ass like a pussy. Steadily. We are rocking in the seat. My face is knocking against the glass. The pleasure is like a low hum. He is stroking so steady, so hard, my tits have been shaken out of the bra. He is pounding me and loving it. I'm giving it back to him. I love it, too. It's so good. We can't stop pumping. We can't.

Where did the rain go? What are those people in the restaurant looking at?

"Johnny! Stop!"

I try to struggle out from under him. But he is holding me by the hair. Hitting it hard. They are looking at the truck. How dark is the tint? What can they see? They see it rocking. They see my face against the glass. Johnny can't stop. He's so turned on. He's swelling in me.

"Johnny!"

He grunts and slams into me hard. He slams again and I feel him pull out. I feel him squirting the rest of it between my cheeks. He lets go of my hair and collapses on top of me. I duck my head down below the glass. I stay there for many minutes with my heart pumping hard.

When I dare lift my head to the window again, everything seems back to normal. Customers are eating. Chanté and Maria are bustling back and forth. Outside, there is so much water on the ground, but the sun is spreading its golden glow over the morning again. Johnny is lying atop me, breathing contentedly, playing with my hair. Every now and then, he kisses my cheek. I nudge him off, and begin to put myself back together. He watches as I tug my underwear up my legs. I say to him, "Anytime you want this . . ."

"You don't have to say that," he says, buckling his belt.

"I mean it. Anytime." I am patting my 'fro back into place. "I mean, you liked it, didn't you? I liked it."

I look at him.

He does not answer, but his silence tells me what the answer is, and I am glad. This is where it begins. It will grow from here. We both know this. We are both hungry.

We will feed each other.

I check myself in the mirror one more time, then open the door, and tiptoe out into the parking lot that has become a lake. I am parked close to the restaurant, and I can see the faces clearly as I pull open my door. The smiles. I can see Chanté's face. I can read her eyes.

Girl, we need to talk.

EDWIDGE DANTICAT

Freda

Haiti, circa 1980

Michel's girlfriend was missing. Crowding his stepmother's living room were the guests who'd been chosen to welcome him. Not her, but him; his grandfather had made this clear.

"We'll see how we like her before we welcome her," the grandfather had said, as soon as Michel had announced their impending visit over the phone from New York.

"What kind of girl is she?" His stepmother had asked on the other extension.

"Just a girl," he'd said.

"What family?" his stepmother Lily, his dead father's fourth wife, persisted, perhaps hoping he'd rattle off the cognomen of one of the many inbred, filthy rich, and socially connected clans that left the island only for lavish vacations or a few years of school abroad. But instead Michel had whispered, "The human family," causing Lily to confess that she was worried he was bringing home a poor black foreigner.

"She's Haitian," he had consoled her.

"Oh God," she'd gasped. "A poor black foreigner who's also Haitian."

From the lowest step of the shiny wooden staircase, Michel scanned the candlelit living room for familiar faces. (For once the candles were a choice and not due to a power outage.) There were his grandfather's old army friends who looked for every opportunity to wear their dark brocade uniforms and stand, stiff-backed, with a drink or cigar in hand carrying on the same conversation they've been having for the last half century. These were the only kind of people whose company his grandfather seemed to enjoy, old men who cashed "zombie" checks every week for several phantom jobs, but felt they had infinite compassion for the poor because they paid their maids and yardmen a few cents above the deplorable pittance doled out by everyone else in their circle. Before he left to attend New York's Columbia University four years ago, Michel had spent endless afternoons and evenings with these men, soaking in—at his grandfather's insistence—their nonstop classist verbiage.

Things had been different when his father, Philippe, was alive. (His own mother had died of cervical cancer when he was one and he had no memory of her.) Even though his dad was also an army man, he took time to read and attend lectures at the Alliance Française or the foreign embassies. Because his father's favorite scholars were not favored by the government he served, he sneaked their books to his only son, building Michel a secret safe in the floor of his bedroom to hide them. It was his father who'd urged him to read beyond his own borders—Che, Marx, Baldwin, Ginsberg—who'd encouraged him to apply to Columbia and study Economics so he could return and help his country. But since his father's car accident, which he suspected wasn't an accident at all, the country had changed a great deal. When Michel arrived at the airport these days, there was always a crowd of cripples and beggars to greet him. This had startled Freda, who'd landed with him, but had left the airport with her aunt and uncle for her own part of the city, promising to meet him later at his house.

Michel had called Freda's aunt's house an hour ago and she'd told him that Freda had already left. He was ashamed of himself for not having gone with Freda to her aunt and uncle's house and could tell from her aunt's abrupt answer that she was offended he hadn't paid them a proper visit or extended a formal invitation to the party.

Michel had been away from Haiti for so long that he was beginning to lose his sense of what his father had called "native courtesy." *Wherever you are, son,* his father liked to say, *you should learn what the native courtesy is and practice it. In some cases it can save your life.*

In some other cases, it can bring you love, he wanted to add to the dialogue he was always carrying on in his head with his dead father, for that's how he'd met Freda, being natively courteous. She was working in a café a few blocks from Columbia. Noticing her accent when she approached him to take his order, he'd begun speaking to her in Creole, which had immediately won her over. That night, he took her out for a student budget dinner of grilled conch and rice and beans at a Haitian restaurant in Harlem. Later, exceeding all his expectations, she'd returned with him to his tiny room in the dorms, had slowly peeled off her blue jeans, tank top, and modest cotton underwear, then slipped under the covers next to him. He could touch her as much as he wanted, she'd told him right up front, but he couldn't enter her.

"What are you, a gate?" he had joked. But he had taken advantage of what then seemed like an extremely generous offer, running his fingers slowly over her cinnamon-toned face and long smooth neck, then massaging endless circles around her wide sable nipples with his tongue. He had cradled her back with his hands and rubbed his face against her stomach until he felt like his skin would burn, but when he lowered his warm cheeks to her thighs, she pressed them tightly together to keep him out, obviously not realizing how much pleasure the strain of her caution was giving him.

But where was she now? Could she be lost? In the endless traffic that snaked through the narrow streets that led all the way from downtown to his house? Had she been robbed? Kidnapped? Was she dead in a gutter? Had she taken the excruciatingly slow public transportation, which practically stopped at every hill and street corner?

He wished he had been able to convince her to rent a cell phone at the airport as he had. This was the only way he was able to reach his grandfather's chauffeur, long after the time he was supposed to be picked up.

*　*　*

Freda's absence was beginning to be noticed—not by his grandfather's friends, who didn't give a damn about him and had just shown up to avoid the old man's easily fired wrath, but by the other guests. Those would be his stepmother's proxy friends, the old ladies, who discreetly sipped glasses of sherry pretending it was some kind of arthritis remedy. Or Lily's peers: fleshy former beauties who still wore their hair in 1950s bouffants, used a glut of white powder on their faces, and streaked too much rouge across their cheeks. And the group that Michel found most bearable, the children of the pale-faced women and their stiff-backed generals, the Cuban, Mexican, or U.S.–educated sons who preferred jeans and a guayabera to a business suit, and the daughters who substituted designer tank tops and dark slacks for evening gowns.

A soft hand was pressing down on his shoulder now, momentarily easing some of his worries. It was his stepmother, his beautiful stepmother. A woman who wore pale make-up and applied excess war paint to her blanched cheeks, but did not really belong to her own tribe. For Lily, a chameleon, was able to blend in, and even become, whatever was around her, without surrendering herself completely. It was the way she'd survived her marriage to Michel's father, an older, eternally sad, once-widowed and twice-divorced intellectual/soldier, who in the name of his government had performed more atrocious acts than anyone in the family was willing to even consider, much less admit. Since Phillipe's death, Lily had kept herself sane by throwing parties and devoting herself fully to Michel and his grandfather.

"They've become my whole life," he often heard her say to her friends who ask how she's endured the years since Phillipe's death. "I focus on them."

His stepmother, his beautiful stepmother, was now sitting on the step next to him, her short red skirt hiked up, way up to her thighs. She was thin and tall and absolutely stunning and every man in the room, married and unmarried alike, desired her. But she wanted nothing to do with any of them. Hadn't even accepted another man's dinner invitation since his father was killed.

"I don't know which one of our friends killed your father," she'd confided to Michel during one of her rare somber moments, when he'd once asked why she wasn't, at least, dating. "I don't want a King David situation, where I'm fucking the man who had my husband murdered."

But these days in our country, death and sex can't be totally divorced, he'd wanted to tell her. Hadn't she already fucked his father, who himself had knocked off a few people? Besides, isn't our raunchiest spirit, Gede, also the same spirit who guards the dead? How had she escaped the twined essence of sex and death all these years since his father's demise?

Deep in his heart, he knew the answer to that. Like Freda, his stepmother was strong, could resist, decline, desist, abstain for a hundred years if she had to. But when that day would come, when she let herself go, she'd have the carnal appetite to kill ten men.

"Where is your girl, darling?" she asked gently, aware that she might bruise him, hurt his feelings.

"I don't know where she is," he said, lowering his head to block out the rest of the room. Somehow he wished he could be alone with Lily, lay his head on her lap and feel her long red fingernails in his hair as he allowed himself to consider the full meaning of Freda's absence. If intentional, Freda's not showing up could mean only one thing, that she had left him. She'd taken the first steps with him, had accepted his invitation home without ever having had him "enter" her, but she couldn't take it any further.

"Darling, why didn't you pick her up or send the chauffeur for her?" Lily asked, lowering her face to meet his gaze.

He didn't know why he hadn't done these things, except that he'd believed Freda when she had told him she'd get herself to his house without assistance. She might have been insulted if he'd insisted on picking her up. He could hear her raising her low, rasping voice ever so slightly to ask him, "Do I have to turn my back on my family to fit into yours?"

"Some of the guests are leaving," Lily said. "I need to make a speech soon." Then gently patting his back, she added, "I'll make a welcome home speech in your honor. I'll tell them how much I love you, your father's only boy. I'll tell them how proud I am that you graduated from Columbia with honors and will return in the fall to start your Ph.D. I'll keep it hidden in my heart how sad I am to have not been able to meet the beautiful girl in your life."

"Thank you, Lily," he said, kissing both her cheeks, which in the dim light appeared illuminated by several bands of ocher rouge and bronze eye shadow.

Even though he'd already heard most of Lily's speech, Michel was moved when she stood at the top of the stairs in front of a room full of her friends and delivered it. After Lily spoke, his grandfather also offered a brief remark.

"We love this boy more than we can tell you," he said, quickly raising his glass, then pulling it down again. Public speaking was not the old man's forte, which made his gesture that much more meaningful to Michel.

Finally it was Michel's turn to speak. He followed his grandfather's example and kept it brief.

"Ever since Papa died," he said, wrapping one arm around Lily's tiny waist and the other around his grandfather's medal-padded shoulder. "I swore to myself that I'd honor him by getting my education and returning here to put it to use. I've only just begun."

But during all the speeches, even his, which in retrospect he thought a bit clichéd, all he could think of was whether or not he would ever see Freda again.

*   *   *

That night, after everyone had gone to bed, Michel kept calling Freda's aunt and uncle's house, but got no answer. No matter how late it was, he would have gone out into the city to look for her, except he had no idea where her aunt and uncle lived, beyond the general fact that their house was somewhere downtown. And "Not too close to you rich folks," as Freda had said.

He was amazed now that he'd asked so few questions about her plans for her time in Haiti. He figured she'd spend a day or two with her aunt and uncle, but most of their vacation with him. Perhaps he'd been too excited about their trip to think all the details through. But could his neglect also mean that she wasn't as crucial to him here as she was in New York, where she was the only person to whom he could speak of his desires and losses in French and Creole? Even during nights when he'd managed to please her by caressing and massaging every bare inch of her body, he never tired of telling her in Creole, the first of their native languages, what he would like to do to her, if only she'd allowed him past the sealed sanctuary of her thighs.

As he lay on his back under a mosquito net, dialing Freda's aunt's number over and over, his bedroom felt unbearingly hot. He raised the mosquito net above him and reattached it to the headboard, but it didn't help. So he got up, opened the louvered terrace door overlooking Lily's rose garden, and allowed the cool night breeze to soothe his naked body. Looking up at the sky, he took in the glow of a small group of stars, something he was never able to see in New York.

Shouldn't you be running all over the capital looking for Freda? a guilty voice hissed from deep in the back of his mind. *Isn't that what you would be doing, instead of standing here calmly looking up at the sky, if you truly loved her?*

Wasn't dialing her aunt and uncle's number every five minutes the same thing? Besides, he thought, people—good and bad alike—had always flocked to *him*. Before Freda, he'd never had to chase anyone or anything. He hoped Freda was all right, that she hadn't been hurt in any way. But if Freda had simply left him, well, screw her. (The little voice in his head hissed *That's right, she won't let you.*) So, lying on the same plush mahogany bed he'd slept in as a boy, he kept a firm hand on what he often jokingly told Freda was "thy rod and thy staff," and nearly kneading himself raw, he imagined Freda begging his forgiveness for having so abruptly and inelegantly deserted him.

*   *   *

At some point during the night, when a cool breeze had raised and lowered the thin white curtain over the louvered door enough times and a few mosquitoes had dug into his skin and fed themselves, Michel realized that he needed to close the terrace door. The inertia of self-pleasure and his longing for Freda made him feel too drained to rise.

He still couldn't sleep. It was too late now to call Freda's aunt and uncle's house. There was no electricity with which to play music, and for illumination he had only the distant moon and stars. So he closed his eyes once more and lay there, feeling the curtain rise and fall like the tips of careful toes landing on a creaky floor.

He wouldn't be able to recall in the morning exactly when he started feeling another presence in the room: a body, breath, the warmth of perfumed skin, the weight of another individual forcing the mattress to slowly cave in next to him. He heard the rattle of chains, not big ones, but very small ones, like two or three necklaces scraping against each other with each turn of a neck. Then there was the tangy smell of basil and caraway mingling with the taste of strawberry-soaked lips, parting his mouth and blanketing his tongue. No matter how much he tried to force them apart, his eyes would not open, the rest of his body also too rigid to budge. He could feel the hurried strokes of long fingernails traveling from his neck and chest, lingering only for a moment at his nipples, to his belly button and finally his crotch. With a firm grasp, the hand smoothed his abundant pubic hair, then quickly forced his thighs apart, greeting a massive erection that had not left him since the first moments he began—as he liked to think of it—flogging his lizard; shaking the dew off his lily.

"Good-bye, Michel." A soft, weary-sounding voice rose out of the motionless darkness.

Before he could process what had been said, the woman, for he was sure now that it was a woman, pinned him down on the bed by pushing her bare chest against his and fluttering her small, round breasts a few inches above his nipples. Her knees were bent, he could feel them rubbing against his outer thigh, and with each slight motion of her body, he imagined a warm triangle drawing him nearer and nearer to the warmth, then heat, then tightness of what she referred to both in French and in Creole as her true home, her *vagin,* her *bòbòt.*

He'd had many dreams like this since he was a teenager. A woman, as elegant as she was curvaceous, with hair that fell in two black curtains down to her breasts, would come to him at night and sit on the edge of his bed. Pale elsewhere yet bronzed in the face, she wore a blue dress, the hem of which she would use to wipe her incessant tears. He would want so much to console her, but he never could, for he would be frozen in his bed, unable to talk, move, or even cry out for help. This dream woman sometimes took the shape of whatever woman he desired but couldn't have at the time. In the beginning it was the maid, then it was a girl he'd developed a crush on in high school. At some point it was even Lily. This time, it was Freda.

In the morning, upon waking, he searched his bed for signs that Freda might have actually been there: stray hairs, discarded undergarments. He sniffed his sheets and pillows for perfumes and body fluids, surveyed his floor for lost earrings or hairpins. But he found nothing, except the gray edge of a newspaper, peeking under his bedroom door. He opened the door, picking up the paper. Greeting him was word that the previous afternoon, a girl and a driver had been killed in a crash, in a taxi heading uphill from downtown.

DARRELL DAWSEY

Luzette

 S he was a sexy Latina, with a mane of dark hair, eyes flashing like embers, 100-watt smile, body by Stairmaster. Afro-Cuban, I guessed. She was the new assistant in my eye doctor's office, a welcome relief from the overweight assistant and the pimple-faced receptionist who usually greeted me. From the moment I walked through the door, I noticed her, all short and compact and fine, her lab coat fighting a losing battle to conceal her voluptuous frame. I tossed her a friendly nod, gave that gorgeous body a quick once-over, and began moving slowly around the office. I was feeling her, but I wasn't going to sweat her.

Turned out, I wouldn't have to.

Her eyes never left me. Everywhere I walked in that office—from the front door to the glass display case—her stare was in hot pursuit. Occasionally, I'd shoot her a glance, just to let her know a brother knew what was up, then look away. I didn't want her feeling too self-conscious. The way I figured it, she'd probably seen me in a movie but was too shy to say anything. I get that a lot: Women'll recognize me, but pretend not to because they don't want anyone to know they watch "that kind of stuff." Instead, they usually just stare. Flattered, I held back a smile and turned my attention to a pair of Gucci frames resting in the Plexiglas display case. Then I settled down in a chair, filled out some paperwork, and waited for them to call me to the counter for my checkup. The whole time, I could feel her smoky eyes burning through my clothes.

At one point during my wait, she walked over, touched my arm, and asked if everything was okay. I grinned and nodded, then watched her as she turned her attention to adding new frames to the display case. In the second her eyes had met mine, I knew that my initial hunch was right. The sense of familiarity was palpable. She recognized me. Cool as she was, for a brief moment, she had registered "the look."

Everyone in my line of work gets "the look" if they stay in it long enough. "The look" is a mixed bag of countenances, one expression folded over others. It's one part recognition, that wide-eyed sense that "Hey, I know you from somewhere." It's also one part realization, when the person figures out exactly *where* they know your face from. (The raised eyebrows tend to give this away.) Then, of course, there are the responses, the knowing laughs or the red-faced titters, the uncomfortable body shifts or the sweaty palms.

As much as I've seen the look, I still never know quite know how to respond to it. Do I smile? Do I wave? Do I turn away?

Maybe one day I'll just walk up, extend my hand, and say, "Hi, I'm a porn actor, perhaps you've seen my work?" After 10 years and 1,100 flicks, I'm not shy about what I do and I'm damn sure not ashamed. I am wary, though. I hate having to sidestep the steaming piles of assumptions people tend to toss in my way. I mean, if it isn't the voyeuristic husbands offering you $2,000 to lick butter off their wives' calves, it's the morality police accusing you of stealing their teenagers' virtue. People are entitled to their opinions about who I am and what I do, but I prefer not to indulge them. I love the advantages my work presents—the parties, the cash, the sex. But for every perk, there's also a disadvantage.

Whatever the case, though, my carping didn't apply to this woman. In her, I saw nothing but sheer carnal curiosity. There were no lewd jokes or autograph requests, no morality speeches or judgmental sneers. Just a "fuck you" stare that triggered chills along my spine. I wasn't about to come on to her too strong. Sure, she may have seen me before, but she may also not really have given a shit. I certainly didn't. I was more preoccupied with figuring out how I'd ask for her phone number when my checkup was done.

The fat assistant called me for my exam. I got up, handed her some paperwork, and followed the dark-haired beauty to the back of the office. She ushered me into an examination room and gestured toward a plush swivel chair. "My name's Luzette," she said as I settled into the seat. She smiled, shook my hand, then began fussing with the eye-exam machines.

She then turned to me and started tossing out the standard pre-exam questions: how was my sight, when was the last time I'd had my eyes checked, blah, blah, blah. Even as I answered, I could see her eyes narrowing, intensifying. Luzette fidgeted in her chair. Her tongue swept quickly across glossed lips. She leaned closer, penlight in hand. Her neck smelled of perfume, her breath like mint. My dick stiffened instantly.

The exam proceeded routinely enough, with me chatting and Luzette guiding me through a battery of tests. She told me a little about herself, when she'd started at the eye doctor's office, what she was hoping to do when she finally left there. Not once did she let on that she might've seen me before. She was cordial, sweet even, but as the exam proceeded, she became more professional. The intensity that I'd felt from her earlier now seemed to have waned. Maybe Luzette wasn't feeling me after all. Maybe I'd just mistaken curiosity for lust. "I'll be right back," she said as she stepped out of the room.

I slumped in my seat, waiting for her to come back and send me home. I began to wonder if I'd been wrong about her, about that look she'd given me. Maybe she was just being nice, just keeping a customer happy. I'd already given up on seducing Luzette when I heard her heels clicking on the hallway floor outside the exam room.

When she walked back into the room, Luzette's expression had changed yet again. The fire had returned to her eyes. Her tongue was now working its way slowly across her top lip. The stare that had threatened to singe me when I had first strolled into the office was back. And this time, it was more intense than ever.

I smiled and stared back. My heartbeat picked up. My dick, which had softened, stirred again.

"So you weren't going to tell me, were you?" Luzette said, closing and locking the door behind her. "You just thought you were going to get out of here without me saying something, huh? I know who you are."

I shrugged. "What was I supposed to say?" I asked. "I don't just go around announcing that I fuck for a living. Not to say that I haven't been seriously considering that option lately."

Luzette chuckled and sat in the chair next to me. She studied my face for a second and then reached out and touched my beard. "Maybe not that, but you could've said something, you know. 'Cause when I saw you, I kept asking myself if you were the guy in all those movies that my boyfriend has. I've seen you I don't know how many times."

I laughed softly and caressed her hand, which was still on my face. I moved down her arm and began rubbing her shoulder. I felt her stiffen. But she didn't withdraw.

"Truthfully, I don't even like most of the men I see in those movies," she continued, her voice a smoky whisper, her strong hands running over my head now. "Most porn is made with guys in mind, not women. It gets so bad I sometimes find myself getting off on the women right along with my boyfriend."

"How so?" I asked.

She laughed again. "I mean, how can the guys who make those movies envision their ideal as some perky blonde with big tits or some chocolate model with a heart-shaped ass and then think we women are secretly pining away for some crystal meth addict wearing nothing but two tattoos, a Budweiser belly, and his black dress socks? What the hell is that all about?"

She leaned in closer, her minty breath wafting under my nose. Her hand had made its way from my head down my shoulder and over to my bicep. "But it seems things are getting a little better for us." She squeezed my arm admiringly. It took all my willpower to resist the childish urge to flex and tell her my gym schedule, but I kept quiet as she continued. "I've been watching you for about three, four years now, and you haven't disappointed me yet. All I can say is, 'bravo.' Looks like somebody finally got the memo."

My dick was rapidly turning to Quikrete. Her caresses were mostly to blame. But I was also turned on by her frankness, her aggressiveness. She wasn't intimidated or deterred by what I do. She wasn't even unduly curious. She just seemed appreciative, like what I did actually mattered in her life. I smiled, struggling to conceal my pleasure.

I wasn't doing anything, though, to hide my arousal. I casually leaned back, so she could get a better view of the bulge in my pants. But her eyes never left mine.

"So do you always fuck like you do in those movies? Just going on and on like that? Or is that just what you do when you're at work?"

"Nah. To tell you the truth, I'm *never* off the clock. Ever."

She pursed her lips and nodded slowly. I was making progress. I reminded myself to move slowly, to just get the number. After that, I was certain I'd see her again.

"So what makes you ask?" I continued. "Your boyfriend doesn't give it to you like you like it or something? Is that why you're all up in his porn stash?"

I was surprised when she shook her head. "No, come on, that's too easy," she said. "I wouldn't be bothered if he couldn't satisfy me. It's not that he's a bad fuck or anything. But we've been together for six years now, and I think we're—I don't know—comfortable with each other, I guess. It's good sex, but routine. We switch it up occasionally to keep things interesting. Watch a few movies. Try to learn new things. But he's familiar to me. I know him, how he feels, what he's thinking, what he wants to try. Sometimes I wonder what it must be like to just get fucked by someone I hardly know, by someone I know will do what I want how I want." She smiled. "I guess that's why I'm into porn. They represent an ideal scenario for me—no strings, no complications, just lots of fun and know-how. It's like getting tips from . . . I dunno . . . the pros, I guess." As she finished these last two words, her gaze finally fell to my crotch.

By now, I wasn't saying much of anything. There are times when a man doesn't need words, when only his body should be speaking for him. This was one of those times. I looked at Luzette, licked my lips, then pulled her closer to me. Phone number be damned. I wanted that pussy. Right then. Right there.

I stood up from my chair and pulled her up with me, wrapping her in my arms. I leaned over and whispered in her ear.

"So what about the other people out in the office?" I asked. "Aren't they going to need this room for something? I don't want you to get into trouble."

She shook her head. "The other assistant is out to lunch, and the receptionist never comes back here. Besides, there's another exam room. We've got this one to ourselves . . . unless you're scared of getting caught."

I hesitated for a second, unsure about her take on the circumstances. Of course, I didn't care if people saw me. I looked at her and figured, *Fuck it.* With that, I slid my tongue into her mouth. Her own embrace tightened around my waist. She ground her pelvis against my dick. We kissed, rubbing each other and grinding our hips together. I moved my hands over her ass, squeezing gently and pulling her hard against me as I nibbled her neck.

I felt her right hand slide from around my waist and down my stomach. Her fingers worked furiously to unfasten my belt and then the button on my blue jeans. I could feel her nails brushing past my pubic hair as she slipped her hand down my underwear. She pulled my dick through the opening of my boxers and rubbed the head against her crotch.

"Mmmmmm," Luzette moaned. Then she stepped back, squeezed my dick, and arched her eyebrows inquisitively. I looked back at her impassively and nodded. She moved toward me once more, kissing my neck, my chest, my stomach.

She then slid down into a crouch and looked up at me, her hand still working over my dick, her eyes pleading. I stroked her hair with one hand, put the other hand on my hip, then leaned back and closed my eyes, as she took my dick in her warm mouth.

She worked the dick like a pro as she deep-throated me. Every now and then she'd look up to tell me how good I tasted to her. Each time she did, I'd just grab the back of her head and shove her mouth back onto my dick. Each time, she jumped back on it without delay.

She must've sucked me for about 10 minutes before I slid out of her mouth. I took her hand and pulled her to her feet. Then I started to unbutton her lab coat.

"Don't worry about the coat," she said. "Take off my pants and fuck me."

I shook my head. I wasn't about to rush through this pussy. I was going to fuck Luzette right. "I want to see your titties," I demanded. "I want to suck them until your nipples get really hard. And then I wanna fuck your tits."

I felt her chest heave. Then she pulled back and the lab coat fell to the floor, revealing her green blouse and form-fitting pants. I could see that her nipples were already hard. When I pinched them with my thumb and forefinger, she moaned and licked her lips.

After slipping off her shirt, I took Luzette's hand and swung her lightly into the examining chair. I pulled a lever, and the chair reclined. Straddling her and then cupping her titties around my dick, I began to pump, slowly at first, thumbing her nipples with every stroke. She bent her head down and stuck her tongue out, trying to lick the head of my dick as it slid between her breasts.

Finally, I stood Luzette up and turned her around. Kissing the nape of her neck, I moved my hands over her breasts and down to her pants. I undid them and let them fall to the floor around her ankles. Pressing against her back, I slid my hand into her panties. They were soaking. Her pussy was dripping, the lips puffy and covered with the same thick juices that were coating my hand.

She breathed hard as I slid my middle finger along the slit of her pussy. I made little circles around her clit and felt her wiggle her ass against my dick. Then I pulled the crotch of her panties to one side and bent her over the exam chair she'd been sitting in.

"You want this dick?" I asked.

Luzette didn't answer, just nodded furiously and ground harder against me. I stooped down until my face was level with her asshole and kissed her full cheeks, biting each lightly. I lapped at her asshole, and then blew hard into it.

"Mmmmpphhhh . . . ," she groaned.

I turned my face into her pussy and began tonguing the slit. I pressed the tip of my tongue against her clit and sucked gently. Normally, I don't fuck with a woman's asshole too much the first time we have sex—many women still don't like to consider their asses as sexual organs, associating anal stimulation with pain—but Luzette seemed like she really wanted to get loose. So I slipped the tip of my middle finger into her anus and waited for the response. Her reaction was to move her ass in little circles, urging me to finger-fuck her harder. My fingers toyed with her a bit more while my tongue was deep inside her pussy.

By now, my mind was as engaged as my body. Every now and then Luzette would moan with sheer pleasure. I could barely contain myself as I thought about how beautiful she was, how badly I'd wanted her when she'd first walked me into the examination room. Now, here I was, my face between her shapely legs, bringing her to climax.

When the anticipation overwhelmed me, I stood up. Luzette was still bent over, legs quivering. "Don't move," I commanded.

I yanked her panties down to her knees, gripped my dick, and moved into her. As wet as she was, her pussy still made for a tight fit. She sucked in her breath as I pushed. "Damn," she groaned. "Damn, damn . . ." I pushed harder.

I felt my dick sliding deeper and deeper, until my pelvis was slamming against her ass. Each stroke made her butt jiggle. She moaned and grunted as I made my dick probe her walls, moving my hips sharply from left to right as I pounded away. I moved faster, watching her ass jump with increasing quickness, enjoying the sound of my flesh slapping against hers. Luzette bent over farther, pushing her face into the seat of the chair to muffle her groans, which were growing louder. I slapped her ass hard for good measure.

Suddenly, I felt her legs start to shake and her ass buck. It was a struggle to stay on, but I managed to keep giving her the dick.

Finally, she unleashed a moan that even the chair couldn't smother, her voice rising and surely falling out into the hallway, but I didn't care. I kept going, driven by the knowledge that I was inside her, that I'd made Luzette cum so hard.

Moments later, I felt myself on the verge of my own orgasm. My skin went cold and hot at the same time. My muscles tightened. Luzette tossed me another of those looks and smiled as I pulled out and came on her ass. I shivered and spasmed. I let loose a deep breath and staggered back against the door, my stomach glistening with our bodily fluids.

I caught my breath after a few seconds, as she adjusted her panties, pulled up her slacks, and put on her lab coat. I followed suit, buckling my own pants and fixing my shirt.

"So when can I call you?" I asked, pulling her into an embrace.

Luzette shook her head, reminding me that she was involved.

I almost roared with laughter. Here I was, chasing a number, trying not to be too forward, and all the time she just wanted to fuck. "But," Luzette added, "I'll see you next time you come in to get your eyes checked, right?"

"Damn straight you will," I said. She smiled broadly. Somehow, I knew we'd fuck again, but it would only be on her terms, on her time. I was a private passion, and not one to be over-indulged. She was writing this script. I just had to make sure not to flub my lines. Somehow, I knew I wouldn't.

Then Luzette unlocked the door and, in her best professionally detached voice, told me I could finish up at the front counter and let me half-stumble past her into the corridor. Luzette's pussy had been like a drug, and I was still buzzing. Hell, I was feeling so good I barely even noticed the receptionist and the fat assistant giggling at me from the examination room across the hall.

TREY ELLIS

Old Story

You try to be unusual, you try to be unforgettable, irreplaceable. Otherwise, what's the damn point? Yet as you get older, one of the many lessons you learn too late is that there is a good reason why a cliché is cliché. The tired script to the late-night cable movie of my life began just as my marriage was ending. I was 39, a father of twin three-year-old boys, and my wife and I hadn't had sex in a month. She was working, or too tired from having worked. I was looking for work or too depressed from having found none.

The house is big and weeks would go by when no one set foot in the guest bedroom off the garage. Since my Internet startup had stopped we needed to lessen our expenditures and babysitters were bleeding us dry. At 10 bucks an hour, dinner and some lousy movie could cost us over 100 bucks. Adriana wasn't our usual babysitter but the pinch hitter. When she asked my then wife if she knew of any cheap apartments in the neighborhood, it was my then wife who suggested she move in with us. In exchange for rent she would sit three or four nights a week and a few hours on the weekends.

I had to be convinced. Not that I prowled the house naked,

but I wanted to know that I could if I wanted to. I was always relieved as soon as a houseguest left. I would sigh and feel that I could drop my host mask. Still, I hadn't worked in so long that we had to lighten our load drastically if we were to survive this slump without·having to sell the house.

Adriana's boyfriend helped her move in. She was 19, a gorgeous caramel-colored Brazilian and a student at the community college studying something different every semester. Her boyfriend was a pimply blond Texan whose Camaro often prevented my garage door from opening. She was so lovely and could do much better than this trashy cowboy (I'm sure he had a mullet before coming to California), but she didn't yet understand her value in the American meat marketplace. He was her "American," the guy she had dreamed of in Buzios, the little seaside resort where she'd grown up.

"I think she's so sexy," said my then wife. "Don't you?"

After ten years you know which are the tests and which are the genuine questions. This smelled like a test.

"She's cute," I told her. "But she could do better than Mr. Achy-Breaky heart."

"Maybe he's great in bed?"

"I don't really want to think about that." We were in bed. I heard his car start up so I went to the balcony and saw that he was strapping on the Domino's Pizza sign to the rusty roof of his car. He delivered pizza a few nights a week while studying marketing at community college. I have an MBA from Stanford. It occurred to me, watching him drive away, the rumble of his engine making the alarm on my Audi chirp but not actually scream, that no matter how superior I felt toward him, he, at least, had a job.

The next morning after my wife left early for work I bathed the twins and poured them cereal. Adriana padded upstairs around eleven, barefoot, bed-headed, yawning, and wearing old sweatpants and probably her boyfriend's T-shirt. She poured herself coffee before she said good morning. I noticed her ass bouncing around in her ratty sweats. I had conjured her image a few times while my then wife and I were making love, but at one time or another, I had conjured up the image of just about every woman I've ever known or seen on TV. This morning, however, I knew Adriana would go to the top of the list.

She joined the twins at the table and I asked her about school. She was thinking about switching to interior design next semester. Marketing, she told me, was too boring. I told her that I had worked in marketing for over 10 years and that she was right.

"How's your boyfriend? What's his name again?"

"Lance."

"How's Lance?"

Her answer was to pucker her lips and force air out of them.

"He seems nice enough."

"He is a boy."

The twins were doing pretty well feeding themselves and they were almost finished. I wiped up Darius, Adriana wiped up Levy, and we sent them to the living room with their fire trucks. Adriana had been babysitting for us for a year but this was the first time we'd ever really spoken.

"What do you mean, he's a boy?"

"He is not very serious. He drinks too much. He does not know what he wants. He is just like the Brazilian boys."

Was this *her* test? Did she want me to say, "You need a real man. An older man to teach you how to fully become a woman"? How tacky. I'd never cheated on my wife—*almost,* several times, but I always pulled myself back from the brink. Besides, she wasn't even twenty-one.

That night my then wife tried to turn away and fall asleep, but I rubbed my erection against her flannel pajamas, then went down on her till she came. Later, inside of her, I closed my eyes and came to the image of me dragging Adriana's sweatpants down and revealing the perfection of her perfect ass.

When she came back from the bathroom my then wife turned on her itty-bitty book light and finished proofreading a report that was due the next day.

*   *   *

When my then wife was out of town servicing a client, I would usually order the Playboy Channel and whack off for hours. I'd lock my door and keep the volume low enough to hear only a rumor of the couples fucking on TV. One time, exhausted from having just come, I went downstairs for some cranberry juice at around two in the morning. The stairway wound down from the master bedroom and the kids' room upstairs to the living area below, and below that to the guestroom and garage. As I was going down the stairs I heard sounds of fucking and my heart nearly stopped. Did I forget to turn off the VCR and was it louder than I had thought? I prayed Adriana was asleep so she hadn't heard me jacking off to porno.

Then I realized that the moaning was coming from her room. I froze where I stood because the floors creak like a haunted house. She was moaning in Portuguese, *"Gostoso! Gostoso! Sim! Sim!"* That used-to-be-mullet-wearing motherfucker was downstairs fucking her. And fucking her well. I burned with jealousy. It sounded like she was multiply orgasmic, coming again and again. I got my juice and tiptoed back to my room. Pizza Delivery Boy left a little while later, then I heard Adriana come upstairs to the kitchen. My heart raced like a teenager's. Should I hurry downstairs and make small talk? Do I even want to see her after she got fucked by somebody else? She might be feeling sexy and . . . and what? What exactly was I hoping for? I didn't know but I hurried downstairs anyway, ready to refill my empty glass, but she had already gone back to her room.

*   *   *

A year later couples' counseling still wasn't working. We were partners in the business of raising the twins but without them we had nothing to talk about and little interest in rediscovering what it was that we used to have. We were in the middle of a session with the counselor when the psychologist said to my wife, "Would you like to share with him what you shared with me?"

They were both so business-like. It was as if they had been discussing how to let me know that I was being fired in such a way that I wouldn't go postal and shoot up the place.

My then wife turned to me. "Vince, you know this isn't working between us. It hasn't been in a very long time. I think we
have to do something concrete about it."

I nodded and held on to my chair.

"I need to be happier. You too. And . . . I've found somebody
who makes me happy again."

I think I closed my eyes. I can't remember for sure. But it felt
like I had closed my eyes and when I opened them again everything in my world had changed.

"Marcus. Tell me it's not Marcus."

Marcus is her boss and my classmate from business school.
There was an undergrad, what was her name? Tammy. We were
both interested but she was only interested in him. My then wife
knew that he was my sworn enemy.

"He's changed. He's not—look, I'm not going to get into that
part with you. I might love him."

"But you don't love me. Anymore."

I didn't know if I loved her either. But Marcus! Ever since my
little company went under I had gotten back into tae kwon do. I
thought about kicking his ass. You get a "kick somebody's ass and
don't go to jail" card after they fuck your wife. But I already felt
like I'd been kicked so much harder than I could ever kick back.

I subsumed my despair in planning the separation. I made
myself as busy as possible for as much of the day as possible because any free time would allow the demons to creep out from
the shadows and cripple me with crying. We decided that since I
wasn't working and Marcus's company was expanding she would
move out and the kids would stay with me. She would see them

every day after work and weekends just like before. They might not even notice the change for a while.

When we told Adriana she just shrugged and asked if she could stay. I said yes. We needed her more than ever. Months went by, I was interviewing a little more frequently, but still no offers. Adriana broke up with her boyfriend about once a month, but then I'd hear her downstairs coming or hear his car going down our narrow street and know that once again she'd taken him back.

My sex life consisted of lap dances at strip clubs, the Playboy Channel—and obsessing over Adriana. For her twentieth birthday her boyfriend had saved up for a hot night out at . . . the Olive Garden. I had just put the twins to bed when I ran into her on the stairs. He was late, as usual. I'd never seen her dressed up before. High heels, a long skirt but slit almost up to her waist, and some wonderful kind of Wonderbra. She was small chested but tonight she was spilling out of her top like honey-wheat bread rising out of a pan.

"How do I look?"

"I think you know how you look."

"Yes. But girls need to hear it from a man."

My cock inflated and I just enjoyed the slow pleasure of it without responding. When I realized that she really was waiting for an answer I stammered, "Nice. You look really . . . nice."

She humpfed and turned to wiggle back down the stairs.

"Happy birthday!" I called after her. "Don't you want your present?"

She skipped back up the stairs. "I love presents," she said.

I should have been tweaking my bio and cv for the millionth time; instead I'd spent most of the day in Macy's StyleSetter section looking for the perfect gift for Adriana. I wanted to get her high-heeled "fuck-me" mules, the kind I have a serious weakness for, but I was wise enough to restrain myself. The last thing I needed was a sexual harassment suit from my nanny. I finally settled on a sweater and some eucalyptus-scented bath salts.

The doorbell rang just as she was tearing into my gifts.

"I love them!" she squealed. Then she kissed my cheek and scampered to the front door.

Sometimes it felt as if the entire universe was pushing me to seduce her. I turned on the TV and there was *The Sound of Music,* and nanny Julie Andrews and whoever played the Von Trapp father were falling in love. The next day they showed *The King and I,* different continent, same old story. When I talked to my friends about my growing obsession they all cautioned me. "Don't shit where you eat. It might not seem like it now but it's much harder to find a good nanny than it is to get laid."

However, every day brought another flirtation. At least I thought it was a flirtation. I could never tell how delusional I was. I remembered all the times when I was single and I thought some girl was giving me the vibe, only to find, after I tried to kiss her and just got her cheek, that she only liked me as a friend.

I said good night to Adriana once and she'd said, "Dream of me." What the hell did that mean? Another time she was about to cut a cucumber up for a salad and she just kept stroking it and waving it in my face and giggling. "When you start dating again I'll tell the girls that you are this big!" I wanted to throw her down and do' her on the kitchen island but I managed to control myself. I ran upstairs and jacked off in the bathroom.

She usually watched TV in her room. Often I could hear the bass from MTV vibrating the floor of the living room. I never told her to turn it down. I imagined her in her underwear bouncing on the bed to Eminem instead of finishing some community college project that was already past due.

One night I sat watching *The Matrix* in the living room, loud like it's gotta be, the home theater thumping the whole room (I had splurged on the system right before I thought my company was going public). I was in my sweatpants, my official divorced-guy diet of frozen barbecue chicken pizza and iced tea in front of me, when Adriana bounced upstairs.

"I love *The Matrix*," she said, collapsing on the couch.

"Would you like some pizza?"

She gobbled it like a guy. A line of mozzarella clung to the curve of her chin.

"You've got some cheese on your chin."

She rubbed and wiped but kept missing the spot.

"Okay?"

"Almost. Down."

"There?"

"Let me see." I hesitated before I touched her face and gently coaxed it toward the glow of the TV. I so wanted to lick the cheese off her face. I casually dropped my left hand in my lap to hide my growing cock and reached with my right to carefully pick off the cheese.

"Obrigada." I loved when she spoke Portuguese and I stared at the piece of cheese, dying to put it in my mouth.

Then I did.

Here eyes flashed surprise, then she turned and watched the rest of the movie in silence.

After it was over and before the next film began there was a card warning of "strong sexual content" coming up. Whatever it was, I was excited to see it but suddenly nervous when Adriana didn't leave. Then *Deviant Desires* began, a straight-to-cable soft-core movie that I'd already seen a depressing number of times. The first image was of a couple screwing on a canopy bed, gauzy drapery billowing in the wind, thin synthesizer music twanging on the soundtrack.

"Um . . . if you want me to turn the . . ." I said.

"Ah! I've seen this one. Have you seen this one?"

"Um, yeah, I think so. But they all kinda look the same."

"Verdade! They always have the same six people."

On the screen the tanned boob-jobbed white girl was pretending to blow this tanned, blond bodybuilder.

"There must be something else on." I moved to change the channel but she stopped me. Her hand felt hot on my arm.

"Could I ask you something, Mr. Roberts."

I'd been asking her ever since she moved in to call me Vince but she never did. This time it made my cock get even harder.

"Sure."

"My boyfriend. Well, he's not really my boyfriend anymore but we . . . you know. Are all American men so quick?"

Was she trying to kill me? Was that her plan? And she always sounded like she was enjoying herself.

"Well," I lowered my voice to sound like a doctor's on TV. "A lot of young guys are so excited that they kind of forget about the woman."

"*Ah é! Esatamente.*"

"I know I was when I first started. That's why I started studying tantra."

"What is that, tantra?"

"It started in India, thousands of years ago. It's kind of a philosophy and a physical practice to bring lovers closer together. The man learns to go for a long time until the woman wants him to finish."

"*Nossa!* Can you do that?"

"I've been studying it for years."

"So then why did your wife leave you?"

My erection left as quickly as it had arrived. "I . . . you'll have to ask her. But there's more to marriage than great sex."

"I don't want to even think about marriage. Not till I am at least twenty-seven."

She got up and took some cookies from the pantry.

"I have some books on tantra if you'd like to show them to your boyfriend."

"I told you, he is not really my boyfriend anymore. But yes. I would like to see the book."

I ran upstairs to my nightstand and chose the tantra book with the least pictures so she would know that I was serious. When I got back downstairs she was gone. I took a deep breath.

She was down in her room. Should I leave the book on the counter up here? Every time I knocked on her door to tell her her mother was on the phone from Brazil, or that the hot water would be off for the afternoon while they installed the new water heater that I could scarcely afford, I felt uneasy and excited at the same time. This time my fist almost trembled as it knocked. Adriana opened the door and looked at me. I shrunk inside, suddenly afraid and ashamed of how desperately I needed to fuck this very young woman.

"Here's the book," I said, then I went back upstairs, two stairs at a time.

* * *

Months passed and Lydia, an old family friend who was moving back from England, where she'd been working, started sleeping on the couch while she looked for a job. I had found some part-time consulting work so I finally had a little money coming in. Lydia was great with the kids and kept pressuring me to get rid of Adriana so she could take over her room. The boyfriend was coming over more and more often. Adriana was now studying pre-physical therapy and was too busy to join me on the couch. And with Lydia cock-blocking me (all my friends said she had a crush on me but I've just never been interested) there was little chance of anything happening. Finally I decided to give Adriana the boot. She took it well and said she'd been thinking of moving in with a Brazilian friend anyway. Three days later she gave me back the tantra book and left.

More time passed. I went out on a couple of dates with

women my age but they almost immediately started talking about marriage. My divorce was not yet final and I was nowhere near ready to settle down again. I finally started to understand the logic behind the cliché of fortyish men dating women 20 years younger. Young women don't expect much more than a good time in that moment, and that's exactly what a recent divorcé is looking for.

I was in my office preparing a report for a new client when the phone rang.

"You missed my twenty-one birthday."

"Adriana?"

"I called and invited you to my birthday. Why didn't you come?"

"I never got a message."

"I don't believe you."

"I swear. But it's good to hear from you. Did you get drunk?"

"Oh yes! My head will never be the same."

"The kids miss you."

"I miss them too."

"When can you come see them?"

"I have class all day now. It's hard. But I want to."

"How about dinner?"

"With the kids? Do they still go to bed at seven? I have class then."

"Or we could go out. I could take you out for your birthday."

"All right."

My cock rose from the dead.

*   *   *

Two days later I drove to her new apartment and picked her up. She was wearing high-heeled Lucite mules and a tight knit mini-dress and plum lipstick on her hypnotic lips.

"Wow! You're so beautiful."

"You never saw me dressed like this before?"

"Not often enough."

She smiled and got in the car. As we drove I filled her in on my dating misadventures and she told me that she had finally and forever dumped Pizza Delivery Boy. I was thrilled by the news.

At the restaurant we waited for our table at the bar. I ordered a vodka martini; she ordered an apple martini. The bartender was a sister, and it might have been my imagination but I thought she gave me a dirty look. She asked Adriana for her ID. She hadn't brought her passport with her so she had to settle for a Coke.

The hostess gave us a choice so I chose a back corner booth on the balcony. At our table the waiter saw my drink and asked Adriana what she'd be having. She and I forced ourselves not to smile. After another martini and Kung Pao chicken I couldn't hold back any longer.

"You know, I always had kind of a crush on you but since you worked for me I didn't dare do anything about it."

"*Nossa!* I had a crush on you too."

"Remember that time we watched *The Matrix*?"

"How could I forget! You ate that piece of cheese right off my face. I was sure that you were going to do something when you came down to my room."

"I wanted to. But I didn't want to disrespect you."

"I wanted you to."

"Really?"

"Of course."

"That would have been so sexy. I used to think about it a lot."

"Me too."

"Can I sit next to you?"

She blushed and looked away. I slid in to her side of the booth and put my arm around her. When she turned to me we finally, finally kissed. When we separated I had to remember to open my eyes. Hers were still closed.

"Wow."

"*Nossa.*"

"I've wanted to do that for so long. This feels like a dream."

"Me too."

I kissed her again, her hand gripping my thigh and mine sliding up her leg. Lost, I was lost, we were both lost till I felt someone tapping me on the shoulder. It was the manager. A brother I kind of knew from around town.

"Um, we've had some complaints."

I just laughed. I was sure he was messing with me. He left and soon we were making out again. Again there was someone tapping me on the shoulder, another manager, also a brother.

"Look," he began. "I'm sorry but some other customers have been complaining."

I looked around the restaurant. Our level was nearly empty and the main level was mainly empty.

"I thought the other brother was kidding too. It's ten-thirty on a Wednesday. We're in a corner."

"What can I tell you? Some folks . . ."

"Player hate," I said. I'd never used the expression before except as a joke. The manager laughed.

"Let's go," said Adriana.

We went back to my house. Lydia went to sleep early, thank God. She would have crucified me if she had seen whom I'd brought home. I expected Adriana to sit on the couch, we'd make out some more, then I'd have to cajole her upstairs into my bed. Instead, she just wound up the stairs, all the way up, stepped out of her shoes, and fell onto my bed. Before I fell on top of her I admired the view.

She was the color of a caramel apple and her brown hair spilled over the pillow.

"I've imagined you in this bed so many times."

Her answer was to stretch out her arms and beckon me with her fingers. I quickly kicked my shoes across the room and fell on her and we kissed as we worked each other's clothes off. When I unclasped her bra I gasped. Her nipples were even more beautiful than I had imagined, harder, darker. I kissed her neck then smelled her, taking her scent into the bottom of me, sucking her nipples hard, kissing her stomach and dragging off her dress and then her panties. She was smaller than my wife, her body so firm and in full bloom. Was I no better than R. Kelly? Twenty-one, she was twenty-one. Barely legal, just like the magazine. The lyric "If loving you is wrong, I don't want to be right" played in my head. I laughed.

"What's so funny?"

"Nothing. Nothing at all. I'm just very, very happy."

I worked my tongue slowly from the inside of her thighs to the outside of her lips and stayed there while she groaned and ground her hips into the bed. She was already so damn wet. Finally I parted her lips with my tongue and lapped gently, listening as her cries got louder and her breath shorter. Only then did I zero in for the kill and suck her clit between my lips and flick it with my firm tongue. She grabbed my head, her stomach jackknifed, and she came. I wiped my wet face on the sheets before I kissed her again. She hugged the life out of me.

Then she smiled mischievously as she kissed down my body and sucked one nipple, then the other. It had been so goddamn long that I gasped and nearly came right then. She continued down and took me in her mouth while stroking my balls. It was almost impossible not to come but after bragging about my tantric staying power I couldn't explode too soon. I clawed the bed and watched my cock disappear into her mouth with one eye closed. Watching with two eyes seemed almost too much, too hard to resist coming. Still I stared hard to burn the image forever into my brain.

Finally I had to grab her head and ease her off me so I'd have some left for fucking her. I put on a condom, laid her on her back, and while I was aiming she grabbed at my ass to shove me in fast and deep. She sucked one nipple while pinching the other with her fingers and her pussy was so tight around my cock I again almost gave up and came. But I remembered my training, concentrated on my breath and on how good everything felt and how I never wanted it to end. I built up a rhythm and got back in control of myself. I held her feet out wide while

I fucked her slowly. I even sucked her toes, which made her make sounds I'd never heard her make with Pizza Boy.

We tried to maneuver to doggy style without falling out but I did. She was on all fours on my bed and I was about to enter her again when I stopped again to admire the view.

"What! What!" she moaned.

"This is just a dream come true."

"Me too. Now fuck me."

So I did and she was noisy but the twins were sound sleepers. I was so happy to have fucked her so well. Then she laid me down on my back and fucked me and pinched my nipples and I hers. She was so wonderful to look at while such intensely terrific feelings radiated out from my cock. I thought about my wife running off with that asshole, about how defeated I had felt, how lost. I thought about how many times I had jerked off to this image and how sure I was that never, ever would it become a reality.

I felt the orgasm rushing toward me like a massive wave in a pitch-black night. I was going to be all right. I was going to survive after all. And when I came, all of me came, my toes, my knees, my hair. My body seemed to briefly pixilate like the crew of *Star Trek* beaming down to another planet, then I returned to earth happier than I'd been in over a year. In the moment just afterward I giggled. What a surprise. I realized that's what life was, pure surprise. Your wife leaves you, the nanny fucks you, a tornado knocks down your house. And if you don't like the surprise on the menu for today, just wait. Another one's coming along soon.

MIKE PHILLIPS

The Little Barton Job

Clifford was a master carpenter, and he had been his own boss for about five years when a contractor he knew called and offered him some work deep in the countryside, in Barton, a village he'd never heard of. The job involved renovating the woodwork in one of those old churches that dotted the English countryside. He knew it would be easy and he thought it would be interesting. But even so, he hesitated because all that he knew about the countryside was that people drove tractors or rode horses and talked funny. He knew also that for two weeks he wasn't likely to see another black person, and thinking about it gave him a creepy feeling of isolation.

In the end he went, partly for the money, and partly because he needed to prove to himself that he could go anywhere and do anything he wanted. In any case, this was his trade, and he couldn't afford to turn down the work. He hadn't always thought this way, but his thirtieth birthday was approaching and he found himself increasingly focused on establishing the business.

Growing up in the city, becoming a carpenter was the last thing on his mind. He'd had a vague idea that he might join the army or become a DJ, but one night back in his early teens, the police stopped him while he was driving a stolen car through the city center. After that his future moved in a completely different direction. After completing a spell in detention, he had decided to train for something—anything—and he'd chosen carpentry mostly because his favorite uncle had been a carpenter and he guessed it would be something he could do.

He hadn't expected to stick with it because he'd never stuck with anything in his life, but when he started training in the carpenter's shop, running the big saw, planing wood, and learning to make joints and pegs, there was something about the work that gripped him. It was so clean, and so absorbing to watch the shapes emerging between his hands. He started to love the smells of the different woods too—oak, beech, and cherry—and the dizzying scent of glue, the first sharp sniff of the day going directly to his brain. In a few years he was qualified for the trade and he started to specialize, fixing and polishing up old furniture for an antique dealer who used him because he was cheap and did a good job. By the time he was offered the job fixing up the old church he wasn't exactly bored, but he was certainly ready for something different.

* * *

Driving out of London, he had the feeling of entering another world. In a couple of hours he was close to the coast and negotiating his way through a narrow lane with barely enough room for two cars to pass. On either side of the road he could see green fields and trees beyond the hedges and in some of them there were sheep grazing or pigs grubbing in the dirt. Clifford hadn't seen anything like it for a long time, and by the time he arrived at the village he felt peaceful and relaxed, as if he was going on holiday.

Barton had a cluster of houses running along the sides of the road, and intersections decorated with signposts announcing the names of various farms. At its center was a typical village green facing a low schoolhouse. That was all, and he guessed that the village consisted of no more than a few hundred people. The church was roughly in the middle near the village green, flanked by a muddy field that doubled as its car park.

It was older than he'd imagined, a pile of gray stone that reared up against the sky, dwarfing the neighboring houses. Inside, it was bigger than he expected, a big hall dominated by the pulpit in one corner, beyond which was a slightly higher level containing a pipe organ, and ending in an impressive altar overshadowed by a huge circular stained-glass window. Clifford stood still, drinking in the sight. He wasn't religious, but he'd been brought up in churches that were very different. Mostly, his mother had taken him to churches in modern buildings made of red brick or concrete and glass, or occasionally a room in the local community center. This was different, with an atmosphere that was almost alive, as if the entire place was breathing out the reverence of centuries.

As he stood there a man and a woman came out of a room near the entrance. The man, Clifford guessed from the long black gown he wore, was the vicar. He was tall, his dark hair streaked with gray, but he looked fit and muscular, the sort of vicar who ran the marathon waving a collection tin. Clifford smiled at the thought. The vicar smiled back at him, shook hands, and introduced his wife, Leslie. She was a tall, thin woman with short blond hair, and Clifford knew immediately that she would be a problem. The feeling was mutual, he thought, because she was frowning.

"You've done this kind of work before?" Leslie asked.

She reminded him of teachers he'd had at school. She was about mid-forties, with an erect posture and a stern look on her face, as if she was about to go into a rage and send you out of the room. "It has to be properly done," she added.

She had the same pale blue eyes as Miss Yelland, a teacher he'd always hated. Miss Yelland had been tall, with spectacular long legs and a tight round bottom, but the expression on her face was always cold and haughty, her eyes fixed and contemptuous.

"That is exactly why they hired me," Clifford said. "If you've got a problem you can phone the contractor and sort it out."

For a moment they glared at each other, the tension stretching between them taut as a piano wire. The vicar hurriedly broke in.

"All my wife meant," he said quickly, "was that we have a very strict deadline. There's an important wedding here in two weeks and the work needs to be finished by then."

"No problem," Clifford told him. "Let me take a look."

He spent the rest of the day assessing what he had to do, pricing the materials, and ordering what he needed. The vicar explained that he serviced four villages. This week they had suspended normal activities in the church so that he could get on with the work in the main body of the hall. However, the work should be finished quickly because the following week would be crowded with preparations for the wedding. He paused, then added that he would be away for most of the week, and his wife would take the responsibility of overseeing Clifford's work. For a moment Clifford thought about objecting, but he couldn't think of a good reason, so he just shrugged.

He set up a workshop in one of the rooms off the main hall and started repairing and replacing some of the paneling and the floorboards. Leslie came by a few times during the first couple of days, but when she saw that he knew his business she drifted out again. In the mornings someone unlocked the church before he got there, and in the evenings she locked up after he left. He was staying in a small hotel nearby, and he went in and out without speaking to anyone except for a brief greeting to the old man at the desk. He took his meals in the pub opposite the church and, bored by the thought of breaking the ice with the farmhands who thronged the bar, he hardly spoke. By the end of the third day he felt as if he existed in a separate universe, like a ghost in the world of the living.

That day Leslie came in as he was packing up his tools, and suddenly he realized that she was the only person in the place he knew. From time to time some of the women from the village came into the church to sweep up or change the flowers, but none of them ever spoke to him. If he wanted to talk to someone, he guessed it would have to be Leslie. Luckily, he had a question. The floor around the pulpit was oak, and sometime during the last century some of the boards had been replaced with a different kind of wood. He could change them back to the original if she wanted, and replace the brass screws with wooden pegs.

She heard him out, staring at him impassively. Then, unexpectedly, she smiled. "Yes. Yes. That sounds like a good idea."

He turned away to pack up his tools but instead of leaving, she stood nearby, looking around.

"That's very meticulous of you," she said suddenly.

He shrugged.

"You said you wanted it done properly."

She was silent for a few seconds and he turned to look at her. Their eyes met, then she looked away, shifted uneasily, and sauntered a few paces along the aisle before twisting around to look at him again. She was wearing a long black skirt that clung to her hips, and with her back to him, the hesitancy of her walk gave a slow-motion effect to the working of her smooth round bottom, the fabric stretching and loosening as she moved.

She hesitated as if she wanted to say something more, but all that came out was good night.

That night, alone in his room, Clifford wondered what she had been about to say. He couldn't guess. Women like Leslie were a mystery to him. It wasn't so much that she was white. He'd grown up going to school with a variety of white kids, and for most of his life he'd lived in the same street as some of the white girls he knew. On the other hand, he'd never had much to do with women older than himself, apart from his mother and a few teachers. Leslie was also the kind of upper-class woman who lived in a world he didn't understand. What would he talk to her about?

Thinking about it, he realized how similar she seemed to his former teacher, Miss Yelland, whose cold face and manner had made her universally disliked among the boys in his class. What he'd never confessed to anyone else was that something about her excited him, and more than once, at home after school, he had masturbated slowly thinking about her long legs and tight breasts. At such times he had imagined himself breaking through the smooth icy surface of her composure, her face contorted in an agony of sexual passion while she begged him to spread her legs, squeeze her breasts, to use her in any way he wanted. At first he had thought of her merely as a middle-aged woman. Now he felt that her age gave her a kind of depth that made her more desirable than any of the girls he knew.

For the first time since he left the city three days before, Clifford found himself masturbating, his hand, almost without his moving it, reaching down to stroke his hard penis. At the same time he was wondering how he could get closer to Leslie. He had no idea why, and he already knew how impossible that would be, but her image seemed to have replaced his old dreams about Miss Yelland.

*   *   *

Everything changed half an hour after he started work in the church on the morning of the next day. He was beginning to unscrew the side panels of the stairs to the pulpit, and when he twisted one of the screws with his screwdriver there was a click and the panel swung open with a faint squeak. It was on hinges, he realized; it had to be some kind of door. He found a flashlight in his tool bag, then stuck his head in for a look.

He'd expected the space to be a small cupboard, but when he pointed the flashlight inside there was a square of wood hanging from one corner and he glimpsed a passage that dropped away abruptly after a few feet. Curious, he climbed in, crawling on his hands and knees through the narrow passageway.

The square of wood was actually a panel that, when shut, concealed the passage. He pushed past and found himself climbing down a short ramp that ended in a square hole. He crawled in on his hands and knees and emerged in a bigger space. When he swung the flashlight around it turned out to be a small room, about eight feet by six. Half of it was occupied by a narrow camp bed. Some papers were piled up in one corner and next to the bed was a candle. That was all. He stood up and bumped his head against the ceiling, then realized that it was only about five feet high, so he had to move around in a crouch.

Clifford lit the candle and looked around. The only decoration in the room was a big wooden cross fixed above the bed. The realization of where he was came swimming up out of his memory. This was a priest's hole. Back in the time when the church was built, Catholics were banned and persecuted, and some families had created hidden rooms like this to conceal their priests.

For a moment he had the shattering thought that he was the first person to stand there for centuries. Then he realized that the camp bed wasn't old enough, and when he looked at the yellowing newspapers in the corner he saw that they came from an assortment of dates in the 1920s. Someone had been there since the 17th century. That much was obvious, but he could also see that the place hadn't been disturbed for nearly a hundred years.

He crawled out slowly, wondering what to do about his discovery, but it wasn't long before the problem was solved for him. Almost as soon as he was back on the floor of the church, he heard Leslie's footsteps and without thinking about it he called out to her.

"I've found something."

"What is it?"

She was wearing a dark gray dress, the hem only a few inches above her knees. He swung the panel open, showed her the hole, and told her about the room he'd found. She bent over, peering in, and for the first time since they'd met, her expression was smiling and animated.

"Amazing," she said. "Well done. This is historic."

She was beaming. Anticipating her disappointment, he told her quickly that the room had been visited and used in recent times. She listened thoughtfully.

"The last vicar was here for nearly forty years," she said. "So was the one before him. I expect before them the vicar or someone else would have known about it, then they went and it was forgotten." She paused, thinking it over. "It doesn't matter. It's the fact that it's there that is important. If it's a genuine priest's hole, people will come from all over to see it."

He nodded back at her, perversely flattered by her enthusiasm. At the same time he found himself thinking that perhaps her standoffish manner had been due to shyness.

She straightened up and walked around a few paces, then, as if struck by a new idea, faced him again.

"The vicar is away for a few more days," she said. "Let's keep this between us for the moment. I want it to be a surprise." He nodded his agreement, and she smiled back at him, as if the thought of keeping the secret between them had inspired a new warmth.

"I'm going in," she said. "Is that all right?"

"I don't know how safe it is. I'd better go first."

She hesitated, then nodded her head in agreement, and they scrambled in one after the other. He swung the flashlight around in front of him so that she could see where she was going, but when they got to the ramp that led down to the room, he heard a bump and a gasp behind him. She had slipped, and he was still on his hands and knees halfway down when she banged into him from behind. After they rolled down the rest of the slope and out of the hatch in a tangle of arms and legs, he found himself lying on top of her. The flashlight had gone out, and for a moment, in the blind dark of the room, he had no idea where they were or what kind of space had they rolled into. All he knew was the feel of her body; her legs splayed apart, her arms outstretched beside her in a posture of surrender, her soft breasts cushioning his chest. Poised between her thighs, he could feel his erection stiff and hard against her and without thinking he pressed down into the heat of her flesh.

Suddenly she moved, twisting under him and shoving violently at his chest.

"No," she said. "Please. No."

Her tone had an odd pleading sound and it struck him that she was frightened. The realization was like a dash of cold water, and he pulled back from her, sitting up against the cot.

"I'm sorry," he said ridiculously. "I was looking for the flashlight."

She didn't reply, but he sensed that she was sitting up and feeling around for the flashlight. In an instant he felt her fingers fluttering on his leg and then she touched his penis and grasped convulsively at it. She must have realized immediately because there was a gasp and she let go as if she'd burnt her fingers. In the same moment, Clifford found the flashlight. He switched it on. Her eyes were screwed up against the light, her skirt up around her waist and her legs wide apart, so that he could see all the way up between them to the slender strip of white. It was only a flash, because she turned away immediately, got up on her knees, and pulled her skirt down. Clifford scrambled over to the corner and lit the candle. When he turned around to look at her she was peering at a cut on her arm from which blood was trickling.

"It's only a scratch," she said. "But I need to clean it up. Can we get out of here?"

Without waiting for a reply she turned and began scrambling out of the hatch and up the ramp. Clifford followed, his eyes drawn irresistibly, in the circle of dim light, to the sight of her buttocks thrusting and straining against the cloth of her dress.

At the end of the passage she sat down to fiddle clumsily with the catch.

"I can't open it," she said.

"It needs the screwdriver," he told her.

She pulled back against the wall, lying back on her side to give him room. They were lying face-to-face, their bodies almost touching, but just before he could unscrew the catch there was the sound of footsteps from outside, and a woman's voice called out.

"Leslie. Leslie."

To judge by the sounds there were two of them, and he guessed that they were a couple of the volunteers who worked in the church. He paused uncertainly, and Leslie reached up and pushed the screwdriver away from the catch. In the same movement her hand found the flashlight, switching it off, and Clifford remembered that she wanted to keep the passage a secret. In addition, he imagined, she wouldn't want to be seen crawling out from under the pulpit in her present disheveled state. Her pride, he guessed, would keep her lying there for as long as it took.

"Leslie," the woman called out again.

It was pitch black inside the passage now. Clifford put the screwdriver down quietly, and his hand came to rest on Leslie's hip. She didn't move, and, absently, as if by their own volition, his fingers started gently stroking the soft cloth of her dress.

"I could have sworn I saw her come in," the first woman said.

"Perhaps she's gone through the side into the car park," another voice replied.

"Look at this," the first woman said again. "He's replacing some of these floorboards."

"About time."

In the dark Clifford could see nothing, but he could hear her breathing, and smell her. His hand moved more firmly around her hip, stroking around the curve of her buttocks. On the other side of the panel the women seemed to be moving around the flooring where he'd been working. His hand cupped the curve of Leslie's thighs, squeezing softly, and he pulled her toward him. In response she made a small sound in her throat, reached down and clutched his hand convulsively, holding it away and trapping it behind her.

"I wonder where he is," one of the women said. "I was going to say hello to him."

Her friend giggled.

"He's an animal."

"Jane! You dirty devil."

"Oh, don't be so politically correct, you hypocrite," Jane said. "I saw you looking."

"Oh, that wasn't it." She paused, her voice hesitant. "I've been in and out without even speaking to him, and the last time he looked at me. He was sort of smiling and I thought he seemed really nice, but I just hadn't spoken because of, I don't why, who he is, I suppose."

"Oooh. That's interesting. But you'll have to get past Miss Bossy Boots if you want to be friendly. I bet she's loving it, giving orders to a big black man like that."

"Stop that. It's not fair," the other woman said sharply, and there was a moment of silence before she spoke again. "But I do know what you mean."

Clifford hardly heard them. He shifted, their two hands linked behind Leslie's back giving him leverage, and lay half on top of her, his stiff cock against her belly. In the dark her breathing was as loud as thunder in his ear, and she gave a faint moan. He shifted again, pressing his cock down between the fork of her thighs, and at first he thought he imagined the movement, but then it was unmistakable. Braced against the wall she was returning the pressure, her crotch squeezing hard against his, grinding in a slow rhythm. Suddenly, she tore her hand from his and pushed his shoulder, shoving him away.

"They've gone," she said in a thin, shaky whisper. "They've gone. Let me out."

She pushed at him again and he could feel her struggling to move away from him. He picked up the screwdriver, his muscles slow and reluctant, and unscrewed the panel. The door opened and they wriggled out. Leslie got up immediately and looked down at herself. Her stockings were torn, with great holes at the knees and calves, and there was blood smeared on her arm.

"Damn," she said.

Without another word she spun around and walked quickly toward the side door.

"Mrs. Whitman," Clifford called out when she'd taken a few steps. Hearing his voice she stopped, as if about to come back, then she seemed to make up her mind and started walking again. In a moment she was gone.

Left alone, Clifford went back to work on the floorboards. He wondered what would happen next. Perhaps, he thought, chilling at the prospect, she would storm back in to accuse him of attacking her or something of the sort. Then he dismissed it. He couldn't see her doing that. It was more likely that she would pretend nothing had happened and go back to treating him with a stiff formality. If she took that line, he decided, he would play along. Anything else might cause him too much trouble. The only problem was that he couldn't stop thinking about her and the way their bodies had been pressed together. Normally the repetitive routine of his work could distract him from anything, but now his mind was in such turmoil that he had to force himself to pay attention.

*   *   *

He had been at work for a couple of hours when he heard footsteps. Somehow he knew they were hers, even though they now seemed different. Usually she walked in a quick and decisive way, but now her steps were slow and loitering, like a tourist who'd dropped in for a leisurely look around.

He didn't look up from what he was doing, and she walked past him and sat on the lowest rung of the stairs to the pulpit before speaking.

"I just thought I'd tell you," she said. "My husband's back on Saturday, and I thought I'd show him the priest's hole then." She hesitated. "Will you be here?"

He had planned to take the weekend off.

"No. After Friday, Monday's the next time you'll see me."

"Fine," she said slowly. "Perhaps you could show me how to get in and out before you go."

"Okay."

Out of the corner of his eye, he saw her stand up. She was wearing jeans this time, and a shirt that covered her arms. He shifted to look up at her and he realized that he had an erection. In fact he couldn't remember whether it had gone down at any time during the last few hours.

"I'm not sure how safe it is," he said. "Maybe I should check the ceiling in there. If it's never been reinforced and the wood is rotten it might come right down once people start going in."

"Yes."

Her voice was faint, as if she couldn't summon up the energy to speak louder. Suddenly he remembered something he'd forgotten for more than two hours.

"The candle. I don't think I put it out."

He swung the panel open and paused at the entrance. He looked back at her.

"Do you want to see if there's any work you want done?"

Their eyes met for a moment, a faint blush reddened her skin, and then she looked away without answering. Clifford waited for a few seconds, then he crawled into the hole. He was nearly at the end of the passage, at the top of the ramp, when he heard her calling out.

"You forgot your flashlight."

He didn't bother to answer. He could already see a faint flickering light. The candle was still burning. He tumbled through the hatch in a hurry, and thanked his lucky stars that he'd remembered. There was still about half an inch of candle left, but the flame was sputtering in the stub of wax near the pile of old newspapers. He picked up the papers and began stacking them on the cot, and he was about to put out the candle when Leslie came through the hatch behind him.

"I thought I'd take another look," she said. "I didn't see anything before."

He didn't reply. She tried to stand up straight and banged her head on the ceiling beams. Rubbing her temples, she sat on the bed and swung the flashlight up into the corners of the room.

"Point it at the ceiling," he told her.

He sat on the bed next to her and played the light carefully over every inch of the ceiling. The beams were old. They must have been reinforced early in the twentieth century, he thought, but they seemed sound enough.

"I'll run a lead in and take a look with a proper light tomorrow," he told her.

The room must have been low on oxygen, because he felt as if he was gasping for breath, his lungs struggling to pull in the air it took to speak. It seemed to be affecting her too, because she merely made a faint sound of assent. The candle went out, and she held the flashlight up, pointing it down at the papers strewn on the cot, and twisting around to bend over them.

"These look interesting," she said.

Her voice was so faint that he could hardly hear. He leaned over as if to look at the newspapers, then put his arms around her from behind. His hands closed over her soft breasts, and he could feel her nipples standing out between his fingers. He squeezed them gently and she gave a long moan.

"They must eighty years old," she whispered.

She leaned back against him. He kissed her neck, running his lips slowly from side to side along the soft skin. The flashlight went out and she turned her head, her lips meeting his gently. Her mouth opened and her tongue touched his, hesitantly at first, then with more urgency as their mouths locked together, his tongue writhing against hers. He swung her around, pushed her backward, and lifted her legs so that she was lying flat on the papers. Without breaking the kiss he unbuttoned her waist-band, zipped the jeans open, and slid his hand under her pants. At the last moment she tensed, took her hand from around his back and reached down as if to stop him, but his fingers were al-ready parting the soft fold of her sex, and instead of pushing his hand away she pressed down on it as if urging him farther in. He took his hand out then and pushed the jeans down over her thighs. She arched her back, lifting off the cot to help him. She kicked her legs as the jeans came down and in one motion he tugged it all off. Now she was naked from the waist down and he could feel the heat of her body in the dark. She felt around the front of his stomach for a moment before she found his erect penis and grasped at it, closing her hand and squeezing.

He pulled at the drawstring in front of his sweatpants and lowered them, freeing his cock. It seemed to leap into her hand and she held it tight for a second, then began stroking it slowly, the foreskin sliding up and down between her fingers. He found her crotch again, and his fingers slid easily into the streaming wet slit. He dabbled in it for a second, thrilled by the soft, fluid feel of it. Then he parted the fold and, tenderly, stroked the hard little nub of flesh at the top. She moaned loudly and pulled at him, urging his body on top of her and spreading her legs wide apart. He moved, guided by the feel of her body and, seemingly without aiming for it, he was in, pushing in slow and hard, then when he could go no farther, moving his cock back and forth deep inside her. She moaned again, and he heard himself mak-ing sounds that matched hers. Then, because he felt himself speeding toward the end and he wanted to make it last, he slowed down, almost stopping his movements, but she kept on, her crotch writhing slowly around his quivering cock, jammed tight inside her.

"Oh, Jesus," she said, her voice high and trembling. "Jesus."

She was moving faster, her body convulsing, her breath gasping and catching in his ear, and he tried to keep still but somehow his cock seemed to be expanding, the grip of her cunt provoking him to push deeper and deeper, and suddenly he was stroking faster and then he knew he couldn't stop it anymore, and he came, his cries echoing in his ears, exploding in her like fireworks sprinkling light over a black sky.

He lay limp on top of her for a few seconds. It might have been much longer, but he'd lost track of time, and he seemed to be emerging from a dream. He wondered whether the noise they were making might have been heard. He had no way of telling how far sound traveled out of the room. Below him she stirred, and he shifted his weight off her, swinging his feet down to the floor. Without speaking they untangled themselves. He found the flashlight, switched it on, and they dressed in silence, avoiding each other's eyes. In a few minutes they were crawling back through the passage into the church.

Glancing at his watch, he was surprised to see that they had been in the hole for more than an hour.

"I'd better get back to work," he said.

"Yes." She hesitated for a moment, then she spoke again. "Thank you."

Clifford went back to work. He felt great, a sense of triumph buoying him up. From time to time he had flashes of memory, of squeezing her soft body beneath his, the long low moans she had uttered in his ear, the strength and passion of her arms around him. Five minutes after she walked out the door he was erect again, and throughout the afternoon, in the middle of tapping in a peg or laying a board, he found himself sitting back on his heels, his hands idle, thinking about what they had done in the darkness of the hole.

The day went by slowly. He was just packing up his tools when he heard footsteps at the front entrance and he looked up expectantly, but instead of Leslie it was the vicar walking down the aisle, his cassock swishing around his ankles.

"Hello," the vicar called out. "How are you doing?"

Seeing Clifford's surprise, he laughed.

"I've had to come back," he said. "My wife has been called away unexpectedly. A sick relative." He looked solemn. "These things happen."

Clifford nodded his agreement, hiding his sense of shock and frustration. It was too much of a coincidence, and lost in his own thoughts, he forgot to tell the vicar about the priest's hole.

* * *

By the next morning he'd decided not to say anything about it. If Leslie came back, he thought, he would let her decide what to do about it. But that was the last he saw of her. In a few days he'd finished the job. Leslie hadn't returned and there was nothing he could do to prolong it. A week after he'd started he was back in London, and that would have been that, except for when the contractor phoned him a month later about another job.

"You know that church you worked on," the man said.

Clifford felt a sinking feeling in the pit of his stomach.

"What's the problem?" he asked.

"No problem," the man said. "Good news for them, in fact. They found a priest's hole below the pulpit a couple of days after you left. It was a secret for years. So you must have brought them luck."

"I guess," he told the contractor. "It was only a matter of time. These little villages are probably all full of secrets."

The man laughed.

"I bet you're right. No one knows what goes on in these places. If only the walls could talk. Eh?"

"Thank God they can't," Clifford said. "Thank God they can't."

Until We Meet Again

*L*ila was still in bed when she heard the bell. She dragged herself up to open the door, admiring how shiny the hardwood floors looked after she did *una limpieza*.

"Don't dare sleep in a new apartment until you burn away the old energy," her aunt Isabel warned Lila, handing over sage, lavender, and rose petals wrapped carefully in aluminum foil.

Lila wasn't sure if she believed in her aunt's *brujeria* but she was determined to change her luck with love. She performed Isabel's cleansing ritual and then followed Feng Shui principles, making sure she arranged her furniture in a way that encouraged partnership.

"I'm here to hook up your phone," the guy yelled through the door.

She opened the door. The phone man was two shades darker than her with a slight accent.

He followed her to the kitchen, where all the phone boxes were.

"New apartment, huh?" he said, smiling.

Lila looked around and wondered if it was safe for her to be alone with him. But they weren't alone. There was something odd about him, as if he walked around with a spirit. Isabel had told her of such people. The haunted ones. He looked younger than Lila but there was something about his eyes—they were brown with yellow flecks—that made him seem older, as if he'd had a hard life. Lila could easily choose to be interested in this man. Why not? He was apparently good with his hands. Didn't blue-collar workers have a reputation that they could do what no man who wears a suit to work could? She started to think about how picky she'd always been, how many lonely nights she'd spent because of it. Lila was tired of dating creative types who spent all their time absorbed with their own ideas. Lila watched his hands, noticing scars and neat cuticles.

"You are quite pensive," he said as he checked her phone line and played with the wires.

"Oh, sorry, did you say something?" she asked him but couldn't shake the feeling that they weren't alone.

"Yes, I asked you if you lived here by yourself."

"No," she lied for her own safety.

"Married?"

"Never been."

"What do you do?" he asked, not looking up at her.

She assumed his questions were part of his installation rou-tine, something to make the time go faster. She wondered if she was supposed to offer him water or a beer.

"I design book covers. I work at home. I mean, I do more than that, but that's what pays the rent."

"When I lived in Haiti I was a painter," he said as he climbed onto a chair to staple the wire against the edges of the wall.

"You're Haitian?" she asked. She should've known. His accent reminded her of a friend's in college.

"And you?"

Lila didn't want to answer him. She was ashamed of the history they shared.

"Does it matter?"

"You should be proud of where you're from," he said, looking through his bag for a tool. "Your native land is your inheritance. Good or bad, you carry it behind the ears."

"I'm Dominican," she said, and instantly regretted it. How could she explain Trujillo, all the racist Dominicans that openly reject and torture Haitians for no other reason than ignorance?

"I love the Dominican Republic. I was there on holiday not so long ago. Punta Cana. Have you been there?"

"No," she said, shocked at his comfort with it all. "So you paint?" She changed the subject.

"I painted. My father had me painting from the moment I could hold a brush. We sold paintings to the vendors in the capital. And when he died my mother and I moved to New York to start again. Painting for me wasn't creative. It was work. I like art, though. Sometimes I go to the museums. It can be very peaceful when the tourists are not around."

"I'm sorry," Lila said, and wondered if he was flirting with her. She couldn't tell if he was just being polite.

"For what?"

"About your father."

"He died when I was eleven. I have a stain over my heart since then. I always feel as if he keeps me company. Strange, no?"

"I sensed we weren't alone." Lila said it and couldn't believe the words came out of her mouth. She was never one to do spiritual speak, but she was feeling him. He was disarming her with his honesty and openness.

"You feel him too?" he asked, surprised.

"I feel something. As if we're not alone."

"My father takes care of me, you know. I don't remember much of him. But he said things that are hard to forget. He told me no matter what happened he would protect me. He said his grandmother had saved his life many times. My father is my ancestor now. It's like an armor. I sometimes think I made him up, like a pretend friend. You ever have one of those?"

Lila laughed. "You mean imaginary."

"*Oui,*" he said, and laughed along with her.

"No, I never did."

"But if you really do sense him, maybe he is real. That is why we need friends. They remind us that we are not as crazy as we think."

"We're not friends," Lila said.

"Then what are we, soul mates?"

"I don't believe in such things," Lila said, looking around for something else he could do. She wasn't ready for him to leave. She wondered if he liked to read books, but was afraid the question would be rude.

"Nice apartment," he said, packing up his tools and looking around at the lavender walls in her living room.

"Thank you," Lila said, wanting to ask for his number and realizing she must be losing her mind. He was the phone guy. What could they possibly have in common? She had arranged her apartment in such a way because she was ready for a serious commitment. She had wasted a lot of her youth on curiosities and flings. Besides, he was Haitian. What would her family think? They would never accept him. Did he even speak Spanish? Would his family ever accept her? Why was she thinking about such things? He was a stranger. They had shared a moment. That's it. Nothing more.

He paused before he opened the door to leave. "Your apartment has good spirits," he said. "You'll be happy here."

Lila closed the door and regretted not asking for his number. How did she know about his father? Maybe it was the leaves she burned that Isabel had concocted for her. Whatever it was that had happened between her and the Verizon man was fleeting. He was gone and she hadn't seized the opportunity to dig deeper.

*   *   *

The next day Lila came home and listened to her messages.

"Hi, Lila, it's me, Jacques. This is a courtesy call to make sure your telephone is working properly. If you have any problems you can call me at 555-5683."

Lila pressed play again. "Hi, Lila, it's me, Jacques . . ."

His name is Jacques. She hadn't even asked. How did he know her name and number? She felt naïve. He knew where she lived, and he had a work order. Of course that was it.

She decided against calling him. It was more fun thinking about him than actually playing anything out. Besides, what if he really was calling out of courtesy?

That night Lila dreamt of Jacques. She was at a dance club. They were dancing.

"Feels dangerous, doesn't it? Two countries in conflict rubbing up against each other and actually liking the way it feels."

"It's you," she said. "The phone man."

"I prefer to be called by my name, Jacques."

"Sorry, Jacques."

"Why haven't you called me?" he asked in the dream. It sounded like a dare.

Lila woke up to the phone ringing. She assumed it was Jacques but it was a telemarketer. No one had her new number yet. She wanted to have her apartment to herself for a while. For years she was the one to entertain gatherings of artists and writers. She was the one to house travelers and offer remedial housing to those in between places. Her old home had become a depot for people in transition. Her new home had a sense of permanence and she wanted to keep it that way.

The thought of being alone made her horny. She touched herself. Her fingers slipped around her clit, under the hood and inside. She was already wet. She thought about Jacques, his hairless chest and his thick legs, and imagined his scent, like cloves and sandalwood. She thought about him nibbling her shoulder, his cock rubbing against her legs, teasing before he entered. She thought about rubbing up against him to a Juan Luis Guerra song and then wondered if he liked merengue, or was he boycotting it because the Dominicans took all the credit for the music that was born in Haiti.

She had to stop thinking of such things, her orgasm was slip-

ping away to a place from which she'd never be able to retrieve it.
Forget the politics, she said to herself. She pushed her thoughts
back to his thick tongue in her mouth. She pulled two pillows
over herself to feel the warmth of something more than her bed-
sheets. She continued to touch herself, pushing two, then three
fingers deep inside, and her mind drifted into a dream. She was
seeing a phone, a large red one. Jacques sitting over it waiting for
her to call. "Damn it," she said, the orgasm retreating back to a far-
away place. It was too late. She had lost her chance. If she didn't
call him it would get worse.

She dialed his number and he answered it before it rang at
his end.

"Hello."

"Hi, this is Lila. I'm looking for Jacques."

"What took you so long?" he asked.

"I've been busy, you know."

"Just this minute I was staring at the phone and saying, 'Call
me, Lila,' and then you called."

"What color is your phone?"

"Red."

"I saw the phone in my dream. Do you think that's crazy?"

"You're a witch, you know."

"I'm not kidding. I saw a red phone."

"It's fate, then."

"I'm serious. I had a dream and you were in it. And you asked
me to call."

"Were we dancing?"

Lila paused. How did he know? It was as if he was feeding

her his thoughts. Maybe he was the witch and he was setting her up. But for what? What could he want from her? Maybe he was back on earth to make right all the wrongs done to his people. That's why he talked about the ancestors and didn't seem afraid of her. That's why he was so forward. He didn't work for Verizon at all. He wasn't even real but a figment of her imagination.

"Hello?"

"Stop playing games. It's not funny."

Jacques paused. "I was teasing. I was thinking we should go out dancing."

"In my dream we were dancing," Lila confessed.

"I want to see you again."

"Where?"

"I can come over to your apartment during lunchtime."

"Okay," Lila said, unsure but curious to find out what was going on. She wondered if having him over at her house was stupid. He'd already been there and he hadn't tried anything. Besides, if she had met him at a bar what would've been different? At least she knew where he worked. And he had installed her phone.

"I will see you at lunch," he said.

"I'm looking forward to it."

Lila ran around cleaning her apartment. She then showered and sprayed perfume on her body.

"What am I, crazy?" she asked herself, but wanted to be ready just in case. She shaved her legs and made the condoms accessible in her drawer. Wanting something to do while she waited, she paid her bills.

The doorbell rang. He was already upstairs. How did he get

into the building? Of course they let him in the building, he's the phone man. No, his name is Jacques; a painter in Haiti who carried his father's mark on his chest. She would be open to what he had to say.

She opened the door and he seemed shorter than she remembered him. And his eyes seemed lighter.

"Can I wash up? I get pretty dirty when I work," he said, as if he had known her forever.

"Yes," she said, and waved him in, pointing him toward the bathroom. "Do you want to order lunch?" she asked nonchalantly.

"I'm not hungry," he said.

A few minutes later, he walked out of the bathroom with a shy smile.

"This is so awkward," she said, not knowing where they should sit.

He stared at her.

"You have pretty eyes," she said.

"*Merci,*" he replied, bowing his head in appreciation.

He stood in front of her and they stared at each other and she felt something strange happening to her. Something was pushing her toward him. She was kissing him and touching him and she hadn't moved at all. Between them was a ball of energy. It was pulsating. She allowed herself to feel it. She allowed the heat to engulf her. She saw him swelling in his pants. He didn't hide it. But he didn't attempt to touch her.

"Perhaps I should come back another day," he said. "It's all happening too fast."

He started walking toward the door.

"But we haven't done anything. What are you talking about?"

"So much has already happened," he said, looking away.

"Why don't you sit?"

"Are you sure?"

"You were the one who insisted on seeing me," Lila said.

"I'm sorry. There is a lot you don't know. My life is very complicated. I don't want to complicate yours."

"Of course there is a lot I don't know. We hardly know each other."

"Fine, I will sit."

He went to the couch. She followed him. He placed his thumb against her cheek, then caressed her neck.

"You're very beautiful. More beautiful than our island. I am also sure you are as dangerous. I am feeling extremely vulnerable right now."

"So am I."

Lila felt she owed him something. It's a terrible way to start anything. She wanted to travel to his land, and make love to him. Heal the pain of their histories. Forget that it ever happened. She wanted to quiet her mother's voice inside her and go with the moment that was begging for a kiss. She leaned toward his lips and bit the bottom half. She sucked them and he sat motionless. Something died. It had been better before she kissed him. She had rushed something he obviously wasn't ready for. He was pulling away.

"Look at me," she said.

"I am looking at you."

"I mean do what you were doing when we were standing.

Open yourself to me. It's the only way I know how to be with you."

"What do you want me to do?" Jacques said in haste and then he pulled her to him. He kissed her and this time it was she who resisted.

"We're trying too hard," he said. "We are either not ready or have waited too long."

"But I just met you," she said.

He laughed. "I feel like I've been here for hours. How long has it been?"

"Ten, fifteen minutes at most."

"I am silly, I know."

"I'm sillier," she said and in the midst of his laugher she tried to kiss him again. This time he let her in. He unclenched his teeth. He loosened his lips. He tasted like mints and despite his claim to be dirty from his job he smelled like soap as if he'd just come out of a shower. He grabbed her waist and pulled her onto his lap. She wrapped her legs around him and thought about loving him. Saw them growing old together and felt as if they were visiting each other again. Maybe that was what a soul mate felt like, as if the future was already the past. She thought about their children. Would they be Haitian or Dominican? Or would they call themselves American and cut the umbilical cord to the countries that made this affair so hard to give in to? She stopped herself thinking such thoughts. She didn't know this man. She didn't know his last name, where he lived, if they could ever make a life together. She knew only about this moment.

He pressed his chest against her breast. He squeezed her nipple, twisting it just so as if he had done it millions of times before. She put her hand over his hardness and throbbed between her legs in anticipation. She wanted to make love. But she didn't want to be the one to take it that far. She wanted him to go after her. To trespass in that way. But he didn't. He kept his hands north of her belly button. He sucked on her tongue and licked her neck and the longer he waited to touch her the hungrier she became. *Damn you*, she thought, *touch me*.

She wanted him to read her mind. She tried to send the message to him with her bites, by grabbing his short hair, by kneading his flesh. She was giving him permission. She wasn't going to hurt him. She would love him. She would accept him for who he was. She would welcome him after he came home from work and listen to his stories about his clients. She would never again think his work less important than hers. She would look into his eyes and see that they are both humans who love each other, despite where they come from or what they do.

He didn't give in to her. He made her ache so much her eyes welled up with tears. He caressed her back. He let her rub against the swelling leaking in his pants. But he protected himself, controlling how far she could go. She was feeling rejected, becoming enraged. What's wrong with you, she wanted to say, knowing very well that she could let what they were doing go only so far. He could sense her fear under all her passion. He was more aware of their future than she was. Could he read her mind? Was he going to places inside of her that she still didn't know of? It was evident in the way he leaned back to look at her. She smiled, trying to hide her impatience. Thinking about the condoms in the drawer.

"We don't need to rush," he said. "There is a better time for this."

He eased her off his lap and stood up, and noticed the small damp spot on his pants.

Lila couldn't believe her eyes. He was walking away from her. What good was Isabel's *limpieza?* What good was all her work? What did her dreams mean?

"But it feels right today," Lila insisted and pulled him to her. Her mouth was near his crotch. She debated whether she should pull out his member and suck on it. She wondered if he was circumcised. Why did she have to work so hard? Why didn't she just let him go? He should be chasing after her.

"I promise I'll be back tomorrow," he said. "I'm already late for work."

"Why not tonight after you're done with work?" Lila asked.

"Tomorrow, I promise." He kissed her on the forehead as if he were the adult and she a child. Then he left.

Lila couldn't get any work done. All her images and drawings seemed phallic. She needed to release herself. She lay down on her belly and started to rub her clit, thinking about Jacques. She came without having to do much work.

She spent her afternoon cutting and pasting on her computer, reminding herself to focus. She could be fulfilled on her own. She didn't need anyone. Not even Jacques. She got disgusted thinking about how many women he might have slept with on the job. How many lonely, desperate women sucked his cock. The thought made her never want to see him again. *Damn you,* she thought. *Don't you dare call me.*

The next day, Jacques didn't call. Lila pretended not to care but she called his number, then hung up on a voice she didn't recognize.

She went about her days pretending Jacques wasn't there scratching at her thoughts. She went out with friends but didn't tell them what happened. She called her Aunt Isabel to tell her she was wrong about her potions.

"Did you think you would find love overnight?" Isabel asked.

"No, but . . . forget it, you would never understand."

"Don't worry, honey, he will call," Isabel said, and that spooked Lila out.

Days later the phone rang. It was Jacques.

"Hi," Lila said in a breathy voice, trying to sound indifferent.

"I am sorry."

"About what?"

"About not calling."

"I hadn't even noticed," she lied.

"I need to see you."

"You can come over if you want."

Lila didn't plan to do anything with him but she shaved her legs and perfumed her body anyway. She made sure her sheets smelled fresh and double-checked the condoms. Just in case, she said to herself.

He knocked softly on the door. She opened it and hurried him in. The last thing she needed was to have her nosy neighbors gossip about her.

Once he was inside, he took a deep breath. He dropped his bag, took off his jacket, and hugged her as if he had been on a long journey.

Lila gave in to his soapy smell and forgot she was mad at him. He kissed her forehead like he did the last time and then her lips. He lifted her up and carried her into the bedroom. And without asking or hesitating he pulled up her skirt, slid down her thong, and licked her inner thighs until she squirmed down so his lips were back at her mouth. She slipped off her shirt, then peeled his off. His chest was hairless like she'd imagined and his skin was soft except for his elbows and the back of his arms. She didn't hesitate to pull out his penis, pushing his pants down with her feet. They were naked and he didn't open his eyes, so she closed hers and he entered her in short thrusts. He slowly opened her up with each thrust, being careful not to hurt her.

As he pushed his tongue deep into her mouth he took her fingers and placed them on her clit, so she could touch herself. She had never touched herself while with a man. He grabbed her hair gently. She felt the pull of it run straight through her body, from her scalp to her crotch. His other hand held her breast, clamping her nipple just so when he felt her shiver with desire. He didn't make a sound, or say anything. She didn't ask him to put a condom on and felt reckless. She couldn't stop herself. She wanted more. She wanted him to come inside of her even though she didn't take the Pill and she could possibly be ovulating. The thought of being impregnated by him made her come. As she came he pulled out and came over her belly and thighs and collapsed over her, breathing hard in her ear.

"I could so easily love you," he whispered.

She didn't think it was the time to ask if he had any diseases. She just enjoyed the release. The laughter inside her heart. The tickle in her feet. She too could easily love him. They were of the same spirit.

*   *   *

He jumped into the shower while she cleaned up the bedroom, trying to erase any trace of their lovemaking. She felt like she had committed a sin of some kind and hated herself for being so irresponsible.

While he dressed, she sat on her bed in her underwear and watched him. She thought about how tight and young his body looked. He was her grandmother's color, a dark café con leche. She really could love him.

"Do you sleep with a lot of your clients?" Lila asked, not wanting to know the truth but intrigued at the possibilities.

"Some," he said. "But I have never met anyone like you."

The answer made her angry. How could you, she wanted to say but didn't.

"Do you usually use a condom?" she asked.

"Always," he said and then went to sit next to her. "There was one other time five years ago. But I have been tested since. I'm sorry I was so careless with you. I just didn't want anything between us. I forgot where I was."

She trusted his answer and wondered who this woman was. She became jealous and wondered if he kept in touch with her.

"She's the mother of my child and in a way my wife," he said, looking away. Lila saw shame on his face.

"So you're married."

"No. But we live together in a house in Brooklyn. My mother

lives upstairs and we have the apartment downstairs. I never loved her but I had to take care of her after I found out she was with my child."

"Why don't you leave her, then?"

"I promised I would never abandon her."

"Not even for me?" Lila said, and couldn't believe she'd said it.

"One day I will move her to Haiti, when my son is more of a man and won't miss his father. Then I will come back for you."

"What if I don't wait?"

He sat next to Lila and laughed at her youth. "We have already grown old together," he said. He was doing it again. Putting thoughts in her head. Hadn't she thought that the last time he had visited her? Or had he read her mind?

"We are just visiting each other once again. I recognized you the day I walked into your apartment. You must have recognized me. History tries to keep us apart. But don't you remember, we are both of the same land?"

Jacques finished putting on his clothes and said he would call when he was ready.

"You can call me whenever you want," he said. "I will always be there for you."

Lila didn't call. She didn't tell her friends. Even when her phone wasn't working she didn't ask Jacques to fix it. Every time Lila saw the phone company's truck she thought of Jacques. She wondered if he was the one driving and would check quickly in the mirror to make sure she looked decent.

KENJI JASPER

Little Get-Togethers

"*T*his is gonna be some real bourgie bullshit," Reynaldo Maat said, tightening one of the still-dreading locks on his crown. It was October 31, 1995, and he felt alone, even standing with his closest brethren. He did *not* want to be there, mixed in with the rest of the student body, done up like their favorite icons from a corrupt culture. Brothers and sisters wasting their time with drink and games while their entire community was in deep crisis.

He usually never went to these kinds of things. When he wasn't arguing with those Eurocentric fools his department called professors, he was in his rooming house on Fair Street, puffing on herbals and mapping out plans to bring black people toward a better day, even if he had to do it all by himself.

The young men surrounding him were equally dedicated to the cause, especially Rey's causes: the Saturday morning breakfast program, the after-school tutoring in the housing projects across from the school, the clothing drive each semester. They were his right-hand men, willing to do whatever it took to make his dreams real.

But they were also young black boys at the beginning of their sophomore year. And young boys, like even their most elderly counterparts, liked to get laid. And this party, in Dejoule' African, was where all the fly sistas would be, as well as the not-so-tight chicks who would be eager to let them hit it after a few drinks and compliments murmured in just the right baritone.

"Bourgie pussy is good as any other," Archie said as the line started to move.

"Whatever," Rey grumbled, feeling the pit of absence deep within him as they each paid the three-dollar cover and slid into the shadows of the club entrance.

It was a costume party and most had adhered to the theme: the expected vampires, witches, ghosts, favorite hoop stars, MC Hammers, and Sean "Puffy" Combses. These brothers and sisters had blown hundreds of dollars in celebration of the most pagan of all holidays.

"It's on!" Jamie yelled in his country tenor, not wasting any time as he started toward the light-skinned cutie on the other side of the club. Her short curvy frame was covered by a catsuit, her face adorned with a feline nose and drawn-on whiskers. Archie wandered toward the bar, where a brown-skinned hottie with a bad weave was packing a wonderful ass beneath the plaid skirt and thigh-highs of her Catholic schoolgirl costume.

Rey anchored himself to one of the walls and watched his boys kick their game. Special Ed's "I Got It Made" brought the dance floor to life. Young hands swayed in the air and secured the waistlines of African beauties. Plastic cups received alcoholic upgrades as green and blue lights washed the place cool.

Rey missed her. God, he missed her. He had been in this very same spot the first time he saw Pauline and that half-Haitian, half-Jacksonville behind jiggling to JT Money at that Florida Club party freshman year. They'd stolen glances at each other all night, and on other nights that followed. They finally talked when they'd ended up on the same train home from Lenox Square Mall. Soon after, their tongues formed a knot in the lobby of the Morehouse James dormitory. Then she allowed him to climb on top of her beneath the sea green Wal-Mart sheets of his dormitory. But it had been there, at Dejoule' African, where their love had begun, and continued, even in her absence.

Pauline had been everything his mother could have asked for: pre-law with post-grad plans for the Ivy League, gray eyes and hips that would make it easy to bear many grandchildren. Plus she'd been baptized at the age of nine, at her own request.

She was only the second girl he'd laid claim to in life. The first, Janay, had been much less savory in the eyes of Mommy Dearest.

Janay was a girl of five feet with hips almost as wide and the biggest titties in Southeast D.C. It was on that starry night at the end of senior year when she took Rey up to the roof of her building. The air gave them gooseflesh as they lay down on the beach towel Rey had stolen from his mother's linen closet. He remembered the warmth as he put two fingers between her sugar walls and felt that sweet and sticky fluid that seemed impossible to wash off.

He was not her first, nor her second, for that matter. But she'd said she loved him. And for Rey that was all that mattered. The sensation was beyond words as he'd entered her, her feminine ankles on both sides of his neck as he squeezed each breast as though it were trying to escape. Her nipples had hardened in his hands as his member explored her wetness unchecked. No latex, no Pill, just her hands pushing him out at just the right time, so that his semen could land between her 38Ds.

He remembered being able to see her breath in the air as she came, not while he was inside of her, but at the moment the long white bullet hit her sternum. She'd twitched and moaned in the grip of orgasm, until she looked up to see that Rey was afraid, his hands shaking as he pulled them away from her. Nobody had told him that girls busted nuts too. So she'd explained it with a smile as they dressed and headed back down to her house to watch BET while her mom was out with the boyfriend of the week. Three weeks later she was gone forever, shipped out to Juvie for robbing that liquor store with her two cousins.

Rey had thought of her often since that night, mostly when he and Pauline were doing it. He would always put her legs on his shoulders and try to make a handful out of her tiny breasts, vainly hoping to re-create that rooftop dream. But it never happened. She just lay there, wanting him to come after the first ten minutes, explaining that she was scared. What if the condom broke? Sex before marriage was a sin.

But that was the only area where he had any complaints. He loved Pauline more than he could say. Tears had stained his pillows for the weeks of nights he'd spent alone since she'd left for Italy. The letters helped, but they were nothing like his hands palming her ass while he slept, nothing like the sweet scent she'd left on his only pair of sheets.

*   *   *

"How come you just standin' here?" a raspy voice inquired. A chill rushed through him and he jumped, startled by this single sound in a room full of noise.

She had been inches from his ear. Her lips and eyes were painted deep black, the rest of her was wrapped in the same color. Thigh-high vinyl boots, fishnet garters, black vinyl skirt, and matching bikini top. Synthetic cornrows stretched tightly down her scalp. Apple martini in one hand, leather riding crop in the other. Rey stopped breathing.

"What?" he asked as she smiled with perfect teeth.

"Had a little too much to smoke, huh?" she said chuckling, referring to his previous blank stare. "That dank got yo' ass all countrified."

"Nah, sista," he replied. "I ain't been blowin' no trees tonight. I'm just doin' my thing."

She looked at Rey and smiled again. "Actually, it doesn't look like you're doing much of anything."

"Do I know you?" Rey asked, slightly annoyed, looking pointedly at her fingers on his dashiki'd shoulder. The sacrament of a woman's touch. "You seem to be a little too interested."

"No," she said. "But that doesn't mean that I don't know you."

"What is this, twenty questions?"

"I've only asked you two so far." She smiled back at him.

Rey felt a strange rush of pleasure at being pursued instead of being the pursuer. Day and night he denounced the enemies of his people, deprogramming boys and girls of the veneer of lies upon which many of their perceptions had been based. So it felt wickedly good to not have a handle on something, to just enjoy the orgasmic flood of submission.

"What do you mean, you know me?" he asked.

"I know your girl," she replied. The stiffening thing in his jeans went slack, the seductive rush fading as her shroud of intrigue dissolved into the familiar. He could hear the music again. The Fugees, "Killing Me Softly."

"Pauline?" he asked, finally getting a lock on his composure.

"You only have one girl. Don't you?"

"Of course," he said. His response should have been wittier, even though he had no real reason to care. "What, you a friend of hers?"

"I wouldn't say that." She grinned before taking a long sip from her drink. "We got a class together."

"Oh really? Which one?"

"Volleyball. But we're in different sections. Same time, same gym, though."

"Oh," he said. His eyes traveled the wonderland of her physique, stopping at the honeyed cleavage exploding from the strap around her torso. Her eyes met his.

"You like it?" she purred.

"Like what?" he replied, quickly cutting his eyes toward the bar.

"This," she said, putting both palms to her ample breasts and pushing them upward. Suddenly he had more saliva than he could swallow. And he was getting stiff again.

"Uh, yeah. It's nice. So you're supposed to be a dominatrix?"

"Wanted to be since I was a little girl."

"I didn't know it was a career choice."

"Hey," she said with a shrug. "You make the world. It doesn't make you."

"You'd make a good philosopher."

"Damn. I was aiming for a prophet."

"It ain't bad to aim high."

"Look," she interrupted. "Are we gonna dance or slapbox with our tongues?"

The girl singing the hook begged Biggie for one more chance as they took the floor, their bodies in just enough synch to make it work. Rey was nervous as he two-stepped to the beat. He hadn't danced in forever. The last time it had been to Stevie Wonder and Marvin Gaye, classics, at one of DJ Brett's parties on Cascade Road. Biggie was for those wannabe players, all the young black boys who dreamed of being exactly what the community did not need.

But the dominatrix before him was so fluid as she ground her pelvis against him, taking him lower than he could go and back up again, smiling all the while. Why didn't Pauline move that way? How come she'd never danced the way she had at that first party when they'd met? Why did they waste calling-card time with hills of words made of nothing, empty talk about what classes she was taking and her dilemma about what she was going to do for Spring Break?

But he loved her so much. And she was a good woman, one who would stand by his side through all that the revolution might bring, a cute little southern thing tailor-made to fit on his arm, no matter the occasion. Pauline didn't smoke or drink and refused to eat dairy or refined sugars. She was perfect for the elaborate fantasy he had constructed for himself.

But Pauline was not at Dejoulé tonight. She was not the one dressed like a harlot and making it look good on the dance floor. Songs changed and sweat streamed from their pores. Within an hour it was he who was holding her glass while she playfully tapped that leather crop against his backside to D'Angelo's "Brown Sugar."

Archie and Jamie had vanished hours before with the objects of their affection. DJ Mars was starting to repeat records, the telltale sign that the party was almost over. The mystery girl took his wrist and led him to a corner, where she brought her painted lips to his ear.

"I didn't know you could move like that," she whispered.

"There's a lot you don't know about me," Rey answered, swaying to the Bacardi in his system.

"I know," she said. "Let me walk you home so you can tell me more."

"Walk me home? Shouldn't it be the other way around?"

"Safety ain't always determined by what you got between your legs."

"True," he slurred, making a note to himself that his liquor tolerance was shit. "Why not? We can talk, sit down and have some tea or something."

"Yeah, right," she said grinning. "Tea."

*   *   *

Ray looked her up and down in the blue light of his bedroom, taking in the firm curves on her divine frame. His dick was even harder than his decision.

"I don't even know your name, sista," he said, closing the door to his room. She pulled the dashiki over his head, then removed the drawstring slacks and tan huaraches.

"Does it really matter?" she asked, breathing heavily as she rose to her feet and removed her top. Her breasts fell less than an inch, perfect melons with tiny, purple nipples. She released the straps at her hips and gravity did the rest, leaving nothing but the black satin that covered her pelvis and the belt and garters that secured it.

Rey started to say something, a question as to whether or not this was the right thing to do, though it would have been only for the sake of his conscience. But her palm covered his lips, implying that silence was best. As she removed the white briefs that covered his nakedness, he thought his final coherent thought before impulse took hold.

Why were they here? Why hadn't he stopped it back at the club when he'd been thinking of Pauline? Why did he feel so helpless now, lying on his back on the full-sized mattress with the splintered box spring? And most important, what was it about helplessness that made him feel so alive, more electric than he'd ever been, brimming over with an excitement he hadn't felt since Janay?

But all thought subsided when lips and tongue surrounded the bulb of him, the unbridled wetness Pauline never allowed him to indulge in. Her range of motion was incredible, as she sucked him toward her tonsils, sending sparks through each and every limb. Her manicured fingers pinched a nipple while the other hand stroked his shaft.

God's face was becoming visible behind his eyes. When he felt that rumbling deep within him, he used his hand to try to push her away, not wanting to violate her in this way. But she slapped his hand away, wanting to keep going. The white mercury rose to the top and continued upward, spilling into her mouth. His face flushed, his head spinning as it hit the mattress.

"Did you like that?" she whispered, wiping her lips with his sheet.

"Yeah," he said, forcing the words out through his own heavy breaths. Every taut muscle had gone loose, a young black male libido fully satisfied. Then reason began to kick in. The questions were returning. Pauline's face was superseding the Lord Almighty's as he thought his six minutes of pleasure were about to expire.

"Good," she said. He raised his head to see her removing her last silken shred of clothing. " 'Cuz it's your turn."

She straddled his face before he could decline, nectar already spilling onto her thighs. Her scent brought his middle leg back to attention and his tongue to the magic spot just below her pelvis. He plunged deep within her and then came out to flick at the pearl in front. The more he did it the louder she moaned above him, making his housemates more and more aware that "Revolutionary Rey" was not keeping company with his usual black queen.

But that didn't stop him from doing his thing. He ground his nails into her fleshy thighs as she came, her body shaking, palms against the wall to keep her from falling over. There was something in their reciprocity that made him let it all go.

There were four rubbers in the desk drawer. And he used them all, entering her from the front and rear, on top, bottom, and that awkward thing they do on their sides in pornos. Teeth worked nipples and clit alike, his tongue to ankles, heels, fingers, and toes.

And she came right back at him, a woman with no name, and no shame, her aim seeming only to push him back to the place that had existed only in his mind on the nights he spent alone, a stroking hand to his hardness as he tried to re-create the stuff of his dreams.

Then he came, into latex, then onto ass, and against her breasts in the position Janay had made famous. Then they both collapsed, fading into the deep sleep of passion well spent, their individual lives existing only on the other side of dawn, a dawn they would not greet together.

* * *

Rey woke just after sunrise, his head clouded and slightly hungover. His sheets were stained with the scent of her. A handwritten Post-it on his monitor screen read: "You're more than she'll ever know."

He burned the note in the blue candle he used for cleansing, washed the sheets, tossed the dashiki, and flooded the space with frankincense. Neither Archie, Jamie, nor anyone else ever asked about that night, or remembered the girl he described.

Sometimes he would sit on the campus quad and spend hours searching for her face and that wonderland of a physique that went with it. But he never found her. Perhaps it had all been in his head, an overblown fantasy enhanced by something extra in the last bag of dank he'd snagged from his dealer. Pauline returned the following semester and life went on, as it should have, on and on, and on, until . . .

"Honey, can you go get the hummus?" Pauline asked, turning her cart toward the produce aisle. She'd changed her hair from box braids to African twists, the current rage at the Fort Greene salon where she spent too much dough getting her hair and nails did.

He could see the excitement in Pauline's eyes. She loved to entertain, to paste on that prefabricated smile and pour Merlot into Waterford goblets, the perfect wine to go with the latest vegetarian dish from *Essence,* the one she'd shared with his mother the last time they went to visit. Sometimes it seemed as if Mama loved her more than the only son she was always lecturing about doing something with his life, even when he had the car, crib, and a cart of degrees to prove otherwise.

"Sure, honey," he answered with a grin. "I'll find you." His wife of seven years nodded and pushed their overflowing cart away from him, arugula and bok choy on her mind.

He sighed as soon as she was out of view, temporarily raising the mask under which he lived, the personification of a Dunbar poem. The world saw him living his dream of an Afrocentric life. He had become a teacher, an educated black man trained to plant jewels in the minds of youth who didn't know the game. It was his job to derail the runaway trains of ignorant perception they believe to be the truth. And he had done it well.

But it had taken its toll on the idealistic views he'd had back in undergrad. He'd had to learn compromise, and to accept the painful fact that things might never be the way he'd seen them in his mind when his 20s were still fresh and new. Such had been the case with Pauline. And there were times when it wore on him.

He caught a glimpse of bootyliciousness as he turned onto aisle four, a little light-skinned shorty of 20, a girl child of four in the cart that she might have spat out, another boy of a few months strapped to her chest. No ring on the left-hand finger. Her onion was a thing of beauty as it swung from side to side like a perfect pendulum.

Rey pictured himself at her home, probably some hole in Bed-Stuy with ratty furniture, the TV on in the other room to entertain the kids while he banged the shit out of her against the wall in the single bedroom where they all slept. He imagined what it might feel like inside walls stretched by the labor of multiple childbirth, so warm that he'd want to disappear inside and stay there forever, at least until it was time to teach his next class.

Her ass vanished from view and the fantasy went along with it. Hummus was on the refrigerated shelf to the left and he snatched it up, suddenly feeling bitter about the latest near-wet dream he'd never have the nerve to make real. Divorce was a bitch, especially when you made yourself the reason for it. Vows were to be taken seriously. And that was that.

But Pauline had been even more still than usual in the sack. He'd often catch her looking over at the clock as he moved inside her, waiting for him to come in their once-every-three-weeks sessions. And when he did she would slide out from under him, lamenting about the day at the office ahead, and then drift off.

"Why the fuck are you with her?" Jamie would gripe during their Friday night pool games on Flatbush Ave. "She can't have no kids. What kind of a hold you think she's got on you?"

Other men might have splintered Jamie's face into a million pieces. But Rey would just look on, telling himself that Jamie could never understand, because he wasn't married. Jamie was running the streets with whores and headcases, while Rey had a good woman. Pauline was a good wife, a wife whom everyone loved at their parties. She knew when to laugh and what to wear, when to be supportive and when to shut up. She was what every man said they wanted in a wife.

"Here you go, baby," Rey said minutes later, handing her the sealed container. He hated that hummus shit. But it didn't hurt him to put it out for the rest of them to suck up.

"Perfect." She smiled, kissing him on the cheek. "Now we can check out."

"So who's coming through tonight?" he asked from behind the wheel of whichever coach they were driving that year. His eyes caught spaghetti straps on the street swelling with cleavage, fudge jugs jingling like LL's baby. Something firm pressed against the crotch of his Dockers, reminding him of the sizable organ he often forgot he had.

"My spesh and her new boyfriend," she answered.

"Spesh" was short for "special," a term of endearment for the senior who had beaten and humiliated her for a semester when she was pledging. She was often heard of, but had never appeared in person. Over the years she had a knack for never ever being where he was at the same time.

"You mean Batgirl?" he joked.

"That's her," she said with a chuckle. "Though you better not say that to her face."

"You know I won't, honey," he replied slyly. "You know I won't."

* * *

A pedestrian journey to the local liquor warehouse. White wine to go with the squash and shallots, maybe a tiny bottle of JD for the walk back. But he knew the wife would check his breath in her own subtle way, a peck on the lips just after the doorbell to make sure all was right as rain. And he wouldn't want to hear about it later. Besides, he'd already downed a better elixir, sticky green mixed into the ball of leaves in boiling water. Add the honey first and the cannabis smell went undetected. He could feel it more and more with each step he took, that feeling of fingers massaging the cells and synapses within his brain.

He stopped with the bag of bottles in hand to see his reflection in a bus stop shelter. Locks long since shaved down to a Caesar, the little pouch slowly making its way over the belt line beneath his overcoat. He'd become a living sketch from his teenage nightmares, the campus activist who hadn't been active since college.

This was not the way it had played on the silver screen in his head. He was supposed to be in Africa learning his lost history, building a family residence with his own sweat, storming the Senate mid-session to take a stand for reparations. And Pauline was supposed to be there right behind him, her belly swollen with yet another child in the army he wanted to build. It had all been in living color back then. Now it was just cold black-and-white stills, images rotting beneath the cellophane of scrapbooks barely viewed.

*   *   *

"Are you going to wear that shirt?" she asked him an hour later. It was a beautiful gray of Egyptian cotton, more than respectable. But Pauline didn't like it. It was too . . . shiny. But there was no time for him to change as the guests could be heard climbing the stairwell. Rey knew her every thought before she thought it, and yet he kept swallowing that blue pill, trapping himself in his own matrix of mediocrity.

He'd often thought of the woman in black and that night so long ago. Of the scent of nylon and the glowing flesh on her thighs, the way he'd buried both heads inside of her, slurping the honey of a goddess in hopes that it might give him eternal life. But it had ended. She had vanished. Now he was married, successful, and without a shred of proof that she'd even existed, until Pauline opened the front door.

Time had hit every friend and former lover he'd seen like a locomotive: spare tires and receding hairlines, sagging tits and stretch marks. But there she was, a decade later, looking exactly the same, only less slutted out. Anne Klein heels with matching hose. Leather skirt and a periwinkle blouse that flaunted the lovely ta-tas underneath. She had come back to him. The power of suggestion had brought his fantasy back into reality.

There were the usual smiles and screams that sistas give in greeting, a light hug that showcased the junk in both of their respective trunks. He imagined the three of them skipping the meal to indulge in a ménage. Then someone came in behind her.

"Damn, girl, you ain't changed a bit," the man said, dressed in that signature jacket/golf shirt combo made popular by most of his fellow alumni. Rey watched his eyes as they moved toward Pauline's behind.

"You know Renee and James, don't you, honey?" Pauline asked. Their eyes met.

"I think I saw you two around," Rey said, shaking her hand as formally as possible.

"Yeah, I think we had gym together," James said, extending his hand. Rey flashed a grin as he then remembered the scrawny little nobody with the patchy beard and no friends, who'd pledged just to be popular.

"I was a year ahead of you," Renee explained, slipping out of her coat. Her cleavage swelled in the V of her blouse. "But I think I remember your face."

Dinner convened. Drinks followed. Idle chatter reigned supreme. Liquor mixed with what was left of the high in Rey's system and he found himself afloat, pulling the right words out of his ass to hold it together. Every time their eyes met, Renee would make some movement, the friction of one nylon crossing over the other, the subtle adjusting of her bra, the swaying of hips and ass as she went to the "little girls'" room.

It all took him back to the bluish tinge of that magical night, of the strength in her quads as they clapped against him in the greatest ride of his single life, the taste of nipples wide and thick, the way she moaned as he took them between tongue and teeth.

It had been more than he'd ever known since. The memory got a rise out of him, a stiffening limb climbing toward his zipper.

He crossed his legs to hide it, but Renee saw, and grinned as if in reaction to something said, the trite joke Pauline made while James continued to look her up and down.

"Real estate's just getting ridiculous in this neighborhood," Pauline proclaimed as Rey poured another round of cognac. His eyes glazed over as he took in what he could no longer have, what he needed more than air in the prison of a world he'd built for himself.

He had to find a way to get her alone, though there was none he could think of. She was an interior decorator. He was a professor. No common ground. No legitimate reason to fraternize in the mind of a wife with superhuman senses. He was doomed, unless he thought of something. Ninety minutes had passed, more than three quarters of the length of time Pauline's little get-togethers usually lasted.

"So you were a year ahead of us?" Rey asked Renee, for another taste of eye contact.

"Yeah, and I spent my last semester abroad. So no one really saw me my senior year."

"But she had plenty of time to pledge me," Pauline joked.

"That I did." Renee laughed.

Rey couldn't forget the months Pauline had spent online, time she'd spent holed up in rooms, communicating with him only through e-mail and answering-machine messages. Only a quickie sex session or two in the duration.

"You were all she used to talk about," Renee continued.

"Every five minutes, 'Reynaldo this, Reynaldo that. Let me tell you about Reynaldo.' She loved you more than anything." She finished the sentence with a smile.

Rey couldn't imagine Pauline talking about him that way, not with all the years he'd spent since, feeling out of place, as if anyone could have held the husband position with the same result. But it made him feel good to remember that it hadn't always been that way, that once upon a time he had excited her enough to tell anyone who would listen. She'd even told her point woman in pledging about her man.

It all might have connected more quickly without the alcohol. He might have been a little more swift without the weed. It came to him only when the dinner guests were rising from their seats, and Pauline was handing them their coats. What had that note he'd burned in the candle said? "You're more than she'll ever know."

Renee had sought him out that night. She had stalked the mouse when the cat was away and trapped him in his own hole. She had used him, used what she knew to get what she wanted, to validate things the naïve pledge had foolishly confided. And he had been a willing accomplice.

It was so evil, so bad, so manipulative. Then she'd disappeared without a trace and played it cool ever since. And here was Pauline, still unaware, making Renee food and serving her drinks. A chill went through him as he shook her boyfriend's hand. Renee offered him a warm hug and subtly ran a nail across his widening love handle, letting him know that it had been good to see him.

Pauline walked them downstairs, while Rey cleared the

glasses from the coffee table, still reeling from the revelation. Then sobriety slowly took hold.

What had he been doing for all of these years? Why had he taken this path when there was another that could have taken him so much closer to the Promised Land? Why hadn't he asked for her number, demanded her name, or awakened to beg her to make their night more like a lifetime?

Why had he chosen the woman someone else had wanted, a choice dictated by a mother who'd never felt a thing for him since the day he came into the world?

"Fuck subtlety," he thought as he staggered toward the door. "Now or never."

He didn't know what he was going to tell her as he trudged down the stairs. The autumn chill bit into him as he reached the street. He looked left and right, searching for Renee, but found only Pauline.

"What are you doing?" she asked, a hand on her hip.

"Where'd they go?" he stuttered. "I wanted to see them off."

"Well," she said, grinning. "They're gone. But I'm here. Why don't we head up and get that kitchen squared away."

Rey strained his eyes scanning the street, thinking that the car might double back, that the object of his secret desires might return for some unnamed reason. But there was nothing, only what he already knew, the life that had once been a dream had morphed into his worst nightmare.

"Yeah," he whispered, almost losing his balance. "Let's square away those dishes."

ASHA BANDELE

My Brother's Wife

When we were young, brand-new teenagers and it was the summer before we entered high school, Marie Masters, Lisa Fisher, Valerie Johnson, and I would have sleepovers. We were going to be split up, sent to different schools, and we wanted to spend as much time together as possible. We each felt as though we were going off into exile or to serve some long, harsh prison sentence.

Most of our days that summer were spent in one of our backyards, or else at the mall, the movie theater, or the Baskin-Robbins. Nights we'd gather in one of our bedrooms and compare horror stories about who had the meanest parents, the biggest breasts, and the most boys who liked them. Lisa always won the mean parent part with nightmarish tales about her grandmother, Ms. Walker, who was raising Lisa after her mother "got sick," a result of the "no-good, lazy-ass drunk" who impregnated her and left her as soon as her stomach got big and "she lost her shape." Two years after he left, someone saw Lisa's mama wandering the neighborhood in her bra and slip. As the story goes, Lisa was found at home, sitting in the middle of the floor in a diaper full of piss and shit. Her grandmother came up to our New Jersey town from Alabama fast as light, and grabbed up the baby before the state claimed her for good.

Ms. Walker told anyone who would listen that she had a second chance with Lisa; that she hadn't watched over Faith, Lisa's mother, closely enough, which is how she'd got mixed up with "that no-good drunk in the first damn place." That wasn't going to happen to Lisa. Every day we'd hear stories from Lisa, pretty, shy, scared Lisa, about her imposing grandmother who made her memorize biblical passages and recite them each morning before breakfast. If she missed even a word, her grandmother was quick to get the yardstick, or worse, send Lisa outside to cut her own switch. And then there were stories about an 8:30 bedtime, unending chores, and a vigilant scrutiny over whom Lisa could befriend.

Perhaps because our parents were members of the same congregation as Ms. Walker, Valerie, Marie, and I made the cut. But we knew we had to be careful. In Ms. Walker's presence, we behaved like the daughters who exist mostly in the prayers of worried mamas and daddies. Of course, once we were alone, those masks cracked, or more accurately, we smashed them to bits with our womanish words and desires—and finally actions.

It was actually Marie, our de facto leader, who suggested it. She said since we were going to high school, obviously it wouldn't be long before we'd have boyfriends, and we didn't want to seem as though we were young, unable to handle their attentions. She suggested we teach each other how to kiss, so when the time came, the boys would be impressed. This seemed to be make sense, but I suspect it appealed to our own unspoken need to be wanted. I suppose the real fear then—in that summer before we were to be separated from each other for the first time since kindergarten—was that we'd go to some new school, some foreign, unfriendly landscape, where no one would want us. We never articulated that fear aloud, but looking back now, I see that it was there, present behind our wide brown eyes and 13-year-old imaginations.

So we partnered: Valerie and Lisa, and Marie and I. We agreed to take turns playing "the man." Marie set it off the first time. We were in her lavender bedroom with the butterfly decals on the walls when she began lecturing us. "When you do agree to kiss him, act reluctant, then blow his mind," Marie instructed, moving toward me. "Like this."

Then Marie, who always won in the big tittie department, slowly sauntered over to me where I sat on her bed. She pushed me back and straddled me, brushing her big breasts against my face, and then kissed me. Prying my lips open slightly and gently with a finger, she licked my lips and then pushed her tongue deep inside my mouth. When she started grinding against me, I began to move too. I closed my eyes and kissed her back. My hands held her by the back of her hair. She reached back, took one of them, slid it up under her shirt. I followed her lead, moving my hand up to her breast, teasing her huge, hard nipples with the tip of my finger. And then it was over.

Marie pulled her slight, cocoa-brown body off my lap, and whispered, "That's enough, Erica." I took a deep breath. I thought I had gone too far, had stepped out of my role and into myself.

Then Marie turned to Valerie and Lisa. "There. See what I mean?" she said, giggling. The other girls started giggling. Then I started to giggle too, but I giggled, I was sure, for quite a different reason. I was nervous, worried they might have seen my desire. Thought they might have somehow sensed the aching, the pulsing between my legs, the warmth and wet that had taken over the center of me. But no one seemed to notice.

Then Marie said she was hungry, and just like that, we were trampling down the stairs to scavenge for cookies and chips in her kitchen. Variations of that night went on all summer long, and when the summer gave way to autumn, so too did we give way, our little group, broken up, gone off to grow and kiss and cuddle with others.

*   *   *

As high school wore on and my sexuality took conscious shape in my head, and I began to date and kiss boys with hard, fast hands, I would think back to Marie. Even with Edward, my first love, my prom date, the boy I thought I surely would marry, Marie was there. I remembered her clearly on the day when I decided I would let him pull down my panties and go all the way inside of me. I thought of Marie that day, thought of her when he touched me.

We'd spoken little, Marie and I, during our years spent in different high schools, with new friends. But on that cool afternoon in Edward's tiny, messy bedroom with its old, dark blue curtains, its no-longer-white walls, its narrow unmade bed, and the Isley Brothers singing "For the Love of You" as the soundtrack to our romance, I took my shirt off slowly and sauntered to Edward the way Marie had come toward me almost four years earlier. I then straddled Edward just as Marie had straddled me that hot, hot summer. I parted his lips with my fingers, sucked his bottom lip, flicked his tongue with my own, and put his hands under my shirt.

Before I knew it I was on my back and he was standing over me with all his clothes off. I'd never seen him naked before. He pushed my skirt up around my waist and pulled my panties down. I lifted my legs so he could take them off. "You sure about this, Erica?" He asked because he loved me, because Edward was a good and gentle soul. But his eyes were pleading, *Don't, baby, please don't change your mind.* I looked at him and said, "I'm ready. Just go slow, okay?"

"Okay," he agreed, lowering himself onto me, pushing my legs back. He kissed me deeply, moved inside of me slowly. I raised my hips to meet him. And in that moment, in that way, I lost my virginity. I was in love with Edward. But I was thinking about Marie.

*   *   *

Edward and I tried to hold on to each other after we headed off to separate universities. He went to Emory as a pre-med student. I ventured west, to UC Berkeley to study literature. After a year, our phone calls, already infrequent after the first semester, stopped altogether. Occasionally we'd email. But mostly we were caught up in our new lives, and romances. I spent the last two years of my college career editing our student literary journal and being wildly in love with a philosophy major from Brooklyn who'd changed his name to Jalil. By my senior year, we were engaged, and when I called my family to tell them, my mother laughed out loud long and hard.

Surprised and then insulted, I demanded—as much as you can demand with your mama—to know what was so funny.

"Well, I guess it's gonna be a double wedding."

"What do you mean?"

"Well, not two hours ago, your brother called and told me the same thing!"

"*What?*" I tried to imagine what sort of woman would marry my brother. Alan was fine, an inheritor of my father's perfect face and big, strong body. But I'd always thought he was cheap, self-centered, and generally annoying. The best two years of my high school life began when I was a sophomore and he headed off to Syracuse on a football scholarship. The house was so much quieter without all those girlfriends of his calling every fifteen seconds. Food was more plentiful. The bathroom stayed clean, and I stopped getting hounded to "loan" money he almost never paid back. Alan getting married. I wondered if the girl was "in a situation" and I'd become an aunt in a few short months.

"He's marrying a young woman who went to Syracuse with him." She paused, and then added, "And you'll never guess who she is." I didn't have a clue and said so.

"Marie. Marie Masters. Remember her? From when you were little? Isn't that funny," my mother said, and started laughing again. I laughed too, but inside, something was churning in my stomach.

"Mom! How could you not tell me he was dating Marie? I didn't even know she went to Syracuse."

"Erica, first of all, change that tone when you talk to me."

"Sorry."

My mother's anger, as usual, quickly subsided. "Listen. You know how your brother is." She sighed. "He didn't tell me either. Never brought her to see me. Apparently they haven't been together *that* long. He did mention once, quite some time ago, that he'd seen her on the campus, but it went in one ear and out the other. You all haven't been friends in so long, and that's when Grandpa was sick, and I just forgot about it. Anyway, he certainly didn't tell me anything except that he was seeing someone he wanted me to meet. Okay? I was just about to call you."

* * *

When Marie and I reunite, we are best friends again, doing everything together. We visit reception halls all across Jersey until we finally settle on the Turner Mansion, an elegant black-owned establishment in Montclair that would be an easy drive from the church. We debate colors for our bridesmaids' dresses, and the proper menu for the reception, agreeing on roast and stuffed Cornish hens, mustard greens, new potatoes, and a premium bar.

The bridesmaids—all 12 of them—wear gold satin gowns with spaghetti straps and a simple bodice we figured they could cut into mini-dresses and wear to a club. Marie and I get different cakes—mine chocolate with vanilla icing, hers lemon with vanilla icing. Our gowns complement each other: The material and beadwork are the same, but the necklines and sleeves are different. We look like twins, I think, when I see us standing shoulder to shoulder in the dressmaker's mirror.

Marie tells me that since she started dating my brother, she'd pried information about me from him. She says she didn't call me because they wanted to work out their relationship before involving anyone else. When she finishes I feel as though I've been kicked in the chest, in the heart.

We laugh about this odd turn of events. I tell her I can't believe she loves my brother, and she says she can't believe it either, but he's not the same annoying kid she remembers from when we used to hang out. She asks me about Jalil, about my writing, where we finally want to settle down. We whisper secrets to each other, about the first time we had sex, about how many men we'd slept with before we met our almost husbands. We say why we love these men, and that it feels so right to be almost family to each other.

We spend one afternoon shedding tears over Lisa. At 16 she got pregnant and ran away to the Bronx with her 30-year-old boyfriend. People said she left because of her grandmother's fatal stroke a month earlier. The word around the neighborhood was that Lisa had four more babies now, and had contracted HIV. Valerie, Marie informed me, had graduated one year early and gone to Oxford. Marie tells me she saw her once a couple of years ago at the Garden State Mall. She said Valerie talked with an English accent and acted like she hadn't grown up in Jersey.

Marie and I talk about the wounds suffered during our separation. About the family members who died, the abortion she

had when she was a senior in high school. About the brief relationship I had during my second year in college with a man who
slapped me so hard I bled and swelled up so badly that I
couldn't go to class for a week. We talked about how lonely it
was when we all split up and went to different high schools. And
we wish that we could have saved Lisa, the sweetest, surely the
most fragile of the four of us. We talk about everything except
the one thing I have carried with me, the one piece of her that
has defined me all these years.

*   *   *

On our wedding day we are together, Marie and I, in her old
room. Our makeup is done, as is our hair, and we are about to
get dressed. Our mothers, who've been flitting about nervously,
finally leave us alone. I am wearing my bra, panties, stockings,
and garter. Marie has on her panties, stockings, and garter, but
hasn't yet put on her bra. I can see her breasts in the dressing
table mirror. They are full, brown, and beautiful, and her nipples
still stand erect. She stands up, walks over to me, hands me her
strapless bra, and asks me to put it on.

"Let me bend forward a little," she offers, "so these big ole titties get all the way in this thing." I bend with her, our hips
touching, and fix the bra around her back.

"Whew!" Marie sighs, straightening up. "Know what that
made me think about? Remember the summer we taught each
other how to kiss?"

I pretend to search my memory, and then I nod.

"Girl, I used to think about that summer sometimes. We were

definitely some sexy little things. You know, I used to actually get turned on. I think it was the intimacy, our friendship and closeness. We knew so much about each other, and then of course you touched me so gently, so openly. I had to work to teach men that later, and I swear, girl, you don't know how many times I'd be dating some knucklehead and think, I just need to get with a woman." Marie laughed, and then she continued, "But you know, I just can't give up the dick. The dick is like crack. Know what I mean?"

"Yeah, girl," I said, hoping I didn't sound like I was lying. I remember thinking then, in that moment, if she had asked, I might have given up the promise of my comfortable life with Jalil, and run away with Marie. Defied expectation, everything. I thought that, and then I pushed the thought away.

*   *   *

We are mothers now, Marie and I. She has two girls, and I have a boy. We live on different coasts. Marie is a stay-at-home mom, and my brother coaches college football. Jalil teaches in San Jose, and I edit a local women's quarterly. Our families gather together on holidays in New Jersey at either my parents' house or else at Marie and Alan's. We live great lives, defying divorce and other mean statistics. We own our homes, attend church, care for our aging parents. Our children listen to hip-hop, and each plays an instrument. They all excel in school; my boy loves to read, and Marie's oldest just skipped fourth grade.

For us, life is filled and fulfilling, and even during the moments when one of us hits a stumbling block, we recover, knowing no life is ever perfect, and neither should we expect it to be. We stumble, and then remember all the reasons not to fall.

And from time to time when my sex life with Jalil hits a lull, and sometimes when it hasn't, I take off my clothes and lie down on my bed. I put my finger on my clit, and begin to rub. I close my eyes and see Marie's beautiful body. I imagine her nipples in my mouth. I imagine what she would taste like. I fantasize about us making love someplace in the home she shares with my brother. And I tell you, I cum so damn hard.

GAR ANTHONY HAYWOOD

Where He's Getting It Now

Lorraine was prepared to cheat on Phorbus for the rest of her life until she discovered the tapes. It wasn't that much of an inconvenience for her. Sneaking around behind her husband's back to get the kind of loving she deserved was a little awkward at times, it was true. But there was a challenge in the deceit that excited her too, and nothing about it afflicted her with the slightest pang of guilt. Why should she feel guilty about something Phorbus had brought upon himself?

Oh, he wasn't a bad husband in the classic sense, perhaps. For sixteen years, Phorbus Gettison had given Lorraine pretty much everything he had to give in the way of love and attention, and if he'd ever even looked at another woman twice, he had done it without his wife noticing. He was an ethical man and partner, well groomed and highly educated, and Lorraine had been happy with him in the beginning. But he was also soft, slow, and almost laughably innocuous, and finally, in the last three years, Lorraine had learned to detest him.

She had sold herself short, she realized now, giving herself up to such a puppy dog of a man when what she really needed was a tiger. Somebody who could not only put her in a big, fine house and hand her the keys to a brand-new Lexus every model year, but could also bring the heat in the bedroom. Make her slippery wet with just a touch of two fingers, then ride her all the way to the wire from every point in the saddle—north, south, east, west—until her sore and spent body had no more sweat to give.

If she cared to look back that far, which she didn't, Lorraine could almost remember Phorbus holding that kind of power over her. At least, she knew she could never have married him if he hadn't been able to approach it. And yet, when she looked at him now, beaten almost speechless by her obvious loss of interest, she couldn't for the life of her imagine him being anything more than serviceable as a lover. Were her memories of a sexually potent Phorbus Gettison all in her head? Had there really been a time when this man, so unfailingly good, kind, and generous, had rocked her world between the sheets?

Lorraine couldn't say for certain one way or the other, and she didn't waste a whole lot of time pondering the question. The past was the past, and whatever Phorbus had been to her once, he wasn't anymore. So she resigned herself to going through the motions of being his wife until either death put an end to her charade, or divorce offered her more in the way of escape than half of what they were worth together. Because Lorraine never settled for half of *anything*. That just wasn't her way. Being married to Phorbus Gettison, who made a very nice living as a graphic artist in Hollywood, afforded her the lifestyle she required if nothing else. She had no interest in living less large just to be free of a man she had already, to all extents and purposes, extricated herself from.

Or so she thought.

Lorraine wasn't accustomed to going through her husband's personal possessions, indifferent to all things about him other than his money, as she'd become. Her stumbling upon the trio of videotapes he had hidden in his office closet had been a jarring stroke of chance. She'd gone up to the office while Phorbus was at work to look for a fresh book of checks, and found the cassettes in an unlocked cashbox, dangling off the edge of an overhead shelf he must have thought she was too short to reach.

The three tapes were labeled in Phorbus's unmistakable hand with a simplicity that immediately tweaked Lorraine's curiosity, and treated her to an offsetting twinge of something she would have never thought her husband could still make her feel: jealousy.

Karen.

Alia.

Ginger.

Lorraine held her breath, ran her hands over each tape in turn like a museum curator examining a priceless artifact. They were former blanks, not pre-recorded. Either copies of other originals, something Phorbus had taped on television, or . . .

Something he had shot with a camera himself.

"Nooo," Lorraine said, whispering to an empty house.

It took her several minutes to move out of the closet, take the tapes downstairs to the master bedroom and the entertainment center there, her mind spilling over with outrageous visions of what she might see when she finally mustered the courage to pop one of the tapes into the VCR. She had never known Phorbus to care for pornography before; that kind of stimulation had always been more to her liking than his. Oh, he might occasionally buy a *Playboy* or two, maybe even a *Penthouse*, but ridiculous as it sounded, she suspected it was only for an article and not the centerfold.

But Lorraine realized now that this wasn't necessarily so. After all, what man openly shared his appreciation for photos or videos of other people slapping skin with his *wife?* If Phorbus were in fact into smut, Lorraine would be the last to know. His home office was a private space she almost never invaded, and for the last several years, she'd been more than happy to give him all the time shuttered up in there he wanted. The room was a veritable warehouse of electronic gadgetry Phorbus used for both work and play: a multimedia PC with high-speed Internet connection, wide-screen TV, VCR, DVD player, even a full stereo system. The truth was, given all his options, there was no end to the kinds of "hobbies" Phorbus might have developed up there without Lorraine's knowledge.

She powered on the television and VCR, eased the tape marked *Alia* into the mouth of the machine, and hit the Play button. Then she took a seat on the corner of the bed, heart in her throat, a tiny ball of anger tumbling about in the pit of her stomach.

The screen snapped to life, and the first thing she noticed was that the tape was homemade, shot with an out-of-frame camera in what looked to be a cheap motel room. Then, in sequence, other realizations dawned on her, each more stunning than the last: it was indeed an amateur sex tape, two middle-aged, physically imperfect black people banging each other silly with the slow, steamy need of crazed adulterers; the man was definitely Phorbus; the woman was definitely *not* Lorraine; and the room, wherever it was, had an odd quality of familiarity.

"Oh, my dear God," Lorraine said.

She let the tape run without interruption for a long time, horror and revulsion slowly sinking in. Phorbus and this short-haired bitch named "Alia," if that was really her name, were doing everything imaginable to each other, turning, rolling, flipping like chickens on a rotisserie so as to leave no erogenous zone unexplored by their mouths and hands, the tips of her breasts and the crown of his penis.

Lorraine would have almost found it funny, watching Phorbus the fool engage in such extended sexual acrobatics, were it not for the fact that, despite herself, she was rapidly becoming aroused by the show. This was the kind of lovemaking Lorraine used to both desire and excel at in her youth, before a marriage she had quit on like a diet she didn't have the patience to stick with anymore had worn her libido down to the nub.

It was hot and passionate sex, stone-hard and desperate, yet almost deathly silent; directions were given with actions, not words. Breasts were offered up for sucking in the cups of two hands, the head of a ready penis was waved like a flag before an open and eager mouth. Lorraine could almost smell the musk in the room as her husband went down on his partner again and again, watching her squirm and moan through eyes gently raised above the dark, sweet canyon between her open legs.

This was Phorbus? *Lorraine's* Phorbus? God*damn* his sorry black ass! And goddamn this cunt he was with, this "Alia," for having the audacity to take from Lorraine's husband something that wasn't hers to take. Where the hell had Phorbus found her? At work? Waiting tables somewhere? And what the hell was the point? Why *her*? Other than their hair and skin coloring— Phorbus's partner in the tape was substantially darker than Lorraine—the two women could have practically passed for sisters. Alia was a little trimmer, perhaps, and maybe younger by a few years, but she and Lorraine were both short, big-boned, and voluptuous. Hell, if the nigger was going to play around, shouldn't it have been with somebody who could offer him something Lorraine couldn't? Some new and different sexual experience he couldn't get from his wife right here at home?

Growing more enraged by the second, Lorraine forced herself to sample the other two tapes in her husband's illicit collection and discovered more of the same. Phorbus in two more nondescript bedrooms, fucking two other black hos with equal, if not greater, ferocity and imagination. "Karen" was a coal-black blonde with silver rings in her navel and right nipple, and "Ginger" was a high-yellow, Afro-wearing throwback to the 70s, tattoos festooned along the length of both arms. And aside from these minor details, that was where the physical distinctions between the pair essentially ended; once again, just like Alia, both women seemed to share the same basic frame with Lorraine, give or take an inch here or a pound there, providing further proof that Phorbus was an idiot, risking Lorraine's wrath to seek something from three strangers Lorraine could have given him in spades, had he only had the guts to ask for or, better yet, demand it.

Lorraine was livid now, but even more incredulous. She could never have guessed that Phorbus was capable of this, of breaking the vows of fidelity he'd made to her on their wedding day. On some level, they both knew, even back then, that Lorraine did hold such potential, that she viewed the promise people made to each other at the altar as mere words of blind faith, no more binding in the face of the hardships likely to befall a married couple than an unsigned contract. But Phorbus . . . Phorbus really believed in things like forever and always, and unwavering monogamy. Men always liked to say their word was their bond, but Phorbus was the only person Lorraine had ever met for whom it was really true. When Phorbus told you something, you could chalk it up as fact and forget about it, because he would either make it so, or die in the attempt.

As furious as she was to have just discovered otherwise, however, Lorraine wasn't really hurt by his deception until she'd gone back to the first tape again, the one featuring her husband and "Alia," and realized why the setting of their adulterous pairing had struck her as familiar: She had been there herself. With Phorbus. It was a motel they used to frequent years ago, before they were married, when sex between them was still new and spontaneous and fraught with the thrill of wanton lust. It was the Hoot Owl on Crenshaw, a bastion of one-night stands she passed by on occasion, but hadn't given so much as a thought to in years. It had been *their* place, hers and Phorbus's. How could the bastard have had the nerve to not only cheat on her, but to do it at the same establishment, perhaps in the very same room, on the very same bed, they had once called their own?

She watched the tape run and burned, heat coming off her

like a rock of glowing charcoal. Seeing Phorbus do things to Alia even Lorraine's present lover, a brainless stud she'd met at church six months ago, never thought to do to her: taking the bitch from behind slowly, deliberately, then turning her around to re-enter her from the front, curling her legs around his waist with his own hands, moving like a man who could wait as long as needed to ensure her satisfaction. His hands shifting modes constantly, brushing skin with a feather-light touch one minute, gripping and pinching flesh like a vise the next. And all through-out, Alia buckling beneath his generous ministrations with little more than a smile and a moan, her voice never once rising above a heavy sigh.

Lorraine finally killed the TV and threw the remote at the blank screen, blinking through a veil of tears that had come out of nowhere to blind her. She did not deserve this. She had been a good wife to Phorbus at first, faithful and loving; it was only when he had proven himself unworthy of her that she had turned cold and adulterous. Was his stifling ordinariness her fault? The pre-dictability others mistook for "reliability" and "loyalty," but which, by any description, only made all her days with him feel the same? With the prospect of living the rest of her life with a man who no longer excited her staring her straight in the face, had she any other choice but to seek that excitement elsewhere?

No, she decided. This was on Phorbus. All of it, both her be-trayal and his, and it was going to cost him dearly. What form it would take, and when, Lorraine could not yet say, but payback was coming. She would see to it.

She would see to it.

Lorraine stopped crying, sat up proud and erect, and took the three tapes back up to her husband's hiding place where she'd found them.

* * *

The inevitable argument came three days later.

Lorraine had said nothing to Phorbus until then, projecting only her usual degree of indifference and disdain toward him despite the constant urge she felt to blow up in his face. It had been like trying to hold a hurricane in a box, but she had managed. And if Phorbus suspected anything amiss, he never let on.

Like many of their squabbles, this one had been about his work, or, more accurately, Lorraine's total lack of interest in it. The latest B-film he had worked on was about to be released, and he wanted her to attend the Century City premiere with him. As usual, Lorraine said no. The kind of movies Phorbus was invariably involved in were big, loud, male-oriented shoot-'em-ups or space operas stuffed with explosions and cataclysmic collisions, and Lorraine was too old and intellectually advanced for that shit.

Besides, Phorbus's hand in a film was never, ever anything actually worth seeing, let alone making a fuss over. A black sky streaked with lightning, a two-lane highway corkscrewing up a craggy mountainside, a mothership depositing alien beings onto an open plain—tiny little pieces of an overall scene—this was what Phorbus toiled eight hours a day at the studio to create? This was his so-called *art*? Lorraine wasn't impressed, and never would be. So she told her husband no, she wasn't going to hold his hand at the premiere of a movie she didn't want to see unless it starred

Denzel Washington, who was contractually obligated to personally greet and French-kiss every female attendee at the door.

"But it's my work, baby," Phorbus said, hurt. "Why can't you ever come with me?"

She never felt anything more than pity for him at times like this. But today, it warmed Lorraine's heart to see the injury in her husband's eyes, knowing this was just the beginning of the suffering she had in store for him, lying, cheating dog that he was.

"Because I have better things to do, that's why."

"Like what?"

"That's my business."

"I'm your husband, Lorraine. We aren't supposed to keep secrets from each other."

Lorraine looked for some sign of irony in Phorbus's expression, but found none. If she hadn't known better, she would have thought he was sincere, that he really did believe that secrets between a husband and wife were out of bounds. She was flabbergasted.

"What did you say?"

"I said we shouldn't keep secrets from each other. I'm your husband, and you're my wife. If we really do love each other—"

"Love? You wanna talk to me about *love?*"

Lorraine lost it. Three days of pretending that the butt-naked trio of Karen, Alia, and Ginger hadn't been filling her head with moans and groans and exhortations to Phorbus to work his tongue on their clits faster and harder had finally proven too much for her to take.

"Nigga, you must be outta your mind. I don't love you. I haven't loved you for *years!*"

Phorbus's jaw threatened to come unhinged from his skull. "What?"

"You heard what I said. *Years.* And it's a damn good thing, isn't it? 'Cause you sure as hell don't love *me.* Do you?"

"I don't understand. Of course I—"

"I found the tapes, Phorbus! All right? So don't stand there and lie to me and say you love me, and respect me, and will always be faithful to me, 'cause we both know that's bullshit, and probably always was."

Her husband's face seemed to torque up in confusion. "Tapes? What tapes are you talkin' about?"

Lorraine had to release a little laugh, because it was either laugh at the man's nerve, acting like he had no clue what she was talking about, or go get a knife from the kitchen right now and cut his fucking heart out.

"*Karen*, Phorbus. *Alia,* Phorbus. You want the third bitch's name too? *Ginger,* Phorbus. All right? Do you know what I'm talkin' about *now?*"

Phorbus looked like a man poured from concrete. He seemed incapable of even blinking a single eye. Lorraine wanted to go on, she *needed* to go on, but she held herself back, choosing to extend her husband's discomfort and speechless stupefaction as long as possible. She watched his face and waited, her gaze begging the question: *So what're you gonna say now, nigga?*

"Oh, my God," Phorbus said. So quietly, she'd almost missed hearing it. And then he did something that changed the course of their lives forever.

He smiled.

Where the smile had come from, or where it was about to lead, Lorraine couldn't begin to guess: But it was enough by itself to set her off, turn the fire already raging inside her way up and beyond any point of her control.

The motherfucker thought this was *funny?*

Lorraine turned, marched out of his office to go downstairs and get the knife.

"Baby, wait!" Phorbus called after her, but it was too late, his voice just a spatter of sound against the blood pounding off the walls of her brain like a jackhammer.

She was halfway down the spiral staircase when Phorbus reached the first step, turned an ankle in his haste to catch her, and fell. Typical Phorbus. His body tumbled past her, grunting and groaning, with the speed and force of an elephant hurled from a cliff, and didn't stop until it hit the floor, landing with a deafening crunch that immediately turned Lorraine's stomach.

Reflexively, she ran down to him, giving no thought to what she was doing, or for whom. She was certain he had to be dead, so contrary to the human form was the orientation of his body, but she was wrong. Phorbus was alive. Blood was seeping in a rush across the tiles beneath his head, and his left arm was practically wound around his neck like a winter scarf, but his eyes were open and his lips were moving. He was trying to speak.

"Oh, Jesus," Lorraine heard herself say.

She took a step forward, started to lean down close to try and make out the words he was struggling to form . . . and then stopped, realizing she didn't really care that much what the message was that he was attempting to convey. Why should she?

Falling down the stairs hadn't changed anything; he was still a lying cheat, he had still betrayed her trust with at least three other women, and she still despised him for it. And Lorraine had another, even more critical thought: If she went to the phone right now to call 9-1-1, and the paramedics arrived in time to save her husband's life, she would only go on to despise him more as a cripple than she ever had as a whole man.

Through eyes fluttering with panic, Phorbus watched his wife straighten up and grow still, standing over him like a silent sentry who might never move again. Arms crossed, expression neutral. And just like that, Phorbus understood that he was dead. Even before Lorraine spoke the last words she would ever offer him.

"Tell it to Alia," she said.

*   *   *

For weeks after the funeral, Lorraine surprised herself by feeling something she never thought she would: loss. Phorbus was gone, and he had deserved to die, but his death had placed a void in her life she could not ignore, no matter how little sense it made to her. In his absence, her husband hardly took on the mantle of a saint in her mind, but those things he had given her as a partner that she had somehow found pleasure in became easier for her to appreciate. His laugh and generosity; the meals he cooked; the chores he did that served no purpose but to make her life, more so than his own, easier; all developed a clarity that was new to Lorraine, and they tugged her heart in directions she didn't care for.

In a desperate attempt to end this revisionist history her memory seemed to be writing about her late husband, she immediately put his things up for sale, hoping her last thought of him would go out the door with the last piece of his personal effects. All the clothes in his closet, and everything in his office—books, furniture, computer equipment, every last paper clip—was put up for sale, and at cut-rate prices so as to move quickly. And it did. When Lorraine's fire sale was over, there was no evidence of Phorbus Gettison's former presence anywhere in her house.

Except for the tapes.

They should have been the first things to go. Her husband shouldn't have been ten minutes in the ground when she tossed them into a roaring fireplace, or crushed them one by one under her feet like roaches she'd found scurrying across her kitchen floor. But it didn't happen. More than once, she had taken the three cassettes from the dresser drawer she'd banished them to, intending to destroy them in some spectacular, soul-cleansing fashion—only to remove them to the VCR instead. She was helpless to explain why.

And sitting there before the television, watching Phorbus fornicate with his three fellow adulterers as wildly and as guiltlessly as ever, her memory of him played yet another cruel trick on her: It corrected her recent perception of the sex she had once had with him as uninspired and dull. That was an illusion. These things he did on tape to three strangers, the sweat-washed worship he paid to their quivering bodies, she now recognized as things he used to do to Lorraine herself, a long time ago, before her loss of respect and affection for him turned her cold to his advances. And as this realization gradually dawned upon her, a point of fact she could no longer lie to herself about, she began to view the tapes with even greater regularity, seeing herself as Phorbus's partner in place of those who actually had been. She would touch herself as the VCR hummed on, the memory of his lovemaking no longer distorted by a screen of prejudice, and feel her nipples harden like stones, her inner thighs grow warm and damp.

Then she would kill the machine and put the tapes away, wondering if she had in fact done the right thing, standing idly by while a man who had played her for a fool slowly died.

*   *   *

The man who had bought Phorbus's computer equipment was a co-worker of his named Jermaine Grant, someone Lorraine had met only twice before, so when he showed up at her door one day a week or so after his purchase, she didn't immediately recognize him.

"Oh, of course," she said when he reintroduced himself.

He entered the house with what looked like a CD case in one hand, and an expression of grave discomfiture drawn on his face, what Lorraine might have expected a surgeon would wear to break the news to the family that a loved one had just expired on the operating table.

"This is going to be a little weird," he said.

"What?" Lorraine asked. "Was something wrong with the computer, or . . . ?"

He failed miserably to smile. "You might say that."

She waited for him to explain, feeling her patience rapidly waning.

"Ms. Gettison, were you aware that all of Phorbus's data files were still on his machine when you sold it to me?"

"Files?"

"The information on his hard disk. All his software applications and work files. Usually, when someone sells a used computer, they erase all the data from the disk first, to make sure whoever buys it doesn't get hold of any personal information they wouldn't want the new owner to have."

"Oh, Jesus." Lorraine finally found a reason to be concerned. "You aren't telling me all our banking stuff was on there? All our account numbers and passwords—"

Grant shook his head. "No, ma'am. That's not the kind of information I'm talking about."

"Then I'm confused. What kind *are* you talking about?"

"I was a great admirer of your husband's work, Ms. Gettison," Grant said, forging ahead. "He was a master of certain CGI techniques I've yet to master. So naturally . . . when I realized the disk on his PC hadn't been cleaned . . ." He shrugged. "I took a look at some of his stuff. And I ended up viewing a few files I'm sure he would have preferred I hadn't." He held the CD case out for Lorraine to take. "I've since erased all the files on the disk and backed them up to DVD." He blushed and said, "I'm sorry."

Lorraine took the disk from his hand, exasperated now. "I'm sorry, but I still don't understand. What are you apologizing for? You're acting like—"

And then it came to her, all at once, what this nervous wreck of a man's bizarre behavior reminded her of: A little boy who'd been caught stealing a peek up his momma's dress. Lorraine completed her sentence: "—like you've seen me *naked*."

Grant tried the smile again, and grew redder still.

"Oh, my Lord," Lorraine said.

"Please forgive me, Ms. Gettison," Grant sputtered. "I never meant to intrude. But the files all had generic names, by the time I realized what they were—"

"What kind of 'files'?" Lorraine demanded. "Speak English!"

"*Video* files. Six of them. It looked like three originals, and three copies he'd added effects to. But naturally, I only saw one, and only five, ten seconds of that, I promise you."

Six files? Video files of Lorraine naked? She couldn't comprehend it. Three originals and three—

Lorraine suddenly felt the blood freeze in her veins. She forced herself to speak.

"Waitaminute. These 'videos' you're talking about. You don't mean of Phorbus in a . . ." She stopped, forced herself to finish the sentence. ". . . in a motel room with three other women?"

Grant didn't seem to know how to answer the question. "It looked like a motel room, yes. But—"

"But *what?*"

"But there was only *one* woman. And it was you. He'd doctored your image to change your hair, and make you a little thinner I suppose, but . . . It was *you*." He watched Lorraine's face slowly disassemble, rushed to undo the damage he feared had just been done. "Again, I'm very sorry. If I had only known . . ."

But she couldn't hear his voice anymore. She couldn't hear anything. The only sound in the world she was aware of now was of the earth beneath her feet, grinding to a permanent and inexorable halt.

* * *

Late that night, Lorraine traced a fingertip along the underside of her right breast, the way time had finally reminded her Phorbus liked to do, and smiled.

There was little consolation now in the knowledge, of course, but it still felt good to know that Phorbus Gettison had been a man of his word, after all. He had promised Lorraine he would be faithful to her forever, and he had been. In the last three years of his life, he had been lied to, laughed at, and completely given up on, giving him every possible reason a man could ever want to run a game on his wife, and still, this was as close as Phorbus could come: fucking Lorraine herself in three different digital disguises. In a video she only now could recall starring in, once upon a time in her distant past, when the idea of making love to someone as "ordinary" as Phorbus Gettison before the lens of a running video camera did not strike her as disgusting and unthinkable.

Lorraine closed her bleary eyes, felt Alia's orgasm run through her like a charge of lightning, then hit the rewind button on the remote and lay back on the bed to wait.

It would be Karen's turn next.

JESSICA CARE MOORE

A New Tale of Two Cities

*I*t was the way he looked at me when I walked into the room. The pale colors of his high ceilings and Ralph Lauren–painted walls bloomed purple lotus petals and covered the space like the ivy of my childhood home. He could trace my sadness, the loss of my father too soon, the neglect from past and present lovers. He was simply my brother, my good friend, and I thought it was just supposed to be that way.

There was a time when another woman caller would have made me jealous, but I never let him see it. He was, after all, one of Harlem's most wanted and his mama had graced him with a name to match his history. Harlem was a tall enough man with a beautiful face blessed with Cherokee cheeks, lush feminine lashes, and long, thick, reddish-brown hair he kept in tight cornrows. He was a pretty nigga, but with enough edge to qualify for thug status. Harlem possessed an old-school pimp vibe, wearing Dobb hats and gator shoes you could find only on 125th Street. He was the guy on the block who could kick it with the street-corner hustler, made sure the elders of the neighborhood were respected, and played big brother to the latchkey kids. Everyone loved Harlem.

I can't believe I'm at his door at midnight,
hoping he didn't have company on the other side.

In our beginning, he would tell me stories of how he'd come home and this certain chick might be posted in his kitchen, completely nude, boiling water and cooking Newman's Own marinara and noodles. He was funny about what brands of food he ate. He'd argue that was what was wrong with our people, always accepting less. He thought watching his diet was important, and he ate only foods that served a purpose. For breakfast, he would eat hard-boiled eggs and wheat toast to help his digestive system. Whatever. We didn't always connect in that way. I was a Midwest girl, but my entire family was from down south. I grew up on mashed potatoes and gravy. Homemade maple syrup, thick-ass grits, scrambled eggs with lots of cheese, and even the culturally taboo pork bacon.

"She climbed through the window, Savannah! Climbed the freakin' fire escape. She's nuts, man!" Then he cracked up. When he laughed he used his whole face, and when he told a story he worked the room like an actor on stage.

She was always in his front row, but invisible, unlike the cute size $7\frac{1}{2}$ shoes lined up near the door of his two-bedroom condo. My size. I had to stop from making a fool of myself one particular morning. Something came over me, and I decided to try on the soft Japanese-style slippers that didn't belong to me and wear them home. I got as far as the sidewalk, then turned around and put them back in their purposeful place on his polished hardwood floor.

A few days later I examined a pair of white leather shell-toe Adidas. The laces were still brand-new bright, and I had a bad-ass jogging suit I could rock 'em with. She was trying to seem down-to-earth and ghetto fabulous, but I saw the stockings and corporate pumps from a mile away. I hated women who peed around their territory so obviously. Fuck it, I thought. She can have the shoe rack.

He was beautiful like Old Harlem—militant, un-gentrified. Harlem's walk was 125th Street confident, before Giuliani banished the West African vendors from the strip. He was never mine and always mine. That's the problem with male friends. In order to stay their homegirl, you can't ever fall in love.

Here I was, nearly 30 years old, standing at the door of a man waiting for him to save me. But not just any man, my friend. I waited for a sign to walk away, but it was too late. I'd already knocked softly and he was opening up a door he'd opened so many times in the past. Only tonight would be different. I straightened my posture and pretended to be thinking of nothing important at all.

I've known my power since I was 11. A self-proclaimed womanist, I started spelling my name with a small *s* after reading dozens of Alice Walker books and *Sisters of the Yam* by bell hooks. I stood there wearing tight red leather pants, dirty south painted on my arms, high black leather boots, deep red lipstick silhouetting a soft flowing Afro, and the invisible word "traitor" across my Sade forehead. I was going against all those self-help columns, *O* magazine bookmarks, Vanzant guidelines, and I Don't Need a Man weekend symposiums. I was a womb activist and I was running to the arms of the enemy to get my head right.

The Breakdown

I'd spent the entire week removing traces of my breakup from the walls, out of my photo albums, from inside the dresser drawers, nine boxes of memories given to the Salvation Army. I was beginning my life over again, and everyone knew it. It was like I'd sent out a press release with the headline: Famous Underground Vocalist Hits a Bad Note in Relationship!

I never expected my live-in boyfriend situation to last forever. I didn't believe in living with men. Always thought they should have their own space, because I definitely needed mine. Maybe it was the good dick, 'cause somehow I got suckered into Rico's dirty underwear on my bathroom floor every morning for two years. Harlem couldn't believe I was "taking in" a lover. I wish he would've fought harder, but I don't think he wanted to seem like he cared. And he knew I liked the idea of being domestic, washing clothes, cooking dinner, picking out cool desserts to share after a late-night movie from Blockbuster. Some regular life–type shit.

Despite my desire for a simple life, I knew I was not a simple woman. After many nights spent driving each other crazy, I decided I had to clean house. Rico had to go. Unfortunately, Rico Medina was a prominent community activist, a celebrity-status public speaker and organizer. It's like I broke MLK's heart or something. I'd never asked to be Coretta or Betty. My least favorite words in the English language became "Poor Rico." The sympathy-pussy posse couldn't wait to get his head on their shoulders.

I was entitled to a nervous breakdown. I painted my walls a deep blood-red with rustic brown trim. I bought long cranberry curtains to cover my windows. Purple tea lights and scented candles took over every room. Chocolate incense in the bathroom, nag champa in the sitting area. Every room in my crib had a prayer corner, an *amen sista-girl you gon' make it* energy, and what my vocal partner Uzuri described as my shrines in honor of all goddesses with broken hearts. Amen.

Opening Night/Closing Night

I was finally prepared to face my music. To push all my energy into my career, instead of hiding from my "public" on the black rock scene of NYC. I had a big show booked at CBGB's with a lineup of some talented young women, singing in the spirit of black rock-and-roll divas like Betty Davis and Tina Turner. I'd rehearsed a drummer that week, hired new backup singers, and would premiere my bass skills in front of all my fans, haters, and your basic nosey art-scene muthafuckas. I was ready to take them all into my witches' brew and then spit them out with black fire.

That was before the sympathetic faces began to haunt me. All those twisted-up looks of worry that followed me backstage. Their condoling hugs, like somebody had died. They didn't know I'd already lost the most important man in my life when my father died. How could this possibly be worse?

Everyone wanted me to seem sadder, to cry uncontrollably in their arms, to write new songs dedicated to my depression and shave my head in honor of the woman I was to become.

Opening night was not going well for me. Hard-rock diva Kali was just exiting the stage after an encore performance. The crowd was zoned out, possessed, overwhelmed by the mix of funk, sweet black pussy, and elegance. Folks had come out to watch and hear me bury myself in my heartbreak and maybe buy the new CD. I felt like Lauryn Hill with no money. I pushed my clothes into an over-sized jean purse, grabbed my bass, and headed for the back. I snuck a peek at the smoke-filled room full of Afro-jiggy folks. Then I slipped outside and faded into the darkness.

So . . . you're supposed to be my boy, right?

He finally opened the door. Music bumped loud from his system. I looked past him to make sure he was alone.

"Do you think it's weird that we're both named after cities?" I asked, walking in behind him. Me coming over was no big deal. I ran through his spot whenever I felt like it. I was hoping he would go into a funny monologue about names and how black folks should stop naming their kids after famous leaders or places hoping they would become deep thinkers. Instead, Harlem just stared at me.

"Must be nice. Your girl is out there grinding in grungy, smoky night clubs and you got your personal assistants ironing your boxers," I joked.

"What's up wit you, Savannah? You look shook, like you heard Kelis singing one of them songs you wrote on the radio. Don't you have a show to do or some men to kill? What are you doing here on the late night?" He opened his fridge and started to make a sandwich. I found a comfortable place on his neatly made bed. He lived like he was in a hotel, and most of the time he was. Some of the "big-boy" producers would get him a room in the city so he could be close to the studio. His place was cozy, with a small gas-burning fireplace in the living room, marble countertops in the kitchen, and heated tiles on his bathroom floor.

I never knew how to really talk to him when we weren't surrounded by the music. He was always talking, the music was always playing, but for the first time everything around us seemed still. I usually just blended in with the rest of his male friends, getting them beers, listening to beats, or watching basketball games. His world was rhythmic, full of uptown, Sugar Hill–type ambiance. His boys gave each other plays like synchronized handclaps, and the room was always clouded by weed smoke. Tonight Harlem looked at me with a decade of memories in his eyes. A curiosity I hadn't seen in years. He was such a ladies' man, but I knew he ultimately wanted more. Harlem was finally letting his guard down and for a moment imagining that *something more* as us.

I lit the black clove cigarette that was dangling from my mouth, biting down softly on my bottom lip, trying to be sexier than usual.

"I'm cool. Just working on the small hole in my lungs," I finally answered, full of sarcasm, blowing smoke circles in the air.

"You know, working on fixing one organ at a time. I'll start on my heart next week." I sounded pitiful, and I knew it. I couldn't believe I'd known him for close to 10 years.

The Meeting

Harlem practically lived in the recording studio when we first met on the D train. He was wearing headphones with an oversized *Scarface* T-shirt, a red hoodie, and black patent leather Adidas. His lack of interest in the sounds around him intrigued me. When I got up the nerve to ask what he was listening to, he ignored me.

"Whachu listening to?" I asked again, not caring that I was interrupting his private conversation with himself. I crossed my legs, then uncrossed them. I smiled defiantly, waiting for him to acknowledge my presence.

"I'm listening to me. My music. Why, you *into* music or just doing a train survey?" His arrogance was sexy and I knew right away I was dealing with a Leo. Of course he was listening to himself, who else exists for a lion?

"Actually I'm a composer of music, you know . . . notes and stuff . . . and I sing rock and roll. You ever heard of that?" I asked with a reflection of his sarcasm.

"Hip-hop is rock and roll, fashizzle," he added, finally taking a moment to take in the person speaking to him. I had on my favorite army-green tank and cutoff bleached jean shorts. My freshly painted gold toenails peeked outside camouflage flip-flops. An ankle bracelet partially covered the tattoo of my daddy's name in cursive black ink. My hair was pulled up in a thick nappy ponytail. No makeup.

"I *am* hip-hop. Yeah . . . that's right! KRS with a twist of Patti Smith flava," I teased him.

"Aiight, fire . . . you wanna listen? I can get your hard-rock opinion of these ghetto metal beats I just finished?"

He stood up and walked toward the cold orange seat next to mine. He smelled like some kinda Muslim oil, sweet, but not feminine. I hoped he could smell my Ivory soap shower and the baby lotion I'd rubbed into my skin.

He was taller and thinner than he'd seemed sitting down. His face was freckled and his nails clean and manicured. His teeth were perfectly straight inside his devilish grin. His mouth was deep pink lined with a natural brown tint. I would find out later that he hated comparisons to anyone but himself, but for an edgy east coast brotha, he had some serious laid-back west coast flavor. I could imagine him driving a pimped-out convertible Impala through Compton, but blasting A Tribe Called Quest.

"I'm Harlem, who you?" he said, looking at me like he was trying to figure me out.

"You may not believe this, but I'm Savannah." I smiled. "Nice to meet you," I answered, bobbing my head to the hardcore coming out of his headphones. He seemed naked without his music. Vulnerable.

"So, you feeling it or what, lil' mama?"

"Yeah, it's nice. You should add some guitars to the hook," I answered, still smiling, looking into eyes that looked back at me with similar intensity.

"Maybe I'll do that, Savannah. Maybe we'll even compose some music together," he said, leaning in toward me. I felt comfortable enough to want to kiss him, but my stop was approaching. My eyes followed his tongue moving across his mouth.

"I gotta go," I said when the train pulled into Lafayette.

I got off with a cute wave; his smile and phone number in my pocket. *That train ride became our history.* The story of how we didn't fall in love. Despite our sexual tension, and appreciation for music, we became friends. His hectic life as an upcoming, highly sought-after producer-slash-songwriter kept him in studios across the country. My late-night lifestyle and international underground cult following, coupled with my independent nature, kept me easily distracted.

Harlem and I exchanged emails and phone calls as well as records. His *Miles Davis* for my *Betty*. My grassroots *Mothers-FavoriteChild* double CD for his *Just Blaze* or *Dr. Dre* instrumentals. He made me feel safe again at rap concerts, got me smoking more herb, and heavily influenced my soundtrack. He was my break beat and I was his electric lady. It was the perfect relationship. Even on the nights we could've both used a stress release, we never went there. We trusted each other. Instead, I filtered out the shallow women and he sniffed out the dogs.

The Day the Music Lived

The Red Hot Chili Peppers banged loud enough to shake the bed. He sang along while biting into his turkey and cheese with extra pickles. "*Take me to a place I love . . . take me all the way.*" He was singing one of my theme songs. He wore white linen pants and a dress shirt. I'd watched Harlem become a beautiful man right before my eyes. Was I crazy? Why had I never pressed up against him, kissed his African nose and mouth? I heard he was great in bed, and I'd never even had a fake drunk moment and given him some. Maybe because I wasn't a drinker and neither was he, really. But I suspected it was because we both knew the best way to lose a friend of the opposite sex is to fuck them.

"Take that out your mouth, baby. You don't need to be sucking those black cancer sticks into your lungs."

"You got something better for me to do?" I laughed, flirting like I normally would. Harlem went to the fridge to make me a tequila shot. I watched him cut the lemons and line the glasses with salt, then he handed me a quick escape. Harlem stood up in front of me and held out his glass.

"Tonight you need a drink," he said. "We need to toast. Can I propose a toast to you, Save-annah?"

Harlem always told me I was destined to save the world, but I first need to save myself. I wanted a drink, but I really just wanted Harlem to fuck me. To want me like all those other women wanted him. I slowly licked the top of the glass, looking directly in his eyes. Harlem could be boyish and intense all at once. I swallowed hard and asked for another. He obliged and followed my lead.

"You never told me about your show, sis. What happened?" Harlem asked, pulling a chair up next to me. You could see all of uptown from his large windows. Even the glow from as far down as 42nd Street.

"Don't call me that," I answered, angrily.

"Don't call you what?" he asked, knowing exactly what I was talking about. "Oh, Save-annah . . . what am I gonna do with you?" he asked, but it seemed like he had a map in his pocket. He knew me so well. Was I so obviously desperate?

"What do you wanna do, Harlem world?" My head was buzzing from the shots, as I sang the Marvin Gaye cut pouring through his speakers.

"I think that you are absolutely beautiful." Harlem seemed to be surprised by his words. But he got up and turned down the lights, and lit a few candles near his bed. I watched, pretending to be unfazed. He sat back down and we just stared at each other for a few awkward seconds. I closed my eyes and took in his scent. I leaned my face in and allowed my cheek to rub against his chin lightly like a purring cat. Our mouths inches from meeting. He pulled back.

"Savannah. I want to make love to you. I've always wanted to." He was asking for permission, but didn't wait for my answer.

Harlem slid out of his chair, onto his knees, and pulled me to the edge of the king-size bed. He unzipped the leather painted to my legs and yanked them down over my high boots.

"Harlem," I whispered, barely able to speak his name. He ignored my apprehension over ruining our good thing.

I was as hot and wet as the Pacific in Maui. He placed his tongue over my excited clit and slowly tasted me for the first time. He gently pulled back my lips and traced my fruit like a new discovery. I pulled his shirt over his head, then fell back into the down comforter, anticipating his next move. Harlem unzipped his pants, then pulled my legs toward his lean body and turned me around. He placed his hand in the middle of my back and I arched on his silent command. He palmed my ass in his hands like he was shaping his world out of my clay. He pushed into my body with slow confidence in his size, then he followed with quick hard drives deep into my ocean.

"What am I gonna do with you?" he asked again, this time half smiling and groaning. Sweat poured off his face and fell on my back. Our pacing was so in sync, so perfect. I was used to being the aggressor in bed. Harlem was taking control like the king of the jungle. He even growled when his body took off, shaking inside of me. When I finally mounted him, I held his arms down hard against our damp surface. He laughed, understanding my need for control, even when I'd felt liberated by losing it. The CD changer flipped to a new selection and I heard my voice singing one of the first songs I ever wrote.

I thought about my show, my music, and the crowd I'd abandoned at the club while I rode Harlem, his hands caressing my nipples as they danced in his face. He pulled me closer to his chest, feeling my worry. He kissed my nose, my eyes, my cheeks, and finally my mouth. He pulled me down on top of him, and pushed deeper inside of me.

"You know you still got time to rock that crowd like you . . ." He whispered as he started to come inside of me. ". . . like you, you need to, baby."

A part of me always had a secret desire to have Harlem all to myself. All those platonic nights we slept together, exchanging musical war stories, popcorn, and dreams. And now that we'd done it, I realized, he was always there for me. Like my bass staring back at me for months before I finally wrapped her strap around my frame.

"You are wonderful," I finally whispered.

"This is only the beginning, Savannah. Take my key and bring your fine ass right back here when you're done with those undeserving L-E-S muthafuckas. I'll be here."

So I pulled myself from the safest place on earth, washed the smell of sex and salt from my body, and grabbed my bass. I was a 10-minute cab ride away from a second orgasm.

I wonder if it'll feel different with everyone watching.

They never knew what hit 'em when I was done. I gave two encore performances before shutting the place down. My throat was hot and scratchy, my pores filled with his sweat and my songs, my fingers hot and buzzing from the strings of my bass. I smiled and fingered the key hanging around my neck, then I slipped through the back door a second time, without looking back.

Ghostwriter

"How's the new book coming along, honey?"

Andrew had been reaching for the bowl of tortilla chips, anticipating dipping a fresh chip in the dish of spicy salsa, his mouth watering in expectation. Danita's question made his mouth go dry.

"The book?" He drummed the table. "It's coming along okay, I guess."

Danita's brow creased—the same look he imagined she gave her clients at the law firm when they tossed a lie her way. Frowning, she folded her arms on the table, leaning forward.

"What page are you on?" she asked.

He cleared his throat. "Well, lately, I've been doing some outlining, working out some of the fuzzy story elements. You know how I write. I need to have a clear sense of direction before I move forward."

"You've been outlining for a long time. Your deadline is only three months away, Andrew."

"I know my deadline, Danita. You don't have to remind me."

"Right, but like you said, I know how you write. You always do several drafts before you're finished, and you haven't even completed a first draft yet. I'm worried about you."

Andrew idly stirred his iced tea. Her concern both touched and annoyed him. For many years, he'd longed for a relationship with a woman like Danita. She was smart, ambitious, loving, pretty. She admired his talent for spinning tales and supported his writing career not for the money and fame it brought him, but because she understood that writing was his labor of love. She wanted him to do well, and he loved her for it.

But sometimes, he wanted her to back off and let him be a neurotic writer—with all the loopy work habits, unpredictable creative impulses, and paralyzing bouts of angst that came with it.

"It's fine," he said. "The book is coming to me slowly. It works that way sometimes."

Danita's lips curled. She didn't believe him; worse, he didn't believe himself.

The book was not coming to him slowly—it was not coming to him at all. His second novel was like a headstrong dog that refused to be either cajoled or punished into obedience. The more he pressed and teased, the more it resisted. It was maddening.

It hadn't been that way with his first novel, *Ghostwriter.* He'd written *Ghostwriter* in a frenzy, burning through 500 pages in only four months. And it was good, damn good. The first agent he queried wanted it; the first publisher they sent it to bought it, plunking down a six-figure advance that enabled him to quit his day job as a programmer. Books by black authors were hot, and industry people were calling him the African-American Stephen King, a derivative label that he despised yet tolerated because it gave the marketing people an effective handle.

Film rights were sold, lucrative foreign rights sales to eight countries followed soon after. *Ghostwriter* had been flying off the shelves since it hit stores five months ago. Readers were clamoring for the next book. His editor was ready for the next book. So was his agent. Add his girlfriend to the list too.

But no one was as ready for the next book as he was, and he couldn't write it. Writer's block, which he had long believed was a myth made up by wannabe authors who'd never finish anything, had fallen like a brick onto his hands, rendering them numb and useless. Each morning, he sat at his brand-new Dell computer, a bright and painfully blank screen staring back at him, and after an hour of fitful typing and story outlining that led nowhere, he'd log on to the Internet and spend the rest of the day surfing the Web under an alias so none of his online writer-buddies could ask him what he was doing, and shouldn't he be working on the next book . . . ?

"Did you hear me, Drew?"

He blinked. "Sorry, I spaced out. What did you say?"

"I said, you need inspiration. Something to get your creative juices flowing."

"Maybe I could start drinking. It's worked for some writers." He chuckled.

She didn't laugh. In the past, she would've found humor in such a joke. He wondered if she was actually worried he just might take up the bottle to loosen his creative muscles.

"Why don't you immerse yourself in a place that fits the stuff you write about?" she said. "Somewhere scary."

"Like your parents' house?"

That time, she did laugh. "Oh, you got jokes now, do you?

No, silly, I mean, you write about ghosts, haunted houses, stuff like that. Why not go somewhere creepy?"

"Like a haunted house?"

Her eyes widened. "The cemetery. At night!"

Andrew laughed, then shook his head. "I know which one you're talking about. Girl, you're crazy."

"It's the perfect place," she said. "And it's so close. You wouldn't even need to drive—"

"Ain't no way in hell I'm walking around a graveyard at night, Danita."

She grinned. "See? That's why I know it would inspire you—because the very idea scares you. It'll put you in the mind-set you need to write your book."

"You're a better lawyer than you are a psychologist," he said, sipping the iced tea, then dipping a tortilla chip into the salsa. His appetite had returned in a rush.

"Make jokes if you want, you know I'm right," she said. "Go to the cemetery for one night, Drew. I know it'll help you beat your writer's block. I can feel it."

"Okay, I'll think about it," he said, which was his way of signaling that it was time to change the subject. Danita and her crazy ideas. Why in the hell would he want to creep around a graveyard at night? What would be next—visiting haunted houses? Participating in séances? Simply because he wrote about such things didn't mean he wanted to experience them first-hand. He didn't need to. His own imagination, nourished over the years with a steady diet of horror flicks, novels, and the nightly news, supplied all the inspiration he needed.

But what had his imagination done for him lately? he had to ask himself. He had been fiddling with the novel for 10 fruitless months, the deadline thundering toward him like a freight train. He could request an extension, but an extra three months would mean nothing if he didn't defeat his block. He knew he had to do something drastic to rekindle his creative spark.

By the time they finished lunch, Andrew had reluctantly decided that Danita was right. He would visit the cemetery tonight.

*   *   *

After his agent sold movie rights to *Ghostwriter,* Andrew moved out of his apartment in Atlanta and purchased a stylish, two-bedroom condo in the Georgia suburb of Marietta. The condominium was located next to Magnolia Memorial Cemetery. He hadn't minded because the condo was great and he got an awesome deal. Besides, he found it oddly fitting for a horror writer to live next to a cemetery; death, his favorite subject matter, was right next door. In fact, the town newspaper had mentioned it when they interviewed him: "Local Horror Writer Finds Inspiration in His Backyard."

Of course, he'd never so much as set foot in there. Why should he? The idea of living near a graveyard was more attractive than the morbid reality.

The reality was that wandering into the cemetery at night scared the hell out of him. He couldn't explain it; it was a primitive fear that seemed to be biologically wired into him, the same way an irrational fear of the dark affected some people. He often wondered if there was a psychological term for graveyard phobia.

An hour before midnight, after spending yet another evening meandering at his keyboard, Andrew stood beside his Nissan Pathfinder. He wore a light jacket and gripped a yellow flashlight. In front of him lay the deep, dark forest. Beyond the woods, the cemetery awaited.

Andrew shivered, but his chill had nothing to do with the cool March breeze that swept across the parking lot.

A pale, full moon gazed down at him. His mind, so attuned to the ominous meanings of full moons, dark forests, and graveyards, churned out a carnival of nightmarish images: hulking werewolves creeping through the forest; rotted corpses struggling out of the earth; phantoms drifting like smoke across headstones . . .

"Okay, cut it out," he said to himself. "Go in there, walk around for a few minutes, and come home. Save the macabre imagery for the book."

He exhaled. Then, heart thrumming, he entered the forest.

Viewed from the lighted parking lot, the woods had appeared to be dark. But when Andrew actually stepped into the forest, it seemed much darker, as if light could not penetrate the area.

He resisted his compulsion to flick on the flashlight. Artificial light would ruin the mood. The whole point of this exercise was to help him tap in to the spirit of the night, if there was such a thing. He carried the flashlight for emergencies.

He crept through the undergrowth, grass crunching beneath his boots. Leaves brushed his face, and twigs probed him like fingers, the darkness alive with the sounds of nocturnal creatures.

The cemetery lay ahead, bathed in soft moonlight and shrouded in mist.

As he stepped out of the woods, a length of barbed wire snagged his jeans.

"Shit." Stepping back, he tore the denim loose from the wire. There goes a pair of good jeans. He noticed, concealed in the shrubbery at the edge of the forest, a low barbed-wire fence that seemed to run the entire length of the woods on this side. Was it there to keep the forest-dwelling creatures out of the cemetery? Or . . . was it there to keep something in the graveyard out of the forest?

He laughed at himself. Danita had been right. This little jaunt was filling his head with all kinds of strange ideas.

He leapt over the fence and into the cemetery. Fog enveloped the area. He noted, on his left, a huge mound of dirt, like a man-made hill. Ahead, he saw countless graves, most marked by footstones on which stood metallic tubes filled with sprays of flowers. The funeral home lay in the distance, barely visible through the mist.

Silence had cloaked the night. He could hear his heart pounding.

"All right," he said to himself. "Walk around for a few, soak up some atmosphere, then go home. That's all I need to do."

He started forward. The churning fog seemed to thicken around him as he moved. He was tempted to turn on the flashlight, but he decided against it. Certainly, a caretaker patrolled the grounds at night. A light shining in the darkness would be a dead giveaway. He could imagine how he'd explain why he was there. "Well, I'm a horror writer, mister. I came here seeking inspiration for my novel. My name is Andrew Graves. Graves is roaming the graveyard, you know? Pretty funny, huh—"

Wrapped in mist and his own thoughts, Andrew didn't see the

dark pit yawning in front of him. He walked into emptiness and fell, screaming, all the way to the bottom of a freshly dug grave.

*   *   *

"Hey, are you okay down there?"

Lying on his side on the hard, damp earth, his head spinning, Andrew thought he was hearing things. It was a woman's voice—soft, musical, soothing. Like something out of a dream.

"Hello?" she called again. "If you're conscious, please say something."

"I'm here," he said shakily, sitting and wincing as pain bolted through his shoulder. He didn't think he had broken any bones, and though his shoulder ached, he knew that it wasn't dislocated. He'd dislocated his shoulder when playing high-school football, and this pain was not nearly as bad as that had been.

He looked up. The woman's face, a featureless black oval, peered down at him.

"Can you stand?" she asked. "Give me your hands and I'll help you climb out of there."

"Okay." Who was this woman? The caretaker?

He stuffed the flashlight into his jacket pocket and struggled to his feet. The hole was six feet deep; the top a couple of inches above his head.

The woman's hands seemed to float toward him through the mist, as if they belonged to a disembodied spirit. His heart stalled . . . and when he moved closer, he saw, clearly, that her hands were ordinary flesh. His imagination was running away with him.

He grasped them—her soft, warm skin sending an unexpected thrill through him—and she pulled him up. He worried that he'd be too heavy for her, but she tugged him upward with ease.

She was a few inches shorter than he was, slim, wrapped in a knee-length, silvery jacket. Her dark hair spilled to her shoulders. In the darkness, he couldn't see much of her face.

"Thanks," he said. "I don't know how I fell in there. I guess I wasn't paying attention to where I was going."

She shook a cigarette out of a pack and struck a match. When she brought the flame near her face, his breath caught in his throat. She was absolutely gorgeous.

She slowly took a draw from her cigarette. "I wasn't going to ask you how you fell in there. I was going to ask you what you're doing here."

"Do you work here?" he said.

She laughed, a low, throaty chuckle. "I asked first."

"So you did," he said. Andrew motioned behind him. "I live in a condo near here. I'm a writer and . . . uh, well, I guess I was looking for some inspiration."

"Why would you of all people need to visit a cemetery for inspiration? Andrew Graves, the best damn horror writer of the decade?"

She laughed at the surprise on his face, then took his hand.

"Come with me, sweetie," she said. "We've got some things to talk about."

Okay, this could be the plotline for a story, he thought. A horror writer crippled with writer's block wanders into a nearby graveyard seeking inspiration. He foolishly walks into an empty grave, and is rescued by a beautiful woman who thinks he's brilliant.

But then what happens?

Feeling like a hapless character in one of his own tales, Andrew followed her.

A dozen yards away, a black granite sarcophagus stood about six feet high. The woman climbed on top and invited him to join her. There, as if in the midst of a picnic, she'd spread a blanket on which stood a bottle of Merlot, a wineglass, a leatherbound notebook, and a shiny Waterford pen.

Her name was Alexandria, and she didn't work at the cemetery. She was a writer, she said, and the solitude of a graveyard at night, stimulated her creativity. He realized that many writers were eccentric, but he had never heard of a writer regarding a cemetery as the ideal place in which to write. It was strange.

He would've made up an excuse to leave, but he stayed for three reasons: One, she claimed to be a huge fan of his, and he needed an ego boost. Two, he felt an instant and profound chemistry with her that had nothing to do with her good looks. Three, well, she *was* heart-achingly beautiful. He made his living with words, and he could not describe the startling impact her beauty had on him. Although he loved his girlfriend, when he looked at Alexandria, he found it hard to remember what Danita even looked like.

He'd never been under a spell, but it must feel exactly like this.

"I've read your novel three times," Alexandria said. "You're so talented, amazingly so. Why would you need to come here for inspiration? That sort of thing is reserved for amateurs like me." She laughed, taking another drag of her cigarette.

Ordinarily, he didn't like to be around smoke, but her smoking didn't bother him. In a way, it added to her appeal, as though she were a film star from decades ago when famous actresses smoked and it was considered glamorous, sexy. Alexandria had an air of grace and sophistication that recalled those fabled silver screen goddesses.

And she'd read his book three times! Now that was flattering. After completing the book, he hadn't wanted to read it even once.

"The first novel came very easily," he said. "Maybe too easily. I got spoiled. Writing this second book is like being thrown in a tub of cold water and having to face the reality that writing isn't always easy. It's work."

"You're damn right it's work." She tapped her leather-bound notebook. "I've been working on this novel for two years, and I'm nowhere near done."

"What's the title?" he said.

"*A Midnight Haunting*," she said. "It's a ghost story, and a love story, all wrapped up into one wondrous, gothic tale."

"Sounds interesting. I'd like to read it when you finish."

"If I ever finish. When I'm most frustrated with it, I think of hiring a ghostwriter to complete it for me. I simply want to be done with it! But I doubt I could ever do that. A ghostwriter would have to be completely filled with my spirit to do any justice to the story. Know what I mean?"

"Definitely. Our work can be so close to us that we have to write it ourselves."

Her eyes were dreamy, her voice a whisper. "My only wish is to complete the novel before I die—and if I die before I'm done, then I'd want to have my ghostwriter finish the tale. But I like to think that I have a full life ahead of me, and that I have plenty of time. I don't have a real deadline like you have."

When she saw him frown, she giggled and said, "Oh, sorry. I'm sure you didn't want to be reminded."

"That's okay, really." He sighed, looking around. Although fog rolled across the gravestones, and the night was as dark as ever, the graveyard did not seem quite as forbidding as before. "You know, I've never hung out at a cemetery. How long do you usually stay here?"

"Until I'm ready to leave." She refilled her wineglass. "I didn't bring another glass since I wasn't expecting company. Would you like some?"

"Sure." She was a relative stranger to him, and here they were drinking from the same glass. He and Danita had not drunk out of the same cup until after they had been dating for a month, at least.

He sipped the wine. It was dry, yet smooth. Delicious warmth spread across his chest. As he reeled from the drink's potency, Alexandria unloosened the belt straps of her jacket and shrugged out of the coat.

Andrew almost dropped the glass.

She wore a skimpy black slip that barely reached past the top of her thighs. Her cleavage swelled out, adorned with a tiny gold crucifix that glittered in the moonlight.

Although the night was cool, probably fifty degrees, Alexandria raised her head to the sky and stretched languorously, as though luxuriating in the moon rays.

"I love night in the cemetery," she said. "To be here with you, my favorite writer, in my special place, is like a dream."

"Is there a caretaker here?" he said. "Someone who might . . . see us?"

"You don't need to worry," she said. "It's only us, and the dead." She laughed.

He laughed too, much harder and longer than he should have. He felt drunk—intoxicated by the wine and by this bizarre, fabulous woman.

They talked long into the night about books, movies, traveling, their families, and countless other subjects. She was fiercely intelligent and shared deep insights that challenged him, moved him. She laughed at his dry wit, and she amused him with her comedic timing.

When their conversation finally dipped into a lull, Alexandria slid closer, pressed her body against his. She took the wine from him and ran her tongue where his lips had touched the glass.

"You inspire me," she whispered, placing her hand against his thigh, squeezing. "I want to be your inspiration too, my brilliant writer."

He closed his hand over hers, brought her slender fingers to his lips, and kissed them.

"You already are," he said.

*   *   *

Sometime later that night—Andrew had lost all track of time—he made his way back home. He stumbled through the door, exhausted, yet excited, nerves jangling. What an incredible night. It had been beyond anything within his ability to imagine.

Now, he needed to write. He had to write. This very minute.

Trembling, he raced to his office and switched on the computer. It proceeded to go through its boot-up cycle. He drummed the desk impatiently.

This wasn't right. He couldn't do this on a machine. That was the problem with this book. It demanded to be handwritten—a purer method of writing.

He found a spiral notebook in the desk drawer.

His Waterford pen, which Danita had given him as a Christmas gift, was in a case on his desk.

With paper and pen in hand, he rushed to the glass dinette table. He uncapped the pen and tore open the notebook.

He wrote non-stop until dawn.

*   *   *

"Drew, you look like you need some rest," Danita said. "Your eyes are bloodshot."

They were at Danita's place, reclining on the living-room sofa. They'd ordered a pizza and were watching a movie; some sappy chick-flick that Danita had insisted on renting. Although Andrew's eyes were on the screen, he saw only mental images of the story he was writing and breathtaking visions of Alexandria.

Danita tapped his shoulder. "Did you hear me? You've been zoning out all evening. Are you okay?"

He glanced at his watch. Nine-thirty. He had a date that evening. At midnight. In the cemetery.

"Drew!"

He looked at Danita. "What?"

"What's wrong with you? You aren't yourself."

"The book is coming to me. Finally. I was up all night, spent most of the day on it too. I don't even remember whether I slept or not. The book is blocking out everything." Everything except Alexandria, that was.

"I see," she said. "Did you take my advice and visit the cemetery?"

"Not yet." He looked away. The cemetery would remain his secret. "The book hit me last night and has been flowing ever since. I've never felt a flow like this. This is unreal."

"Hmm." Her eyes held a trace of suspicion, then she sighed, her suspicion giving way to resignation. "This is what I get for dating a writer. Occasional weird moods and temporary obsession. But I love you anyway." She leaned forward and kissed him.

He quickly broke off the kiss and stood up. "Danita, I've gotta go."

"To write?"

"It's taking me over, calling to me. I don't know how else to explain it. I'm . . . under a spell."

"I won't pretend that I understand, Drew," she said. "Because I don't. But handle your business."

Driving back to his home in Marietta, he swung into the parking lot of Tom's Beverage Depot. He bought five bottles of Merlot—the same French label he and Alexandria had shared.

He also bought a carton of Newport cigarettes. Her favorite.

*   *   *

At midnight, they found each other at their special meeting place: the empty grave he had fallen into the first night they met.

"I missed you," Alexandria said, pulling him into her embrace. He wound his fingers through her silky hair. He could hold her forever. He never wanted to leave her. She inspired him. She excited him. She understood him. She loved him.

Before meeting Alexandria, if anyone had asked him whether it was possible to fall in love within minutes of meeting someone, he would've called that person a hopelessly romantic fool.

Now, he knew better.

Wrapped in each other's arms, they went to their spot on the big granite tomb.

Later, when he returned home, his creative batteries more powerfully charged than ever, he scribbled in his notebook for twelve hours straight.

* * *

For five days, the book was Andrew's world, and Alexandria was his sun. They met each night at midnight, always in the cemetery, always at the same location. Once they embraced, time spun out like spools of thread, became meaningless. They drank wine, talked, made love, drank wine, talked, made love . . .

Within five days, he had filled the notebook's five hundred pages with words. The novel was done.

He couldn't wait to tell Alexandria.

A few minutes before midnight, he dashed out of his condo and into the woods. He followed the path that he had created during his previous trips, then jumped over the barbed-wire fence and into the cemetery.

It was midnight when he arrived at the grave, their meeting

spot. But Alexandria wasn't there. Odd. She was always on time.

He also noticed that the hole was no longer empty. It had been filled, a gravestone embedded at the head, and a wreath of bright flowers placed atop it.

Well, it was about time someone was buried there. He could've broken his neck when he'd fallen into it on that first night.

Out of curiosity, he flicked on his flashlight. He focused the beam on the headstone.

Reading it, he was seized by such shock that he dropped the flashlight.

"No," he said in a choked voice. He bent to retrieve the flash-light—and crashed to his knees.

"No, no, no, no, no." Like a blind man, he crawled across the grass, fumbling for the light. He grabbed it, then shined it on the inscription.

ALEXANDRIA BENTLEY
BELOVED DAUGHTER. GIFTED WRITER.
JANUARY 18, 1976—MARCH 5, 2001

Hot tears scalded his skin. He had to think. This would've been the sixth night he had spent with Alexandria. They had first met around midnight of March 7 . . . two days after she had died . . .

"Impossible," he said. He fought to stand. Staggering, he went to the black granite monument on which they had spent so many hours. He peered over the top of it.

The surface was bare. There was no blanket, no wine, no cigarette ash.

He had touched her, kissed her, loved her. Here. Right. Here.

"Impossible!" he shouted.

Then he ran out of the cemetery.

* * *

Danita was knocking at the door of his condo when he ran out of the forest.

"Where are you coming from?" she yelled. "Jesus, Drew, I've been worried sick about you. You haven't returned my calls, you've been acting distant, I haven't seen you in days. What's going on?"

He didn't answer, just unlocked the door and brushed past her.

Danita slammed the door. "Dammit, Drew, talk to—What have you been doing in here?" She gasped, looking around the living room.

Blinking, he scratched his head—and saw what had been invisible to him for days. Wineglasses and bottles of Merlot littering the coffee table. Empty packs of Newport cigarettes scattered everywhere. Saucers, bowls, and cups brimming with ashes and cigarette butts.

"I don't . . . know." He was groggy and disoriented, as if he had awakened only minutes ago from a deep slumber. "I've been writing a novel. Done with it now." He grabbed the spiral notebook off the dinette table and handed it to her.

Confused and anxious, Danita opened the notebook.

"What is this?" she asked, flipping through the pages. "What the hell is this?" She turned back to the first page, smacked it, and shoved it toward him.

He looked at it.

A Midnight Haunting

A Novel by Alexandria Bentley

"Oh, Jesus," he said, and fell onto the sofa.

Alexandria's words, spoken during their fateful first meeting, came to him:

I think of hiring a ghostwriter to complete it for me . . . A ghostwriter would have to be completely filled with my spirit to do any justice to the story . . . My only wish is to complete the novel before I die—and if I die before I'm done, then I'd want to have my ghostwriter finish the tale . . .

"Drew?" Danita said. She stepped toward him hesitantly.

He stared at the title page. Then he lowered his face to the pages and wept, his tears mingling with the ink . . . running in black streams down the paper.

SANDRA JACKSON-OPOKU

Iguana Stew

*T*he door flew open at my first faint knock. She leaned toward me for a kiss, a dainty dark-skinned woman holding a skimpy robe closed with one hand and a champagne glass with the other. The fruity scent of liquor reached my nose before her lips met my cheek. I kissed her back, touched that she seemed so happy to see me.

Cedella flashed a dimpled grin and tugged me into the room.

"Here it is, my home away from home. The ghetto meets Park Avenue."

I was shocked at the ravaged luxury of the overfurnished penthouse suite. Piles of clothing were heaped on the unmade beds. Surfaces were littered with room service trays and plates of half-eaten food. A magnum of Pol Roger champagne reclined in a wine cooler on the crowded desk. Cedella freshened her drink from a half-empty bottle of Chambord.

"What's the celebration, Cedella?"

"It's all about you, Queasy. How long has it been, darling? Ten, twelve years?"

She pushed a pile of clothing to the floor, beckoned me onto a bed, then plopped down next to me. A green oriental print that looked like silk was loosely belted at her waist. I caught no glimpse of nylon or lace underneath. It seemed she might be naked under that green silk. She leaned toward me, grasping my hand.

"Thanks for coming to see me, Queasy."

"That's 'Kway-SEE.'"

"KWEE-zee. Just what I said."

"Ready for the interview?"

"Oh, sure, sure." Cedella waved her champagne glass. "Ask away. My life's an open book. I've got a surprise for you, too. You'll find it provocative to say the least."

"Fine. I'll check your voice levels, then we'll get started."

"Here's something to chew on while you're setting up. I'm preparing a Las Vegas revue for the end of the year. Isn't that wild?"

I was confused.

"What, are you designing the costumes or something?"

"Of course not, silly. I haven't fooled with fashion design in years. I'm making my musical comeback, darling. A few torch songs, some Cole Porter classics. Don't you just love those old songs?"

"If you like that sort of thing. I didn't realize you were a singer."

"Oh, sure. In fact, I'm thinking about dubbing up a posthumous duet of 'The Farmer in the Dell' with Hector."

"Cedella." I shook my head in disbelief. "You're amazing."

"True." She nodded sagely. "I'm what you call a Renaissance woman. I've been an artist ever since I was a little girl, weaving words in straw and sisal. One of these days they'll be calling me Dr. Guzman. Did you know I'm an ABD in theology, Brown University?"

"All but dissertation? No, Cedella. I didn't know that."

"Marriage interrupted my education, but one day I'm going back to finish my dissertation and get my Ph.D. I've also been known to do a little fashion and interior design. You've seen the new decor at Hector's loft? That was all my work, a surprise anniversary gift for that African gal of his. And of course, I've always loved to sing."

"But breaking into show business at this stage in your life won't be easy."

"I've sung before, but they never took me seriously because of who I married. My own priorities were different then. I was a regular geisha, making Hector's bath and testing the water. Scrubbing his back and washing his hair. Setting out his clothing the night before. I was into total mothering once the twins arrived. Now that Hector's gone and the kids are grown, it's time to do something for Cedella. You know what it means to put your dreams on hold, right, Queasy?"

"I suppose I can imagine. My little one is still young yet."

"I'm not talking about parenthood. I'm talking about marriage, living in the shadow of a illustrious mate. Of course," she added with a sudden grin, "Alma Peeples is no Hector Guzman."

Her tone hadn't changed and she was still smiling. I couldn't tell if it had been an offhanded comment or a pointed barb.

"Alma is a talent in her own right," I said. "Though I wouldn't exactly say I was living in her shadow."

"Well, just between friends, I think you've got loads more writing talent than Alma. Loads."

Control was squirming from my grasp. I wondered what would be lost if I got up and left right then.

"Thanks for the . . . vote of confidence, Cedella."

"Dell."

"What?"

"Call me Dell, all my friends do. It was Hector's pet name for me. You remember his soca version of 'The Farmer in the Dell.'"

The Farmer takes a wife
The wife takes a knife . . .

"Yes, I remember," I interrupted. "Hector's version was on the off-color side, as I recall. Something about a cheating woman and an illegitimate child, wasn't it?"

"Not at all." She shook her head. "That's a common misconception. It was actually inspired by a naughty little love game of ours. Hector would play the randy farmer, I was the lusty wife . . ."

"Enough." I shuddered. "I get the picture."

If I suspected it before, it was now confirmed. It was in her body language, the way she kept patting her face. If I sniffed hard enough, I could probably detect the scent of lies.

"Hadn't it been at least a decade since you two were together?"

Cedella laughed airily and waved her hand, sending the charms at her wrist tinkling.

"Don't be naive, darling. Divorce doesn't have to mean the end of a love affair."

"Really? Even with Hector remarrying so soon?"

"I always was, and always will be his Mrs. Guzman. The one who gave him children to carry his blood into the next generation . . ."

I fiddled with the controls of the tape recorder, half-listening.

". . . I'm the one he walked up the aisle with in a white veil. What did he marry that woman in, I ask you? She was bareheaded in a rag, that's what. A little piece of African rag like something I would sleep in . . ."

Cedella seemed suddenly to become two things in the same body, a spoiled child morphing into a spiteful woman. She settled against a bank of pillows, snuggling into the bedclothes like a kitten.

When the first lie slid from her mouth as slick as grease, my antennae went up. I waited for the next one, then yet again another. My early years as a general assignment reporter had taught me that a single lie can be forgiven. A second, if fairly innocuous, could also be overlooked. But once that third lie popped up, you were looking tainted testimony full in the mouth.

Cedella paused to sip from her ubiquitous champagne glass. The silk robe parted, revealing glimpses of a pert breast, a smooth thigh, a curved knee. She sat so close to me that I could smell her scent. However much she lied, she still smelled good.

Alarmed at the sudden erection swelling in my pants, I took my machine and switched over to the other bed. The swelling subsided but didn't disappear. It would continue to plague me like a faint, persistent itch.

"The tape is rolling," I reminded her.

She sat up bolt upright at the edge of the bed, tucking her feet neatly beneath her.

"Okay, first I want to get a really nice head shot. Do you know a good photographer? Then we'll blanket the media with press releases, maybe line up some talk show appearances."

I shook my head, clicking the off button.

"Cedella, what on earth are you talking about?"

"My show business comeback," she sniffed. "I've been looking for someone with your credentials to help me launch a publicity campaign."

Was this the "surprise" she'd hinted at earlier?

"I'm a journalist and music critic," I objected. "Show biz publicity is not my forte."

"Nonsense. You've done lots of work for Hector over the years."

"What, the occasional liner note? Besides, I wouldn't have the time for a project like this. If I follow through with his biography, that's where I'll need to focus my time and energy."

"Oh, Queasy, what an excellent idea! I could help, you know. A coffee table pictorial would really be nice. I've got tons of photos from birthday parties with the kids, vacation snapshots, our wedding photos, although they're a little on the risqué side."

"Actually," I explained. "I was thinking more of a musical biography."

"Well, you can't tell Hector's story without me in it. Everything he became, he owes to me. I'm sure he's told you that many times."

"I can't say that he ever did."

"It's true. I was his muse. You remember his first hit song, 'Brown Girl, Blue Island'? I starred in the music video. It was one of Hector's first love songs to me."

"'Brown Girl, Blue Island,' huh? I never knew you were an island girl."

Cedella paused and began playing with her hair. Another lie was on its way.

"We first met in *Rhode* Island, which isn't an actual island, but that's Hector's sense of humor for you. Although, to tell you the truth, I did spend some time in the Bahamas as a wee gal in pigtails."

"Yes, I can hear it," I nodded. "You sounded quite Caribbean for a minute, there."

"Oh, there's very little West Indian left in me. I've been wandering ever since I was a young thing with big dreams and itchy feet."

*   *   *

I've moved around so much, there was never a place I could say, yes, that's me—a West Indian, an American, a Canadian. When people ask where I'm from, I never know what to answer. It's all my father's fault, although I don't blame him for it.

Daddy was a part-time Pentecostal preacher who made his living as an itinerant mechanic. He'd fix up all the air conditioners and fridges he could find on one island, then we'd move on to the next. It seems that every move took us deeper into the ring of out islands.

We finally settled on Mayaguana, as far out as you could get and still be in the Bahamas. I'd take the mail boat to Nassau on weekends and school holidays to help my gran at her market stall. She was a French market mammy, a vendor at the Straw Market in Nassau. When I heard it was torched to the ground, I broke down and wept. It was like losing the last thing that connected me to my past.

My job was to count money, run errands, and sew words in sisal on the handwoven straw goods. That's when I knew I had a little of the artist in me. I picked up enough French, German, and Dutch to say, "Welcome, pretty lady. Your name on a basket?"

Aurelie Daudinot was a sophisticated woman, even though she spoke English with a thick accent. Daudinot? French, not Haitian, mind you. God forbid all that voodoo should be running through my bloodlines. My gran came from France, not Haiti. No, I do not know why a person would leave France to come struggle in the Straw Market. Maybe she was like me, always wanting to travel. Maybe she packed her dreams on the mail boat and sailed from one island to the next.

She wasn't one of those frowzy market women in out-of-style dresses. No, my gran was always turned out. She may have been a market woman, but she knew how to dress herself.

And Queasy, she could sell ice to the Eskimos and make a profit. She'd sit there in her tailored dresses and hats, her head held high like a queen. If you present yourself well, people believe your goods must be quality. Tourists would pay a dollar just to take her picture. She was respected by the other market mammies, always coming to her for loans and favors. Does that sound to you like a common Haitian refugee? I think not.

No, Queasy, I am not lying. I am spinning story. Okay, maybe Gran did stretch the truth a little. It's not my lie, but I do understand. Those Haitians from the District, who would want be seen like that? Bad street boys, illiterate old women, all of them dirt poor.

You make too much of a little thing, Queasy. What's the difference if my Gran was born in Haiti or somewhere off the coast of France? The point is that she became something better, just like me.

I lived on an island you could walk across and back in the space of an afternoon. There was a villa in Old Hooper's Bay where my father worked on the air conditioning system that was always breaking down. It was hardly any tourists, just Bahamians from New Providence and Paradise Island, coming a-country for the weekend.

The place was overrun with iguana and hutia, a little rat rabbit you wouldn't find anyplace but Mayaguana. There was nothing to do but read expired newspapers at the petty shop in Betsy Bay or wander along the beach and collect conch shells I could decorate and sell in Nassau for a few pennies.

How did they get to calling me Story Gal? Well, whenever I'd been to Gran's, I came back loaded with gifts, new shoes, smart dresses. Compared to girls back home, I looked like a fashion plate from a Paris magazine.

I'd tell my schoolmates I'd been away to France. Not lying, Queasy. Spinning story. It was how I practiced for the life I wanted to live one day. When I talked about climbing the Eiffel Tower or walking the Champs-Élysées, it felt like I'd really been there. Anytime I met a French person in the Straw Market, I would beg them to send me a postcard from home. I would take my postcards and put them all together in a photo album. People would crowd around to see my pictures and hear my stories.

"Story Gal," my father would scold. "If you don't stop telling so much story, your soul will be damned to hell. God surely doesn't love a liar."

I didn't think of it as lies, Queasy. I was making stories for myself, embroidering my dull life with dreams, words like sisal sewn in straw.

I read my O levels at the age of 17 and moved to Nassau against my parents' wishes. It used to be so much fun sitting at my gran's elbow as a little girl, watching all the tourists passing by, trying to get them to stop at our stall.

"Hello, pretty lady. Come over, fine sir. Your name on a basket, please?"

It now seemed coarse and common to be begging up these posh white people. As an educated woman I thought I had better options.

There were advertisements in the papers for "Office girl wanted. Must be of good appearance."

Mind you, it was high-color gals they wanted for the banks, shops, and offices. I found that out. The only job for me was just like I had been doing all my life, waiting on white people. I got hired at The Yellow Bird, a little cafe on Parliament Street.

I don't know what it is about these white guys, they always seem drawn to me. A guy in his fifties, Pierre Delacroix, used to be lunching at The Yellow Bird. I would always catch him staring at me. He sat at my table every day.

In Bahamas, we used to call lunch dinner.

"How's your dinner today, Pierre?" I'd always ask.

He would complain about the food, just to have a chance to chat me up. I asked him one day, "If you don't like the food, then why you keep coming back?" He said it was so bland and ordinary that he

*hardly knew he was eating Bahamian. He told me he was waiting for
me to serve him something special.*

You know how some men can't bear to admit they want you? They
will only give you negative attention, like the boys at school who dip
your plaits in the inkwell.

He spoke with an accent I thought was French, so that attracted
me to him. I would get Pierre to fall in love, marry me, and take me
back to Paris with him. I'd give those peasants on Mayaguana something to see, a photo album full of real photos. I saw myself in the gardens of Tuileries, dressed up fancy in a fluffy white wedding gown.

It would never happen if I couldn't get him to see me as something
other than the girl who brought his dinner. "Come back here the same
time tomorrow, Pierre. I'll have some real Bahamian meat for you."

Next day early morning, I went to Potter's Cay. It's a local market
beneath the Paradise Island bridge where you can get just about anything Bahamian to eat, fresh and cheap—conch, fish, seafood, produce. I looked all around until I found a nice live iguana selling at a
good price. I took it to The Yellow Bird in a basket, killed it, skinned it,
cut it up, and made iguana, country style.

The nerves on iguana take a long time to die. You lift up the lid and
the meat is twitching and jerking like it got somewhere to go. You have
to cook it slow, stew it down in boiling water with salt, onions, sweet
pepper, garlic, and seasoning. Then serve it up with a nice plate of
peas and rice.

Oh, don't turn your nose up, Queasy. You just don't know how delicious is iguana stew. Once it cooks up in a nice gravy, you'd never
know that soft, clean meat was once a loathsome creature. The taste is
a cross between stewed chicken and hutia.

So Pierre came in at lunch as usual, ate his Bahamian meat, and fell in love with it. It wasn't until he fell in love with this Bahamian meat, that I told him what he'd eaten was iguana stew.

Oh, Queasy, you should have seen his face.

"But this is impossible!" He turned perfectly green and clutched his belly. "I have eaten reptile?"

Of course, he forgave me. He loved me by then. He was not like these island men who always want to stick it in you bare, don't care about you getting the pox or pregnant. Pierre never made love to me without first putting on his "French letter." He knew that I was young and clean, and he wanted to protect me.

He showed me a life that I had never seen before. Diplomatic parties, dinner on the town, romantic picnics at the Botanical Gardens. For the first time in my life I saw the Bahamas the tourists came there for.

It turned out that he wasn't French at all, but a clerk at the Canadian Consulate. Pierre was sent back home before the year was up, and tried to kiss me off with a few dollars, like he'd spent a weekend with a hotel tart. I wouldn't let him off the hook that easy.

I told Gran that we were engaged to be married, but his money was tied up in Canada. She reached into her bosom and peeled off a roll of Yankee greenbacks. That was her bank, a little purse tucked into her bosom.

Some of the money went as a bribe for my visitor's visa. The rest went to buy my airplane ticket. Pierre was surprised to see me in Montreal, but he took me in. The relationship didn't last, but I did. I'd finally gotten away from the islands, and I wasn't going back because of an old man with a weak nature.

* * *

Despite the fact that we were the only ones in the room, Cedella cupped her hand to my ear and whispered loudly into it.

"Man problems, if you know what I mean."

"What, he couldn't get it up?"

Cedella giggled.

"Not on a regular basis. Personally, I think he was a little on the gay side. Now, Hector, he was a real man. Not a gay bone in his body. And did you ever see his equipment?"

And off she went again, dancing through the mud of her memories. I let her chatter on unchallenged. I felt peculiarly sordid and listless, as though I were being spat upon but couldn't summon the energy to wipe myself clean.

". . . and a white liver to match, oversexed as he was. God knows, I've caught him in any number of compromising positions over the years . . ."

There was something cloying about her little-girl voice, as sweet, syrupy, and debilitating as the black currant liquor she stirred into endless glasses of Pol Roger.

". . . come back from snorkeling and she's lying in our bed, naked to the world. Some little whore, ready to do God knows what with my husband, who was probably off fooling around on the other side of the island . . ."

I sat there watching the tape counter click off the numbers. I nodded at the right places as she rambled on, but I had stopped listening. My mind skipped ahead to what else I had planned for that day. The erection twitched listlessly in my pants, like a half-dead snake. Maybe it wasn't swollen with lust, but infected with all the lies floating around the room.

"So I'm standing there with the twins at my side going, 'What the hell?' With a man like that, every slut out there between seventeen and seventy wanting to bed him . . ."

I felt as if I were drunk on Kir Royales, although I hadn't touched a drop. Maybe the fumes had gotten to me.

". . . thinks she's going to take my man with her looking like that, and me looking like this? You're a man, Queasy. What do you think?"

I shook my head to clear it. The recorder had stopped at the end of the tape, but I couldn't summon the energy to flip it over. Cedella was standing before me, pivoting on her heel like a beauty pageant contestant. The belt on her robe loosened another notch, showing yet a wider view of her naked torso.

"Doesn't this body look pretty good to be damned near fifty? Especially after having twins?"

"Yeah, you look great. You're coming undone, though."

The compliment had been crudely solicited, but it was genuine. I quickly averted my gaze as she opened her robe and re-belted it. My slumbering erection sprang back to life, and I put a hand in my pocket to hold it still. My eyes strayed back of their own volition. I found myself mentally comparing her to the woman whose body I knew best.

Alma was always fretting about her figure. When she was thin, she worried about the relative smallness of her breasts. I would assure her they were perfect, just enough to hold in the palm of my hand.

Now that they spilled from the cups of her bras, she worried about their growing size, their slight sag. Sometimes I grew tired of reassurance.

When Alma began to point out flaws, I found myself looking at them critically. Once she went on and on about her love handles. I suggested a weight room at the local YMCA. I was still apologizing days later.

Women, I realized, didn't want their flaws confirmed. They only bring them to light so that the laser of the loved one's assurances can burn them away. Instant liposuction.

Cedella's breasts were clearly outlined beneath the thin material of her dressing gown. They seemed perky for a woman her age. I wondered how she'd made it into her late forties without them falling, or whether they'd been surgically altered to stay upright.

Alma's breasts had grown heavy with pregnancy and nursing, never returning to their former proportions.

I wondered whether Cedella breastfed her twins. And if so, whether it was done in tandem or one at a time.

When Alma didn't remove her makeup before making love, I'd find smudges of lipstick on my flaccid penis afterward.

I saw Cedella's lipsticked mouth moving a mile a minute, and wondered whether and how often she'd gone down on Hector.

Alma would fret from time to time that childbirth had stretched her out inside.

I found myself wondering idly if Cedella was still tight down there. I noted the narrowness of her hips and wondered how she could have given birth to twins and still have a body like a kid herself.

I shook my head to disperse the random, deviant thoughts floating through my mind like airborne soot. It was true what Mama used to say, "An idle mind is the devil's workshop."

I popped out the cassette and reached for my briefcase. Cedella's hand shot forward, grabbing the handle.

"I know you aren't thinking of leaving, Queasy."

"It's getting late, Cedella. I'm going to have to call it a day."

"But haven't you forgotten something?" She reached into her pocket and brought out a handful of miniature tape cassettes. She stood riffling through them like cards in a deck, her dimples deepening in a teasing grin.

"What have you got there?" I asked warily.

"Lend me your machine and you'll hear for yourself. I have conclusive proof of who killed Hector."

I reluctantly handed over the recorder.

"What makes you think someone killed Hector? The coroner says he died from natural causes."

I watched her fit the cassette into the chamber.

"Come on, Queasy. You think he was murdered too. Otherwise you wouldn't be doing all this snooping around. Imagine if you wind up cracking the case. Your book will shoot to the top of the bestseller list. I won't claim any credit myself. I'll let you tell the whole world who murdered my husband."

She clicked the Play button, held the machine to her ear, nodded with satisfaction, then turned up the volume.

Although the voice that floated out was a familiar one, there was something decidedly different about it. A slightly higher pitch. A disquieting anxiety that I'd rarely heard expressed. Several seconds elapsed before I recognized it as my wife's voice.

Alma: Just what do you want, Hector? Why do you keep calling here?

Hector: I need to talk to you. I thought we were going to do this thing.

Alma: Do what thing? I haven't the faintest idea what you're talking about.

Hector: You know. What you promised me.

Alma: I promised you nothing, Hector. I only said I'd see what I could manage.

Hector: What? You need to dodge your old man, right?

Alma: I'm sure that your old lady's keeping him busy enough, Hector.

Hector: We need to finish what we started, Alma. An hour of your time, that's all I ask.

Alma: Oh, all right. I'll do it, if only to get you out of my hair. When this is over, you're never to bother me again.

Hector: Where shall we meet? Can you come up here to my place?

Alma: Hell, no. Why should I have to drive all the way up there? Besides, I don't want to be alone with you.

Hector: Why, Alma? Don't trust yourself?

Alma: You keep that up and we're calling the whole thing off. I want to meet in a neutral place. Make it seven tomorrow night. There's a hotel not far from me . . .

Cedella reached for the controls, stopping the tape in mid-sentence. She leaned across the passage separating our beds, watching expectantly.

"I don't know what you want me to say, Cedella."

"Isn't that proof enough for you? The night my husband dies, your wife is arranging to meet him somewhere."

"That's bullshit, Cedella. Alma was nowhere near Hector on the night he died."

Cedella stuck out her chin defiantly. She tilted the Pol Roger bottle, bottoms up. Empty. She sucked her teeth in annoyance and filled her glass with straight Chambord. I realized that she'd finished an entire bottle of champagne by herself, yet showed no obvious signs of intoxication save the expanding balloon of lies and the loosening dressing gown.

"Let me ask you a question, Cedella. Where'd that tape come from?"

Cedella's dimples creased into an infectious smile. She looked like a child who had done something exceptionally well, and was waiting to be congratulated for it.

"Well, just between you and me," she confided. "When Hector had me in to redo his loft, I asked a guy I know to slip in a few bugs here and there."

"Do you realize that wiretapping is a federal offense?"

The smile turned into a childish pout.

"I was only trying to protect my husband."

Cedella sat on the opposite bed, beaming at me. I couldn't imagine a more innocent, artless smile.

"How'd you talk Hector into letting you in his home? It must have taken some doing."

"Actually, it did," she admitted. "The wife was out of town for an extended period. I begged Hector to let me do the job for free, all he had to pay for was material and labor. I told him that I needed to build a portfolio to show to prospective clients. If he liked the work, maybe he'd refer me to some of his well-heeled friends. It was the perfect cover story."

Cedella eased back, batting her eyelashes and sipping Chambord. With all of her movement and manic fidgeting, Cedella's dressing gown had grown progressively looser since she'd tightened it. Maybe all that liquor had finally taken effect. She seemed blissfully unaware of how far it hung open in the front. She lurched forward to touch my arm and her breast popped out.

It had been years since I'd seen another woman's naked breast. Cedella glanced up to catch my reaction, and I suddenly knew that all the provocative peeks and flashes of skin had been deliberate. The head of my penis throbbed, seeming to nod in affirmation. It felt ready to burst in an explosion of flesh, booze, and lies. I felt like an animal teetering on the edges of a steel-jawed trap. Caught dick first, trying to break away.

The ringing of the telephone released me. Cedella snatched it up quickly, one breast still exposed.

"What is it?" she barked, then softened her tone. "Oh, it's you. Did you get it? Good. Just give me another fifteen minutes, then come on up."

When she placed the phone on its rest, I sprang to my feet.

"I can see you've got things to do. I won't waste any more of your time."

"Talk to me, Queasy," Cedella murmured, "tell me what you think. Didn't you find that conversation between Alma and Hector the least bit suspicious?"

"I refuse to believe my wife had anything going on with Hector, much less played a role in his death. It's time for me to leave."

As I prepared to leave a cassette tape went tumbling to the floor. I leaned over and picked it up. Cedella grabbed my hand, pressed it to her naked breast, and held it there. My palm tingled, more from the hard edges of the cassette than contact with her skin.

"I didn't mean to upset you, darling," she murmured. "Are you sure you want to leave just this minute? Can't I convince you to stay a bit longer?"

Her face was sharp above her soft, silk-wrapped body. Her dimples deepened purposefully, although she wasn't smiling.

"No," I said, pulling my hand away. "I really need to get going."

"Suit yourself." She shrugged the breast into hiding, then tilted back her glass and drained the contents. "I practically served myself up on a silver platter, and you don't give me so much as a second look. You obviously aren't much of a man."

I couldn't control the image that sprang to my mind of Cedella with an apple in her open mouth, one tit hanging from her open dressing gown, reclining on a bed of lettuce atop a silver platter. I couldn't help it. Laughter rose from my belly in waves, erupting from my mouth in harsh guffaws.

"Just what in the hell do you find so funny?"

"Just life," I managed to sputter. "Life with an apple in her mouth."

Cedella's face grew harder still, her dimples frozen like commas in her soft brown cheeks. She stalked over to the door and flung it open, pointing to the hallway outside.

"Get out!"

I slid past Cedella. The door slamming shut behind me snapped the string of my laughter. I wiped tears from the corner of my eyes and headed toward the elevator. I met a familiar face when the doors opened in the lobby. Short and slight like his mother, pale and blond like his father, Sonny Guzman struggled with a case of Pol Roger.

"I know you," he murmured.

"Sonny, that box looks heavy. Why not let the bellhop handle that?"

He continued to regard me, glassy-eyed.

"Here." I took one end of the box, guiding him onto the elevator. "I'll help you."

"Who are you?" he asked as the door slid shut, trapping me inside.

"It's your Uncle Kwesi. Your father's old friend. Don't you recognize me?"

He nodded finally.

"Kway-see," he repeated carefully. "Mummy always says it wrong."

"Yes, I know."

He reached toward the row of numbers, then looked at me apologetically.

"Would you happen to know where I'm going, Uncle Kwesi?"

My heart seized in a paroxysm of sympathy. Poor Sonny, the

one they called Hector's Moon Calf, was rumored to be everything from drug addicted to mentally defective. I felt I understood him somehow. I'd been addled in Cedella's presence after
just a couple of hours. I couldn't imagine having her for a
mother. I would have given Sonny a hug if I wasn't holding my
end of the box. I pushed the button.

"Your mother's suite, Sonny. I'll ride up with you, but I'm not
going back in."

Sonny's foggy blue eyes shot me such a look of shrewd
scrutiny, I felt like he could read my mind.

"You and Mummy?"

"Oh, no," I hastily reassured him. "Nothing's going on between me and your mother. I was interviewing her."

When the doors opened, Sonny tottered into the hallway, forgetting to take up his end of the load. I struggled out after him,
lugging the heavy box. A door squeaked open at the end of the
corridor.

"Sonny," a voice called, soft and syrupy sweet. "Hurry up,
darling. Mummy needs her drink."

I didn't want another run-in with Cedella. I leaned toward
Sonny, transferring the box into his frail arms. I watched him
turn and stagger down the hallway. Cedella stepped into the corridor, clutching an empty champagne glass.

"Well, I'll be damned," Cedella sang. Her dimples deepened,
winking like the points of a very sharp hook. She leaned against
the doorjamb. "I knew you'd change your mind. Sonny, you
might have to give your mummy and Uncle Queasy a few minutes alone."

I shook my head, backing away. The growing firmness in my groin felt more like betrayal than bliss.

To think that Cedella would have had me there in her sloppy room. A fifteen-minute fuck on an unmade bed, with her shattered son waiting outside the door.

Before actually leaving the Waldorf, I stopped in the men's room, detoured by the overwhelming desire to wash my hands.

I wound up giving myself a hand job instead.

REGINALD HARRIS

Easy

One more set of lifts, a few more squats, and then I can get out of here. Too many New Year's newbies in here this evening. Too much socializing, not enough focus. You'd think Kathleen would appreciate me working out like this, trying to take care of myself. You'd think she'd understand the amount of steam I need to blow off, how I don't want to bring too much crap from work home with me. I still find myself yelling at her for no reason sometimes, or snapping at the kids, even after hitting the gym three, four times a week. It would be a lot worse if I didn't come in here and push these weights around. There's just so much to do and not enough time, too many briefs and deadlines for too few junior partners. What does Kathleen think would happen to her if I didn't try to keep up with all that?

The cars, the house, getting the kids into private schools . . . you'd think that maybe, just *may*-be she'd appreciate all the things I've done. My folks did all right, better than the wrecks they both had for parents, that's for sure. But they always felt their pasts breathing hard down their necks like a hot wind. They were permanently scared, as if we all lived on the edge of a cliff. I didn't have the well-connected family that Kathleen and her racist bastard brother had. We had to work for everything.

That's why I'm working so hard, coming in early, a few extra hours on the weekend, trying to make partner. It's what my folks always wanted for me, the kind of goal they'd plotted for me and pushed me toward. Now, it's my turn. I have to give my family the things they deserve, got to keep Kathleen living in the style to which she's accustomed. Sure she married me to stick it to her family, but she also knew I was a solid guy and could provide for her. I have to make some kind of cushion for the kids too. I don't want them to feel the pressure I felt from my folks. I can see Kathleen doesn't have a clue about how tough the world's gonna be on our half-black kids. How could she? That white skin of hers has saved her from so much.

All she does is complain. I'm never home. I'm always working. I don't spend enough time with her, or the kids. We never make love. And now she's accused me of having an *affair*? She doesn't know, she just does *not* know. After all I've done, all I do, to remain faithful. We wouldn't have a home if I wasn't out there pushing, pushing, pushing every day.

"Excuse me, do you mind if I work in?"

I don't recognize this guy. He looks young, like one of the neighborhood toughs who hang out here all the time like this was their local rec center. "No, man, go right ahead."

"Thanks, brother."

On the edge of downtown and not too outrageously priced, this is the kind of gym where you get all kinds. I'm here often enough to know most of the regulars—I guess that makes me a regular too. Like over there, the guy standing next to the mirror, writing down the number of his weights and reps in a little record book. He's staring at me, just like always. We do that black-man head-nod thing to each other. He never says anything, but I see him looking. He always seems to be watching when I do crunches on the incline board. Each time I rise up, there he is, eyes blazing like suns coming up over the horizon of my knees, wearing that maroon Scales U team T-shirt again, and blue baggy basketball shorts. He always wears black socks and either high-tops or boots to work out in, like he just walks in off the street and starts lifting. It's the high-tops today.

Okay, so, yeah, I've been watching him too. Something about him reminds me of someone I went to school with. I've seen him play basketball with the young guys, running, jumping. When he comes up to the exercise floor to do his curls and lifts his form is perfect. His lats, deltoids, and biceps bulge, the muscles straining under the pressure of the weights. He does it, he really works it, and it's paying off. He's toned up really nicely.

And she thinks I have a woman on the side.

I must have been staring too hard this time. Here he comes. Let me get busy. What's my max this week for the shoulder shrug anyway?

"You using these sixties?"

"Go ahead."

He sticks out his hand. "Stephon, man."

I guess I can be friendly. "Hey, Stephon. Vincent."

"'Zup, Vin?"

I shake my head. "Not much," I whisper, lifting a pair of

80-pound free weights from the rack. He nods, picks up a set of weights, and walks back to the mirror.

Stephon, huh? Well, Stephon, if you want to stare at anyone, you should be looking at the guy over there at the station next to you doing squats, not me. That short, brickhouse-looking guy; now, that guy is ripped. He should be in a body-building contest. Sometimes I wish I looked like that, damn, muscle on top of muscle. Nice. I'm okay, I suppose. My stomach's still relatively flat, and cutting my hair short keeps those first gray ones from being too noticeable. Shaving off the moustache helped too, although now when I look in the mirror in the morning I hardly know who I am anymore. It'd been so long since I'd seen my upper lip. Makes people think I'm ten years younger than I am—a little hair was a small price to pay for that. I'll never be on the cover of a men's fitness magazine, but I'm okay.

That little cannonball, though, he's in here all the time, working out with those other black guys. They're all cops, I think. All three of them are tight, with fantastic definition. They even work their legs too, which so many guys forget. That light-skinned one always wears a pair of sweats that hug his ass like a second skin. He's really hairy too, like a yellow bear. I've figured out those guys must work together, be assigned to the same station house or something. They move so easily, spotting each other, flowing around each other like they've been doing this for years. I wish I were smooth like that.

Sometimes it gets so noisy in here, with the music and the TV sets, the sound of guys playing basketball and the clang of weights, no matter how hard I try I get distracted. I keep forgetting to bring a radio or my CDs. Maybe next time.

That Stephon guy—what's with him? He keeps staring at me. We play this game all the time. I glance at him in the mirror, he checks me out as he walks by, same thing every time. He's harmless, I guess. I like humoring him just to give him a little thrill, you know? Like the one night we took it all the way out into the parking lot, staring at each other as we left. It was fun, nodding and grinning at each other as we drove away in opposite directions. Just a silly game. He carries himself well, but I see guys like that in here all the time. I know what he wants. Even at work, either the mail guy or one of the partners, they watch me all the time. Like they know something. What do they think they know?

Kathleen thinks she knows something too. She thinks I'm screwing around with women. Well, let her think that. It's better that way. As if I had time for an affair, the way I'm carrying everything around on top of me all the time—the house, the job, the kids, and her, everything everyone expects from me all piled up on my head, until it starts sagging down around my ears. Who could blame me for wanting to set it all down, even for a little while? For wanting some kind of release; a place where I can let it all go and just *be*.

"I know you from someplace, man, I know it." Stephon had walked up right next to me when I wasn't paying attention.

"Someplace other than from here, you mean?"

"Yeah. You live around here?"

"No, I'm out in Windsor Hills. I work for Welles, Schlamme, though, two blocks down on Park."

Stephon nodded his head vigorously, making his dreadlocks bounce around his shoulders. "See, I knew it. I'm at Big Apple, right around the corner from y'all. I bet I seen you in there, eating."

I knew he couldn't be in corporate America with that hair. "I've been in there a couple times, sure. The firm has you guys cater all their meetings."

"Yeah, well, I manage the carry-out side of things over there. Maybe you should say something when you stop in for lunch one day. I'll hook you up."

"Maybe I will."

"Cool." Again a quick grin, more like a flash of light. Stephon nods, mouthing the words "I knew it" as he walks away, looking down into his workout book for the next exercise on his schedule for the day.

Oh, Kathleen, why did you get me started thinking about this crap? Who has time for any outside shit anyway? And women? You're the only woman I ever wanted. I mean, sure, everybody fools around in high school, college. This guy on the college track team, Jeffery and I, a couple of others, used to do it all the time. Get together at someone's house after school before their parents got home, or else in the shower or locker room after practice was over and everyone else had left. It was no big deal. What else you gonna do with all those raging hormones and pent-up frustration?

Girls were taught to be prissy and keep their legs closed, but they feel it too. Some of them put out, but mainly guys have to make do with jerking off in the middle of the night. Guys in the military understand that, needing to have a friend to help you out. Don't ask, don't tell, nobody cares. Even in law school. Now, there I was surprised. And Catholic school too. No one would believe what goes on in some of those bathrooms. But, you know . . . that's men for you. Always looking for something "other," a little bit of extra on the side. You're supposed to grow out of that kind of thing. Get serious, settle down, raise a family. Marry your college sweetheart. Start a career. All that other stuff, you just put that away. Leave it behind. Forget about it. It was easy to give that up, no big deal. I can go either way.

There's always a bunch of new guys in here after the first of the year, eager to get rid of holiday pounds. They're easy to spot: too friendly, always looking around to make sure they're holding the weights correctly, sporting their coordinated workout gear and brand-new athletic shoes. They're dedicated—until they begin to think coming in on the regular is boring because they don't see fast results. Or else they push themselves too hard and pull something, then wake up in the morning with throbbing muscles. Most won't make it to February, March at the latest, I bet. It takes commitment to persevere. Keep on going and going and stay the course no matter what if you want to change.

Check out that older man and the young guy with him. He knows everybody's looking, wondering how such an old guy can have that young buck with him. I bet they don't think about how hard he has to work to keep Youngblood happy. Maybe he's always wondering if tonight's the night he's going to lose him to someone younger. Nobody wants to be one of those old men you see out drinking too much, grabbing on every ass they see, paying thugs for the privilege of sucking them off while they sit back watching women with huge tits in a porno. All the men in here are thinking about is how amazing it is to watch the young guy slowly caress himself as he oils up after a shower, then slips into his clothes.

I grab my towel and head for the locker room. Stephon is finishing up too, and walks up the stairs to the locker room with me. Looks like I've made a new friend.

"You married, Vin?"

"Yeah."

"Why are you laughing?"

"I'm sorry. Nobody calls me 'Vin,' that's all."

"Hell—Vin Diesel, right? He's who everybody in here wants to look like, right? Or else The Rock. They the guys getting all the play now, you know."

"Yeah, I guess you're right."

I don't know what else to say, so we climb the stairs and head down the hall in silence. I don't feel any obligation and I don't have to say anything, really. He came up to me, right? Then why is my heart pounding?

"And 'Vincent' is kinda formal. Or do you go by 'Vince'?"

"No, no, 'Vin' is okay. I like it, actually."

"Then 'Vin' it is, brotha."

Of the long rows of gray-green lockers lined up like soldiers, I always take one in the back, away from the novices and the socializing. Unless he's put his things in one of the lockers close to mine, I'll be able to shake Stephon loose.

"Married with kids too, I bet."

"Two kids. How'd you know?"

"No reason, Vin. You just look settled, is all."

I grunt. "Yeah, like a house. Settled into its foundations."

"It can't be that bad."

"It's not like being single, Stephon, I can tell you that." I start to head toward my locker.

"Sure, of course not. But even single guys don't want to be alone all the time. We need to hook up sometimes, you know."

"Yeah, I guess you would." I call out from the end of the room. I unlock my locker and strip off my gear. No steam today, just straight to the shower and then home.

There have been days when Stephon's gone so far as to stare at me in the shower. He'll probably do it again today. I don't play that shit. Let him do whatever the fuck he wants to do—it's on him, not me. One thing he does do, as always, is walk around the locker room naked, long rope of dick swinging, making even the straight guys take notice, confirming all the white guys' fears about black men. It's embarrassing. I don't feel the need to put on a free show. I wrap a towel around myself and head to the shower.

"Nice ass," Stephon whispers when I walk in, as he tries to hide that thing between his legs waking up. What's wrong with the guy? He's really off the chain tonight. I ignore him and turn on the water. Stephon must sweat a lot when he works out, because I can almost taste his funk, spilling from his armpits and crotch as the water hits him. I don't know why I hadn't noticed it before. Something about his smell mixed with the too-sweet soap of the shower overwhelms me. I can't breathe, as if I'd been in the sauna too long trying to inhale the damp air.

I turn toward him and Stephon smiles slightly, unveiling a line of ivory between his plum-colored lips. His skin is dark and smooth. As he lathers up, the soap slides down his hairless chest and legs like tiny marshmallows swirling in a cup of hot chocolate. His large sleepy-looking eyes remain steady on me until someone else comes into the shower area. Then he turns to face the wall. I step from the stall, grab my towel and dry off. I face the wall as I towel off so the plump globes of his ass will stop calling me. I hate to admit it, but there's a pull to all this bullshit that excites me, a dick-hardening thrill to doing wrong in public, and the possibility of getting caught.

After his shower, Stephon walks over to me in the locker room, naked except for the towel hanging casually over his shoulder.

"Think we're gonna make the playoffs this year? Or you not into sports?"

I keep my eyes focused on his eyes. I don't look at the residue of dampness still on his shoulders. I ignore the one drop of water slowly rolling down his chest, down his stomach, into his crotch hair. "I, uh, I try to keep up. But I don't know about them this year. They've been playing really lousy ball lately. Can't seem to keep it up, keep it together. They always seem to fall apart at the end."

"Maybe you should stop by sometime after the gym. We can catch a game. Bought myself a w-i-d-e-screen for Christmas," he says, opening his arms.

"They're playing Monday night, aren't they?"

Stephon nods. "Next week, yeah. But the team they're tied

for second with plays tonight, though. If they lose . . ." He grins.

"Let me think about it." I turn away and continue dressing.

*   *   *

Why do we label people, anyway? As if we were things: This is an ottoman, that's a side chair. He's this or that. Isn't that how discrimination begins, with labels and stereotypes? Why do we need names for different types of people? Better to think about what kind of person you are. Who you are, how you treat people. Things are just the way they are. People do things because it feels good. It stops feeling good, they stop doing it, that's all. Labeling people puts them into a box. A label makes it easier to stick them in some closet somewhere and forget about them.

"Hit me up on the cell sometime, okay?" Stephon says on the way to the parking lot, holding out a slip of paper.

"Yeah, yeah, sure, I sure will. It was nice talking to you." I look at what he's handed me, but don't really see it. The writing might as well be in hieroglyphics.

"Same here, man, same here. And don't forget about that game."

"Next week, right? Monday?"

"Yeah . . . Or tonight . . ."

*   *   *

Freeway construction has everything fouled up so it'll be another long drive home. At least I don't have to make any stops. With no detour to make I can get home early for a change. Even though I'm lifting weights, I always leave the gym feeling loose and relaxed. I go in tense and come out flowing. She doesn't understand that at all. Kathleen thinks I'm tense at home, let her see what I'd be like if I didn't come down here after dealing with crackers and their deadlines for eight hours. Just because I don't come right home doesn't mean I'm fooling around.

There was a time once, maybe. Once, when I felt as though my life had shattered into fragments. Pieces of myself lay strewn about everywhere, broken mirrors with my face inside. What tips things over the edge when things fall apart like that? Who knows? I have no idea how my life wound up unraveling. I had to take the strands of my self, re-knit them, and put them back in place. Slowly life gets pieced back together. But it always turns different, off-center. Incomplete.

Next week . . . Or tonight . . .

It would be easy. Just follow him home. Sit in the basement, have a couple beers, the game on the big TV. Let his hand accidentally brush my leg. Later you can both blame it on the alcohol, being tired from working out, the end of the week, the wife not putting out, the shots of cheerleaders and the players' wives, all of them blond just like Kathleen. The sudden hard-on is "just one of those things." Every guy knows the damned thing has a mind of its own.

He'll take a swig of beer and say, *"Maybe I can help?"*

So you lean back, and let him do all the work, undoing your belt and zipper, pulling it out of the slit in your boxers. Let your legs spread as wide as a net when his warm, wet mouth takes you in.

Yeah, Stephon, that's it . . . Aww shit . . .

How long has it been, anyway? You deserve a little pleasure. Kathleen says she doesn't like it, does it with reluctance. She can't suck for shit, anyway, so you don't even ask anymore. And that time in the park, well, the kid was just too scared of getting caught, that's all.

You like that, man?

Hell, yeah. Keep doing it just like that.

He didn't know what he was doing. Stephon, though, one look at those big dick-sucking lips and you know: He's a pro.

It always feels so strange, holding another man in your hand, another person's blood pulsing right there in your hand. My fingers gripping, pulling, sliding up and down on it. Hard not to compare: Short guy, big piece—where's the justice in that? And if I were to decide to return the favor, bend over, put my lips around his big thing? Well, that's just to show I'm a good guy, right, a pal? To let him know how much I appreciate what he's doing for me.

And if he wants you to fuck him? Or he wants to fuck you? That's just between the two of you, right? No one has to know what you did to each other, who did what to whom. It's really been a long time since you've gone up in a man, been knee-deep in something really tight, or had someone inside you. And it always felt so good. Like being at the end of the world. No one can expect you to ask your wife to bend over and spread 'em, or to stick something up your ass, now can they? Of course not.

Kathleen's about as far from a freak as you can get. The guy
looks healthy too, and works out all the time, just like you do.
You two don't have to worry about not having any rubbers. It
would make it seem like this is something you both do all the
time, and it's not. This is just one of those things, a one-time-
only thing. Wrapping yourself in plastic just ruins the way it
feels, anyway.

   Damn. That was nice.

   Better than nice. It's been a while . . . Thanks a lot.

   Fuck, man, thank you. You like to wore me right out.

   I guess that means you're too tired to go again, huh?

   Come here, and let me show you "too tired" . . .

*   *   *

I know how wrong it is. That's why I try not to do it. But what
good is knowing right from wrong when it's four A.M. and your
skin is burning? The wife softly snoring, TV still on from when
you both passed out, you carefully sneak out of bed, tiptoe in to
make sure the kids are okay, and then head into the den. Watch
something on cable, read, anything to keep from thinking too
much. Anything to stop the ache, to keep from wanting them.
Anything to stop yourself from seeing them working out, lifting,
stretching, drenched in sweat. If you drift off you might find
yourself longing for the feel of callused hands, the rough lick of
a tongue. You don't want that. You don't want the dreams of a
firm hand on the back of your neck pushing your head down.

   Waking up, it feels like you have little ships inside your veins,
straining to set sail. The cushion is a damp island of sweat and

tears. The room returns to focus, swirling back into the familiar. Around you the house seems empty, cold air breathing against your face as you head back upstairs. Kathleen doesn't even know you'd left. Try to fall back into sleep quickly, before the spell is broken. In this bed the only dreams you have are of running through the streets without your shoes, or of standing up in a meeting and watching helplessly as everything you own falls from your pockets. Maybe it would be better if you just stopped dreaming altogether.

Maybe it's wrong, maybe not. Feelings have to come from somewhere. Who knows? All I know is this: I know I'm not one of *them*. I'm not like those guys at work, thinking they've got people fooled while everyone talks about what they were doing down in the sub-basement. I'm not like those guys at the gym who think it's some kind of bar at happy hour, always laughing and grinning in your face, playing at working out. I'm not like that guy who lived across the street from us when I was growing up, the one with the curled hair and painted nails. I don't talk like that, walk like that, act like that. I see guys like that coming one way and I go the other. I don't relate to them, don't go to their parties or parades, and am never going to call myself by some stupid label. I'm not a name, I'm not a type, and what I do and feel is my own business. I'm me.

"See ya around, Vin."

"Yeah . . . uh, Stephon. See you next time."

"You can hit me up on the cell anytime, okay?"

"Sure, sure, no problem."

"And don't forget that game Monday night."

*   *   *

Just the other day I saw one of the guys I knew in college,
Jeffery. I doubt that he saw me, but who knows. I was with
Kathleen and the kids, taking them out for pizza. It was early
one evening, the setting sun fading, the sky a pale pink on one
side of the city, deepening turquoise on the other, my favorite
time of the day. I had to stop at an ATM for cash, and there he
was, walking away as we drove up. Jeffery always held himself
so stiffly in school, his body tight as a fist, but now, I almost
didn't recognize him. His whole demeanor had changed. He had
become casual, open, relaxed. He turned to the guy with him
and laughed, cupping his hand around the back of the other
guy's neck, as if he were about to pull him into a kiss. His whole
body seemed surrounded by light.

Who knows what his life is really like, what path he chose.
All the moments of his life can't be like that, no one's is. And yet,
whatever he did, it seemed to be working for him. He's lucky.
Some people can't do that. Their paths are set, laid out from the
start. You put your life on a grid, like a workout chart, so you
can see your progress, forward movement. To keep it from spinning out of control. I always knew I'd be here, living this kind of
life. It's what I was told I should have, and all I've ever wanted.
Even if sometimes I think all I want one day is to be able to hear
myself, the sound of my own voice, without the echo of what
someone else wants always behind it.

"Vincent?"

Kathleen places her dry, hot hand in the center of my back.

"Are you all right, honey?"

I should say something.

"What's wrong?"

I have to say something. Let it all go.

"What is it?"

I turn to her and open my mouth. I try to speak, to hear the sound of my own voice. Nothing comes out.

"Tell me."

Tell her? Tell her what? The truth, a lie? My dreams? Let everything out? What I did? What I want to do? What I might do one day, or wish I'd done, but it's too late? We've been married for years, share everything, and know each other so well, it should be easy, right? Right here, everything you've ever wanted. It should be *so* easy.

So how come it never is?

JERVEY TERVALON

Always Running

They say you can't go home again, and why the hell would you want to? But what do you do when Home shows up at your door and you can't talk him into going back where he belongs? And you're not sure that you even want to? What do you say when Home is having a mid-life crisis and needs to get a grip? Or when Home looks at you like only you can save him and you know you ain't up for saving nobody but yourself?

Home sits there reading the *New York Times* like he wants to read the ink off the paper. Home is drowning and hoping I'll save him from all that guilt he's wallowing in. I can see it in the way his shoulders sit high and rigid, the way his mouth is hard and tight, not like how I remember it back in the day when he was the teacher who had funny and interesting things to say.

Home has been living with me for a week, camping out on the couch, waiting for me to invite him into the bedroom for a free one. Men think that when your life gets shitty, all you need to do is fuck and bam, like magic, it's all good.

Men believe some ridiculous shit.

I really need to get rid of him before he starts to get the idea that I'm gonna break down and hand over the pussy, gift-wrapped with a cherry on top.

I admit I can't tell him to go even when he knows he should.

"Margot, you know I could get a motel by the wharf. It's nice and not too expensive," he said.

What did I do, but tell him to shut up.

I like having him here. It's wrong, I know that. He's married. He needs to be back with his wife, not crashing with me. Stay, that's what I want him to do, but I'm wrong.

I'm so wrong.

I do like seeing him twisted up in the blanket when I go off to work, watching CNN, not saying much unless he's shouting about that stupid frat-boy president.

Most of the time he just sits there with his feet resting on the coffee table, thinking.

I could tell from his expression that he was caught up in his own grief about where his life was going.

I knew that expression well, because I had been wearing it on my face for so long that I had to take it to the cleaners.

Life's like that, and then you end up living on somebody's couch. Home found me and my couch, but when I was in his position, I couldn't even find a box to sit my ass on.

I guess making friends wasn't my strong suit. Anyway, three days is long enough to be a guest, longer than that and you're as welcome as a stinking fish.

But you got to feel for the man, he's gone through bad times.

I need to be generous, the kind of person who can let herself be put out. For once in my life I was willing to be inconvenienced. For once I was not going to be a bitch.

I won't even ask him to split the rent.

He'll have to buy dinner and breakfast, but I'll let him slide on lunch. I don't eat lunch.

I needed company and I had a good thing with him, like having a potted plant in the house, or maybe a good-looking dog for security.

Yeah, he's not bad-looking, well trained too, keeps the toilet seat down, cleans up after himself, and never making a move on me, but then I had to ruin it.

I poisoned the well, got the waters churning. Whatever that was inside his head that kept him under wraps burned out.

It was about lust.

Maybe it had always been about lust with him and he didn't know how to let go. I guess I got him started.

* * *

I call him Home because he was my homeroom teacher when I was a senior in high school. Back then I knew he was straight up in love with me, but he never said a word about it. Not like some of them freaks they call teachers. Shit, I had been propositioned so many times by the track coach that when I'd run into him on campus I'd say, "Hell, no!" and keep walking. He should've been glad I didn't sue his ass.

I had to give Michaels that, though, he was professional. Only his eyes would convey what he was feeling, 'specially when I wore something outrageous. Not like that sick-ass sociology teacher who kept pictures of naked girls in his briefcase. Yeah, I heard he was good to go if you needed forty dollars.

I should've known better. I should've dropped dimes on their asses, but back then I thought if a girl got into that madness she did it because she wanted it. Back then I watched out for only one person's ass and that was mine.

Now, I know. It ain't that simple.

Back then I was mad at the world, in it to win it. If you can't hang, get out the game.

I wanted men to hit on me so I could come back with "I don't got the time."

Gave me a sense of power.

I liked being a cruel bitch, 'cause I was one. Really, was there any other way to be?

Back in the 'hood, brothers could not be trusted unless you wanted to be publically humiliated, or even worse. I remember one silly-ass girl in my honors English class who thought she could kick it with a high roller and when she tried to leave him, he took back the car and the gold chains and posted photos all over campus of her naked and doing him. Oh, yeah, fools carried those photos around like trophies. Thank God it was close to graduation. She got her diploma in the mail.

That's why I don't play. A woman has got to be strong or she'll get beat down by life like a porn star with AIDS.

I just assumed (still do) most men are dogs and I was right about that 99.9 percent of the time.

But Home, Michaels, wasn't a dog. I flirted a little bit with him. He didn't fall for it, though, even when I was legal and in college. He stayed cool. I chalked it up to his being married and righteous, though most of the married men I knew were bigger dogs than the unmarried ones.

When Michaels called to see how I was doing, he talked about school, my situation with my parents, about my knucklehead boyfriend.

He never let it slip that he wanted to hit it. He wanted to hit it, no doubt. If he had it would have ruined everything.

It always did.

That's why I don't go to church now, because that minister asked to lick my pussy.

I told him I was going to tell everybody about his sanctimonious, perverted ass and he said to me with a straight face, "Now, don't overreact. Let's be discreet and pray for deliverance."

Conflict is easier for me than relationships. Relationships are about letting down your guard, letting go. But I'll tell you straight up, that's not me.

'Cause what's true in life is this: When you slip, everybody watches you fall.

*   *   *

Funny thing, when Michaels showed up I needed something good to come into my life to keep me from thinking about what I'd done to myself. Sometimes I get myself into trouble because I got habits that I can't shake. I don't even know if I really want to shake them, but this one habit I need to get under control.

I lie.

It's easy to lie if lying gets you what you need.

I lied with a straight face because it was the easiest thing to do. I'll admit that. I'm not proud about it, but it's true. I lie because sometimes it's easier than telling the truth.

I lied about being pregnant.

Back then I had a place in the Oakland Hills right off Fruitvale, below the Mormon Temple. I loved my neighborhood, my view, my solitude. I liked my situation, even though working as a counselor at the Catholic College of Moraga was fucked up. Nothing like being one of the few black people in a sea of white faces to make you feel like a freak. Every time I'd see a black person on campus I'd feel too happy for words. All the black folks knew each other and got along 'cause we had a common enemy—ignorant white people. Then somebody mentioned the coach of the basketball team, said that he was handsome and intelligent and unmarried and I needed to meet him. When I finally did, it took me just a minute to recognize him.

Back when I was a teenager, spending a week checking out college at UC Santa Cruz, we'd dated. But I couldn't get with his program—he was stuck on himself, a Pan-African Oreo. You know how they are. Plus, he was king of the white girls.

He had some kind of power over them, especially the blondes.

Those bitches dropped their drawers soon as they saw him coming. Moses couldn't part the Red Sea any quicker than he got them white girls to spread their legs.

I knew there was no hope we could make that work, so I bailed on him.

Did that whole throw-the-number-in-the-toilet thing. Flushed and flushed again. When I ran into him I'd just turn my head and pretend he was a big-ass sheet of glass with legs.

He was my invisible man of Santa Cruz.

When he realized that I wasn't going to kick it with him, he went on back to being king of the white girls.

I was surprised as shit when we hooked up ten years later.

But not too surprised that two years after that we were done for good.

*   *   *

Jamaal caught me when I was about to lose my mind working with them Catholics. Man, I can't stand to see men in black robes, makes me want to scream. Brother Jones and Brother Jack, you'd think they were all in the Black Panthers. And talk about being stuck up, those Christian Brothers were some arrogant sons of bitches, like they knew the truth and everybody else was just suckers. That shit got me so sick. All they wanted me to do was counsel the black ballers to make sure they didn't kill anybody or rape a white woman. Problem was all they had was white women on that campus. The best player on the team told me he didn't really want to play because he was more interested in his classes than basketball, but that if he quit, he'd lose his scholarship.

Those Christian Brothers were all about black brothers balling for their recruiting pleasure. White boys want to go to a school with a good sports program so their friends won't think their school is gay. Truth is, I thought all the Christian Brothers were gay. They bring me onto a campus where all the black folks are on athletic scholarships to keep them feeling good about being at some silly-ass college where they say they want you, but you know it's just 'cause they need a basketball team with a winning record. I wasn't happy to see Jamaal on that small campus, but to my surprise, time seemed to have calmed his ass down.

He was easy to work with, polite, and all those months I didn't see him with *one* white girl. Then he asked me to a reggae concert. Blame it on the contact high, because soon enough we were fucking.

I had to be high, 'cause that campus was too small to hide anything from anybody, and everybody would know we were going out. I hate for people to be in my business.

It was a mistake, but you know you got to live with them.

*   *   *

When he moved in with me I stopped taking my birth control pills like some fool. I guess I was thinking this was it, life was about as good as it was gonna get. I needed to grab on to my piece of the rock and hold on.

Jamaal is fine, college educated, and gainfully employed, runs five miles a day, and reads books. I ain't stupid, so I went for it.

When I missed my period I was happy.

Happy until I drove out to campus to see him after practice, thinking we could have dinner, tell him the news. I walked into the gym. The ballers were still running drills. Then I saw a pretty blonde sitting next to Jamaal holding a clipboard. When she looked up at him and smiled, I just knew they were fucking.

They were fucking.

I turned my ass around and went home. When he showed up, he went straight to the refrigerator for a beer.

"You want to go out for a burger?"

"Naw, you go."

He shrugged, and went into the bathroom. He came running out clutching the pregnancy kit I'd left on the sink.

"What's up with this?"

"It's nothing."

"What, you pregnant?"

"Did I say that?"

He looked confused.

"The strip is blue so it says here you're pregnant."

"Don't believe everything you read. How you know I left it there?"

"Who else would have? Why are you being so evil about everything?"

I shrugged.

He looked at the blue strip again. "Are you sure you ain't pregnant?"

"What if I am?" I said. "You want to get married?"

Suddenly his eyes narrowed.

"Is that what you want?"

"Well, if it's your baby, and we live together, what do you think?"

Jamaal sat down on the couch looking like a little boy who just found out his pit bull was a punk.

"I just don't think we should rush into this. It's a big deal."

"Oh, so having a baby ain't a big deal?"

"I didn't say that."

"Of course you didn't. You're not gonna be the one carrying a load to term. And when you get tired of playing house you can bail. I'll be the one stuck with the crumb snatcher."

Jamaal jumped up so fast I thought his head would hit the ceiling.

"I don't get this. You so damn moody. One day you're happy with me, the next day you're all pissed."

"Don't put words in my mouth."

"Then suddenly you want to get married like I got nothing to say about it."

"Yeah, Jamaal. You got lots to say about it. I'm not doubting that."

"You just mad 'cause I don't want to rush shit and you got to act a bitch about it."

"Nigga, please! I don't even want to marry your ass. I just wanted to see what kind of dog you were. Yeah, I was just trying to trick you. See how you would act. Now I know. I don't want you living with me. This is over."

Jamaal's eyes narrowed. He turned around, went into the bedroom, packed his bags, and headed to the front door, then without a look back, he walked out.

Maybe I had been wrong about him, maybe not. But it was done and I had to live with it.

Pregnant or not.

*   *   *

Santa Cruz is like a corpse: It might look good, but it's still dead and I like it like that. I came back here because I needed to be somewhere as dead as I felt. I needed space; space to be alone.

I didn't need another man to break me down.

But I don't have to worry about that here. I'm the invisible girl among the pines and oaks, along the beach. Those blond dot-com types walk right by me and it wouldn't matter if I was straight-up naked.

They got their own ideas of what a woman is, and it's not me.

A friend had hipped me to a job opening at UC Santa Cruz in the counseling office, developing programs to make colored kids comfortable. I was now a expert in the field of making black folks comfortable around white folks when the white folks outnumber the black folks five hundred to one. It was cool, though, almost double the money those cheap-ass Christian Brothers had paid me.

Yeah, I get my share of knucklehead girls straight from South Central or Oakland who end up in a place like Santa Cruz and think their lives are over.

For them, the dorms are too open, even with security doors and alarms everywhere. Or they've never seen so many white people, not even on TV. And all those trees. Yeah, I remember how those trees scared the shit out of me. Sure, I admit it, I thought Freddy Krueger was behind each and every one of them. Nobody ever got me to go hiking, and don't even talk about camping. These young black girls, and a lot of them Latinas, come here to Santa Cruz from ghettos and barrios and their worlds get rocked.

I do my best to get them to see that it's more than trees and hippies and all that.

Let them know it's about a world where they can grow safely

into adults. Where they can learn how to be independent, and that's good. They've got to know being independent is the best thing.

I get 50 grand for being troop leader to my own little gang of Brownies.

"Naw, girl, you don't have to worry about white girl gangs in Santa Cruz," I said to Keshia.

"No, don't get all freaked out if a white boy asks you out. Just do what you feel," I told Luwanda.

*   *   *

Michaels distracts me from how alone I am here. When I come in and I see him watching TV I feel good, like maybe he belongs here.

"Hey," I say, and he almost falls on his ass.

"I didn't hear you come in," he says.

Michaels has his UCLA sweatshirt on, and his shoes are sandy. Must have been down walking on the beach, watching the waves.

"Yeah, I'm majoring in Ninja studies."

He looks out the big window with the view of the bay, if you ignored the wires and TV antennas.

"You okay?" I ask.

He gives me a loopy smile and shrugs.

"I called home. She won't talk to me."

"Don't sweat it. She'll come around."

He shakes his head.

"I'm cool. I'll just go for another walk."

He rushes out, not even bothering to take his jacket on a cold-ass winter day.

Michaels surprises me. I never thought he'd be the type to walk out on his wife. But I guess I didn't think he'd be the kind of man who got married. I didn't know him that well to be trying to figure him out nohow. I thought he understood me, and that was just as good as me knowing him.

I knew he had a thing for me from his sly glances and from how he called on me to help him grade papers and run errands back in high school. If I got too close too him, he'd blush. He had it worse than most men. But he never did nothing 'bout it even if he was my teacher. He wouldn't even flirt with me, even when I flirted first. That's why I called him boring. He wouldn't take the bait.

I want to know what happened to him, but he's not talking.

* * *

I got one homegirl up here and she ain't even black. Martha works with me in the counseling office. She stopped by yesterday and was very surprised to see Michaels sitting on the couch like he lived there.

I didn't try to explain when we walked to the Starbucks.

"Are you two a couple?" she asked.

"No," I said, then pulled my hoodie over my head to block the breeze off the bay.

"What's he doing here?"

"He cooling out. He busted up with his wife."

"Well, he looks like he could afford a motel room."

"But he's staying here."

"So, what's it like? He looks a little old for you."

I shrugged. "Yeah, I guess so."

"What's the deal with him? He's going to be your sugar daddy?"

"No, we're friends."

"And you took him in? Wow, I didn't know you were that nice."

"I'm not. You know I'm a bitch."

"Yeah, sure you are." She smiled.

She didn't have to believe me. I had spent too long learning how be a bitch to give up on it at this late date. Yeah, you know how that goes. You plan your life to be a certain way, and then your plans get all fucked up and you wonder, damn, where did I go wrong?

I felt that as soon as Michaels ended up in my bed.

It was the food poisoning.

I've got to leave cheap-ass burritos alone. Once I stopped throwing up, I got the chills something fierce and all I wanted to do was rest. After sleeping for 11 straight hours I felt a whole lot better.

Michaels came in with soup and flu remedies and there I was, covered up in blankets, hoping my breath wouldn't kill him.

"Maybe I should get you to the doctor."

"No, don't worry about me. I'm over the worst of it, even the chills."

He nodded, and pulled up a chair and started reading next to my bed. I was happy for the company and dozed off and on, waking to see him there, keeping an eye on me. It must have been about midnight when I told him to stretch out on the bed.

"Come on, Michaels. I'm not contagious."

He smiled and continued reading.

"I need a back rub," I said.

I guess I needed more attention. It was an open invitation for him to kick it with me. I rolled on my back, slipped off my sweatshirt, and I heard that fat book of his hit the floor.

I felt his warm hands on my back as he worked my shoulders, then he slowly slid his hands to my ass. I guess he thought he was squeezing the Charmin the way he worked my cheeks. I can't say I didn't like it. I rolled over and pulled him down on top of me.

Then I came to my senses.

"Hey, we can't do this."

"What?" He says, totally confused.

I got up and headed for the shower. I let the hot water run, steaming up the bathroom while I sat on the toilet trying to figure out what I was doing. Two and a half months pregnant and I still didn't know what the hell I was gonna do. Even so, I didn't need to be a knocked-up home wrecker. If he was gonna get a divorce then it would be all good, but not now. Now was wrong. I must've been drunk off of the flu medicine.

I showered and put on my robe and went out.

Michaels was on the couch packing his clothes, looking sheepish.

"What are you doing?"

"I'm leaving."

"What? You headed back to your wife?"

He laughed.

"That's over, but I'm not comfortable with this."

"What do you mean?"

"I don't want to make my life any more complicated."

"You mean I make your life more complicated?"

"Try being married for ten years and then it's over and you don't really know why. Last thing I need is to ruin my relationship with you."

I shrugged and patted the couch for him to sit down.

"I don't need this either. I got more than enough complication in my life."

He sat down next to me. I hadn't gained much weight, but I wondered if he noticed my belly starting to show. Anyway, we sat there for a while. Then he turned his head toward me and we kissed.

Why was I lying to myself?

I wanted to. I got out of my robe and he pushed me back and we went at it like we were back in high school doing the worst possible thing. Least, now it was about self-respect and not him going to jail for statutory rape. I let him lick me until we couldn't stand it anymore and then we fucked and when he came he started to laugh like it was all very funny.

I was already pregnant, I couldn't go for a double or nothing.

I started to laugh too, but I didn't let him in on my secret.

I had to have my secrets because I was always on the verge of running from another man.

Always running. Always running.

Narrow is my bed, wide is my road.

LISA TEASLEY

Voiceover

Steamed trout, Thai lemongrass chicken, oyster mushrooms, and coconut rice cool on a tray on the living room floor. Serena Peters-Alls carefully splays her long cocoa limbs under her husband, Alfred Alls, who roughly yanks down her pink lace drawers. They are TV-flash-lit in the dark as he grinds their way through to the springs of the navy-striped couch bed. Serena shifts weight to the plush of her left cheek, saving the wear on her delicate, raw tailbone. With an awkwardly outstretched arm, she manages to snatch her panties out of the peanut sauce.

Propped by his elbows, Alfred grabs on to fistfuls of hair at the nape of Serena's neck. The expression of ecstasy on her face barely betrays the grimace she'd rather make. She fitfully moans so he will speed up his thrusts. He comes, apologizing as always for beating the clock. He crawls down to put his face between her thighs, exhales heavily before noisily licking her up. Serena fantasizes that she is a woman who climaxes when forced.

Three years ago, a week before the wedding, Serena agreed with Alfred that there would be no television in the bedroom, no missed opportunities for making love by falling asleep to a flashing screen. But lately they've found themselves eating on the

249

couch in front of TiVo or DVD, rather than sitting across from each other at the elegant oak dining table. Whether the program is good, passing, or bordering on unbearable, Serena makes sure they commit to the end, usually without interruption or interaction. By the time they get to bed, Serena is snoring moments after her head hits the pillow. Tonight—for the sake of their faltering marriage—she dares to be different.

Until this moment, watching Alfred as he too-swiftly slips from between her legs after her exaggerated orgasm, Serena realizes she never questioned their union. Neither does she admit that she has orchestrated these sexless TV nights to relieve the bed burns on her butt, which have become an overwhelming pain and nuisance. She uses Retinol to remove the layers of darkened, bruised skin at the very base of her spine, which only adds to the fragility and sensitivity of the area. Every time she and Alfred assume the missionary position, the friction causes new blisters that she Band-Aids for a week, waiting for them to bust and ooze. She then wears long, loose dresses with no underwear for the breeze, so they can scab and flake off.

It is during this fresh mid-week Band-Aid burn cycle, after the disappointing Thai food night, that she decides to take a "business trip" from Los Angeles to Seattle. Serena tells Alfred she has a voiceover gig there, but the bulk of her work doing commercials and animation is in L.A., with the exception of a few Claymation spots in Portland.

Alfred has never been a suspicious husband, and Serena has never given him reason to be. Not much of a flirt, she doesn't know her eyes are capable of holding power over men. She maintains a direct stare and an open body language, even in times of threatening situations. Serena considers her voice to be her best feature only because it makes her such a splendid living. However, money wasn't the draw for Alfred, as he has enough of his own, being a leading economist and investor. Rather, he finds her inspiring, particularly in her apparent unshakable confidence in the face of a competitor or adversary.

Serena never uses her direct stare as a means of seduction, and she doesn't spend time weighing her options, heading straight for what she believes was always meant for her. Because of scant distractions—Serena won't allow herself many—she has had relatively few men to which she can compare the unusual (almost cruel) vigor with which her husband bangs her in bed.

* * *

A month later, she finds herself at the Pike Place Market on a rare warm and dry day for November in Seattle. Serena wanders through aisles of lush produce, stopping to ogle the ripely feminine turnips; engorged phallic squash; glossy, pubescent white pumpkins; and fluorescent purple flesh bell peppers. She buys a large basket at the corner stand, deciding a cornucopia of sensuous vegetables is a far better gift for her aunt than a bouquet of fall flowers. Her aunt is not the one Serena hopes to please anyway, but rather her young, gangbanging cousin, Randy, recently sent to stay with his father's sister in hopes of keeping him from the heat of new trouble. Three weeks earlier, Randy's best friend was found boxed and chopped up in neat parts in a warehouse in Long Beach.

Serena—always close to Randy's father—has been especially attentive to her uncle since her mother died of breast cancer five years ago. Her mother was her uncle's most beloved sibling, and Serena is the one child of the extended family who has truly made it on her own to the next level of success. Hoping her influence will rub off, her uncle has urged Serena to encourage Randy, his youngest boy, whose only interest outside of making quick, dangerous money the one way he knows how, is his relatively secret love of cooking. Even when Randy was a kid, he had forsaken cartoons for the Saturday morning PBS cooking shows. All of this Serena surely could have shared with Alfred, if it weren't for the fact of her 20-year-long guilt. When she was a late-blooming 15 and Randy was 10, she led him into their grandmother's closet so he could feel up her new, period-swollen titties.

In the cool Seattle evening, Serena climbs the hill in her nondescript, mid-size rental car to her aunt's bland, upscale housing development of Somerset. She is scared, rather than stifled or bored as she tells herself. *At least,* she says aloud, *there are trees over 100 years old.* She rolls down the window to take in the air she imagines the trees make only for her. Serena feels a prickle in her nose like she might sneeze, but it is more the change of temperature from within. The breeze is sharp and clean, but the heat inside her chest tickles her throat, and her heart thumps as it did before her very first voiceover gig. But once at the mike, as she does in every sound studio, she envisions a more glorious physical version of herself. (Though few would ever consider her unattractive.) The point, she insists, is to believe in the mo-

ment that you are more than what you are, and this she does
nervously, as she scans the addresses on curbs, doors, and mail-
boxes, the numbers alive, jumping, and switching places as if
she had dyslexia.

To her utter amazement, it is Randy who opens the door. Serena blurts out hello, and he takes her in his arms the way you
might a beloved teacher. She can hug only with one arm, as the
other hand holds the vegetable basket, and she butts the toe of
her smart burgundy pump on the threshold as she enters. He
takes the basket from her, as she lifts the heel of her shoe to ex-
amine the scuff. When she looks up at him with embarrassment,
he smiles with warmth for a cousin as well as with appreciation
for a woman. *No, I am not mistaken,* she says to herself.

He leads her back to the sewing room, where their aunt Dossy
is obsessively patternmaking. The two wall-to-wall closets are
packed with old clothes, and there are more piles in each corner.
Dossy barely turns around to greet Serena. She cocks her head,
offering her cheek, which Serena kisses. When she looks up, she
sees that Randy has disappeared.

"So how's that husband of yours?" Dossy asks, not taking her
eyes off her vest pattern.

"Alfred? He's just fine," Serena says, backing away, looking for
a window that opens.

"So you got a commercial up here? What you doing without
him?"

"Yes, a commercial. He can't get away just now. You know, his
analysis of the economy is getting a lot of attention these days."

"Always wondered why we need people like him to tell us

that things are in the crapper, we already know that shit," she says, as her scissors crunch through the fabric. Serena swallows hard, bears down on her jaw.

"Can I get you something to drink, Aunt Dossy?"

"No thanks, honey. Make yourself at home. I think Randy's already called out for a pizza."

"Pizza?"

"What's wrong with pizza, child? You one of those weirdoes that don't eat it?"

"No, no," Serena says, touching her throat with three fingers. "It's just I brought a basket of vegetables for Randy, as I know how much he loves to cook."

"Rim? He hasn't cooked shit since he got here," Dossy says, flipping her left hand, still bent over the pattern.

"But Uncle Dan's always talking about Randy's scrumptious gourmet meals!" Serena exclaims too loudly, then covers her mouth with her palm. Suddenly she wants to make a nasty face at Dossy, who might turn around to catch it.

"Dan." Dossy flips her hand again, and chuckles. "He thinks that boy walks with God." She laughs out loud now. "It's a mystery to me."

Serena clears her throat, and assumes the sophisticated tone that she'd use for a car ad. "Why don't I go see what Randy's up to."

"You do that," Dossy says, turning around to look at her, then laughs.

Serena clutches the collar of her white shirt as she makes her way down the hall, but then she doubles back to the bathroom.

The shelves are pristine, with shells, perfume bottles, and various talcum powders arranged in old lady charm. The toilet has a white fur cover, and the bathmat is a pink shag circle. Serena sits, turning on the faucet to help her pee faster. She quietly berates herself for not drinking more water, taking better care of her throat. She decides she'll ask Randy for some tea and lemon, and they can sit in the crisp, cool air on the balcony and catch up.

She looks in the mirror, licks her finger, and slicks up her eyebrows. She opens her eyes wide. The veins, marks, and sun blisters in the whites make her overly self-conscious. She sticks out her tongue, checks that it's clean, covers her mouth and breathes to smell her breath. *You're not so bad,* she says aloud to the mirror, admiring the natural shape and outline of her lips, the sweetness of her chin, the warm bronze undertone to her dark skin. She pulls on her shirt to tuck it in, pats her stomach, turns to the side, but can't quite see in the mirror as low as her waist. She touches the pleats of her burgundy skirt, then clicks her heels.

The doorbell rings, she hears Randy's footfalls on the linoleum, and she rushes to meet him at the door to contribute. She doesn't notice the pizza guy's striped shirt or the grape stain on his temple, since she is taking in the sexy, grown manner of her younger cousin. He's not little anymore, she thinks. He's a man.

"Aunt Dossy got this," Randy says, refusing her money and taking the pizza into the dining room, where he's already set the table.

"Here I come," Dossy calls, taking her glasses off, which hang on a chain. She crosses the hall swiftly in her navy blue Keds, drawstring-waist jeans, and mustard-colored sweater. She has a skunk's single streak of gray in her hair.

"Wow, I feel like I'm really seeing you for the first time," Serena says. "The light's so dim in there. You've lost so much weight, Aunt Dossy!"

Dossy gives Serena the look she would give an insolent child. "Get me a beer, will you, Rim." She roughly pulls out and plops down on one of the white spindle-backed chairs with tied-on vinyl pink and gray floral cushions.

"What'll you have, Serena?" Randy asks, his voice husky and gentlemanly, his lush midnight eyes sparkling.

"A glass of red would be nice, whatever you have. Merlot or cabernet would be fine." Serena swallows, pressing her lap with the paper napkin, wishing it were cloth.

"There's an old bottle of something under there in the bar, Rim." Dossy flips her hand, and looks at Serena, who stares back at her aunt with challenge.

"So what did you say that commercial was for up here?"

"I didn't. I'm here for an animation voiceover," Serena says, looking directly into her aunt's slanted eyes, laced with salt-and-pepper lashes. If it weren't for the gray or the moles on Dossy's face she wouldn't look much older than forty.

"Uh-hmph," Dossy says, grabbing the beer from Randy's hand. He stands there and uncorks the dusty bottle of wine as Dossy opens the pizza box.

Serena clears her throat. "Hmmm, fresh basil and garlic, this smells wonderful," she says, looking up at Randy.

"How many toppings did you order, Rim?" Dossy knits her brows together.

"Four."

"The coupon allows only for three, didn't I tell you that?"

"The guy took the coupon anyway, Auntie." Randy sits down, scoots his chair in like a proper but scolded child. Serena sighs with embarrassment and impatience.

"So, how do you like Seattle?" Serena asks, looking at Randy.

"It's okay," he answers with a full mouth. Serena looks down at her lap, then leans in to the table and takes a bite.

"Rim needs a job," Dossy says with disgust, picking the mushrooms off her slice.

"What have you been looking for?"

"There's an organic market not too far that needs some help," Randy says, looking at Serena, who brightens.

"He's waiting for the Holy Ghost to call him back," Dossy says, shaking her head.

"Uncle Dan says you're interested in being a chef. You know, a job like that could be perfect for you, while you enroll in cooking school. There must be some great ones here."

Dossy laughs in rolling girlish flutters, the sound of which seems to tickle her all the more, so she just keeps going. Serena ignores her.

"I don't know," Randy says.

"We should get together tomorrow in town. I'll take you to a fine lunch, and we can brainstorm together."

"Brain-*storm*," Dossy says, still laughing. "Where you think this child's s'posed to get the money for *chef* school, girl?"

"I don't know, we'll figure something out," she says, defiantly looking Dossy in the eyes.

*   *   *

The following day, Serena walks carefully in the rain down the cobblestone alley of Pike Street to a brick wall covered with countless colorful dabs of chewed gum. If it weren't such an unusual sight, it would be revolting, she thinks as she makes her way past to the door. It's quiet, dark, and romantic for a pre-noon date at the Alibi Room. She sits near the window, eyeing all the film scripts, event postcards, and flyers stacked in the corner, then peers back toward the kitchen, happy to see a black face.

Alfred calls, as if to punctuate her guilt, and she pretends she is on break at a café across from the sound studio, almost convincing herself. He asks about her butt burn ("How's the ouchie?" as he puts it), which is only the third time he's asked about a problem she's had off and on for three years. She drums the table with her French-manicured nails, getting rid of her husband as she spots her date.

Twenty minutes late, Randy hurries in, dressed in pressed baggie jeans and an oversized canvas hooded jacket. Though Serena had planned for them to meet for coffee, then browse the area for Help Wanted signs before lunch, his dangerously sweet smell and the menu seduces her to change plans. She orders spicy jalapeño and carrot bisque, a stack of portobellos with pesto, parmesan, and yam mash. Randy wolfs down his red beans, rice, and pecan cornbread. After cruising the Pike Place market with two job applications in her black attaché, they run together through the rain only to find that her rental car has been towed.

Walking fifteen blocks through the light sprinkle under a fold-up umbrella, Serena debates how far she should take things with her younger cousin. With a mere five years on him, she still feels like the wiser 15-year-old to his baby-like 10. Visions of self-help books, trashy talk shows, and incestuous, retarded hill-billy offspring dance in her head.

She gets into a screaming match with the young and lewdly painted Chinese woman behind the tow desk, who says she can't give Serena the car unless she shows her rental agreement (which is in the glove compartment). Randy remains quiet when Serena shocks herself by throwing the rental keys—aiming for the girl's neck but missing—and slapping down her rental gold card for emphasis, on the desk. The woman barks that she will call the police, but when Serena stares her down, she calmly calls to verify her card instead.

As they get in the car, the rain pouring, Serena doesn't know in which direction she should head. She asks for directions to Dossy's Somerset neighborhood, though wanting badly to take Randy back with her to the hotel. He's as confused as she is as to which way is the freeway, so she pulls over to find the map. As she reaches behind her to the backseat, leaning slightly forward, her hair brushes his wet jacket. Overpowering her is the erotic smell of the rain, his skin, the car's dank interior, already musky as sex.

His caramel skin flushes with heat as she noisily ruffles the map open. He leans in to look with her for the street they're on. There is a single drop of rain on his finger, which she purposefully touches to feel it melt on her own. Their mouths meet and hungrily mesh together in a mess of tongue and teeth. He puts his hand on her breast, squeezing the nipple so hard it burns between her legs. She takes his hand, puts it inside her pants, which she unzips for ease. She is so wet, wetter than she'd ever been with Alfred, and the Serena she's always known would have been ashamed of that. In the moment, as they climb into the backseat, limbs knock, clothes peel off in loosened buttons and small rips. As he enters her, Serena feels dizzily hot, happy, and desperately relieved to have once again gone straight for what she always wanted.

*   *   *

Nothing is more awkward than dropping Randy back at her aunt's after having passionately fucked him in the backseat of her rental, stifled by the steamed windows, the pounding of the rain, and the pounding inside her chest. He says nothing to her as he opens the passenger door, now feeling some gravity as well, she thinks. *These kind of things happen, it's not such a very big deal*, she says aloud, as he gallops toward the front door and she pulls off without looking back.

In the hotel room, Serena orders Pay-per-View porno, and makes herself come again before sleep. In the morning, she calls her aunt's house and is relieved to get Randy on the phone. She imagines she is a woman in control of her life, she envisions herself in a sound studio, doing a sexy but authoritative voiceover, when she asks him if he has filled out the job applications. She is too thrilled, she thinks, when he says he has, and too eager, furthermore, when she rushes in that she will pick him up to deliver them.

There is an ever-so-slightly cocky lilt to his lips when he smiles hello, and she does not kiss him as he climbs into the car. Afraid of being towed again, she waits, listening to the car stereo for 40 minutes. He returns with a small bunch of near-wilting, rust-colored daisies, and tells her he had a good talk with the manager, who said he would refer him to the owner. She places the daisies on the backseat, suspecting him of having grabbed them from the store's two-day-old stash, and of lying about the manager, and everything else. With no conscious rationale whatsoever, contempt builds inside that Serena mistakes for rage. When he asks her what's the matter, as she turns on the engine, she snaps back that all is perfect. Her cell phone rings in traffic, and she lets it go to message as she tries her best to find the freeway on-ramp.

Cursing herself for taking him all the way back to Aunt Dossy's rather than the hotel, where she imagines sitting on his face, Serena dreams she is someone else when she goes into the house after him. The sewing machine hums from Dossy's room as Randy signals her from the hall, and they tiptoe past. His room is empty and beige, clothes strewn about. He turns to her with a brief, embarrassed expression on his face. Not only lust but also compassion overcomes her, as she remembers the recent loss of his best friend. Wondering if she's ever been anything but totally self-centered, she grabs him by the wrist, pulls him into the cedar-smelling walk-in closet, and unbuttons his pants. He closes the closet door behind them, and down they go for a sloppily cramped but deliciously naughty 69.

"Rim, you in there!" Dossy bangs on the bedroom door just before Serena can come. She's on her back, trying not to rub the butt burn that is Band-Aid–free but softly scabbed.

"Just a minute, Auntie, I'm not dressed!" Randy calls, Serena imagining his teeth again with braces. She remembers the hot, bubbling tomato smells of the stewed chicken sauce; she can see her mother at the card table with Randy's father; and she starts to cry right there in the closet, the pain fresh and sharp again over her mother's death, any thought of coming long gone.

"Shit," Randy hisses, pushing his way out of the closet, pulling on his pants so fast he trips but catches himself before falling.

"Why's the door locked!" Dossy calls.

"Goddamn it, Auntie, I'm not a child!" he yells. Serena still cries, shuddering, half-naked, lying in a ball on the carpeted floor of the closet.

"I need help." She bangs the door. "Why is Serena's car out there?" Dossy bangs again. Randy opens up once Serena shuts herself behind the closet door.

After what feels like hours to her, but is actually 20 minutes, Randy returns to shuffle Serena out of the house, now that he has helped Dossy with a fallen shelf and she is safely in an Epsom salt bath. He is calm again, having told Dossy that Serena lent him the car, having no use for it since she has an all-evening voiceover session, the studio being minutes from the hotel.

Serena rubs her red eyes, sorry that he is such a smooth liar. He grabs her by the neck as if to choke her, but kisses her roughly instead. He pushes her down on his bed, and with his hand over her mouth, bangs her butt raw into the old-fashioned, white, nubby-knit spread.

* * *

Back at the hotel, it is Serena's last night in Seattle. She opens the window wide, and breathes in. Room service knocks on the door, and she holds her robe together at the throat. The waiter puts the tray on the bed, and she imagines herself the kind of woman who would open the robe, show him her ravished body, and the way to pleasure her best. Instead she signs the bill, adding a hefty tip, then looks him in the eye in that direct way she has. He smiles uncomfortably, nods, then tells her that if there's anything else she needs at all, to just ask for Tim.

She goes through the Pay-per-View movie list as she eats the risotto, not caring for her striped bass, and drinks her white zinfandel too fast. *Why leave the hotel room key on his bed? Dumb, dumb, dumb,* she says aloud, slapping the tray, but spilling nothing since her glass is empty. She shifts the menu to porn and, embarrassed to have already seen three of them, she thinks of Alfred, who she realizes has always simply wanted her attention. Serena grabs her cell, dials home, and when he picks up, she breathily, excitedly asks, "How about a little phone sex?"

GREG TATE

A Ballistic Affair

*I*n Marina's experience, the boys with the guns were always the most beautiful boys, the most game boys. The only boys she wanted to talk to at parties, the only ones she could see herself going home with at the end of the night.

Marina always demanded they wear their little buddies to bed. She loved the feel of grooved, tippled metal grazing her stomach, breasts, and ribs.

She lived to absorb the love taps a weapon's icy weight doled out when her one-night beaus took to tossing and tumbling her around. One fellow, a true professional, revered among his cronies as a killer's killer, brought three sidearms when he came to bang her: the .38 he kept strapped across his chest, the .22 he'd taped to his thigh, and this old-school miniature, tubular zip gun of a thing which he kept clipped to the Prince Albert piercing clamped onto his phallus. (She told best female friend Duck that she had never, ever, in her frothy recollection, come harder.)

Marina didn't keep any guns in the house. They meant nothing to her if they didn't come with a warm male body attached. There was one guy who spoke of a desire to rub his unholstered

weapon's barrel around and around her clitoris and then pump
its clipless stock on her labia majora, but she refused him. She
liked the idea but instinct told her to save it for a less gung-ho
guy—the kind of guy who'd have to be convinced that was such
a good idea.

*   *   *

Marina refused to acknowledge her taste in men as a fetish. She
remembered having sex and even enjoying it without guns being
flashed or being used to fondle her, and when her work required
it she could even manage a projectile orgasm without a firearm
grinding against her ribs. For this reason she refused to counte-
nance the notion that the pleasure she took from sex with gun-
men made her some kind of addictive, freaky gun moll.

As always with Negroes, it's the reductive label that they hate
(straight, bi, gay, dominant, submissive, fetish freak) more than
the act itself. This is why we so commonly hear things like "I
fuck men but I'm not gay" and so forth. Labels tend to read like
prison sentences to blackfolk who often find their freedom in
fluid states of being. This would be particularly true of blackfolk
like Marina who fancy themselves a breed apart.

Her, a fetishist? She just couldn't see it, no matter how often
friends called upon Freud for backup. It helped that what she
knew about fetishes, in a clinical sense, was next to nil. This is
why, to her mind, if there were no elaborate rules and no special
makeup or studded leather harnesses, and no feverish theater of
the repressed mind going on when there were small arms center
stage, then she was no fetishist. Far as she was concerned it was

simple: She just liked boinking guys with guns strapped on because she mightily liked the feeling of those hard, slick, powerful, life-determining things bumping and jumping her bones.

She would admit to loving the element of risk involved. Some of her guys wanted to remove their bullets first, and she would let them; that was no biggie for her. Registering the click of the safety was as close as she came to security measures. What she didn't always like was the extreme roughness of some of the more stubbled grips or when some of the left-handed guys wore their pieces with the grip pointed inward, as that made her feel like her titties were being hammered against.

The few and far between occasions when she had slept with women let her know her taste in girls ran toward nothing more deadly than spiky jewelry and small blades—preferably unsheathed, since she didn't mind a few nicks and cuts here and there and favored the shiver she caught whenever she spied small streaks of blood splattering the sheets. Nothing her regular cleaning lady wasn't used to or couldn't emotionally handle. In her time with Marina that poor woman had had to clean up far worse stains, though none worse than those left behind after her Guinness book escapade—a 48-hour stunt involving live chickens, lusty robot zombies, Roman candles, and a stereotypically correct Talking Hottentot Booty doll. This performance is now officially recorded as the world's longest continuous work of performance art.

One critic even went so far as to describe the piece as "bridging the gap between Yoruba, necrophilia, and the African genome," that fanciful description being much to the disgust of her Yoruba-practicing father, mother, and two older brothers, all of whom were forced to hear about it at a self-congratulatory dinner in the Hamptons Marina threw for herself after *not* being nominated for a Tony award that same year. ("I mean, really; a Tony, Duck? I mean, c'mon, how monumentally uncool is that? The day I quit the business is the day they hand me a Tony. I mean, I've had my un-acceptance speech ready for years.")

If Marina would not admit to being a textbook fetishist, she would acknowledge being a very wild girl. "Yes, I'm that perfect heretic that stereotype tells us every upright preacher's daughter must turn out to be."

* * *

Marina had long ago decided that embracing the stigma of being seen as a godly man's wild child demanded much from her outrageous imagination. In her late 20s she became fond of telling friends and always-kept-distant relations how "Having discovered my role early in life I decided to give it all I had. What was left, I gave to off-off Broadway." Her current show was a faux-feminist extrapolation, *The Virtues and Varieties of Our Virgin Mother's Orgasm*. In it she and 27 other women portrayed a composite of orgasmic states that had been dutifully researched by Marina and co-writer Duck over a five-year span in several predominantly Catholic countries. Holy and unholy states of ecstasy were all given their due in the course of the performance's three-hour run.

Marina herself played two roles in the production. In the opening minutes she played a kidnapped nun named Mariah, who develops Stockholm syndrome and has sex-starved visions of dressing her captors in robes and habits and humping them to death. In the second act she came on in the role of an East Harlem woman not so unlike herself who was going for the Guinness Book world record in projectile orgasm.

Though all of Marina's understudies required a fluid-shooting harness and unsightly catheter tubes taped near their private parts, Marina was a natural at long-distance female ejaculation. On her best nights she could fling her bodily fluids just a few inches shy of the light array mounted 10 feet above the set. According to the skit's plot, the day the Guinness film crew arrived they'd find her character's prone form set to erupt like a volcanic geyser or a gushing whale spout, one all-too-ready to shoot off at a moment's notice and head its spew directly for the heart of the sun, or at least the set's back-projected facsimile.

Somewhere during the middle of the run Marina was approached by the enterprising young photographer and filmmaker Aron Dearborne to star in a fictional documentary he was shooting on a group he described as "the Afro-Victorians." This motley crew of scenesters based their exploits on a mutual exploration and exploitation of Wharton's (and Scorsese's) *The Age of Innocence* and Chester Himes's scandalous Harlem Renaissance novel, *Pinktoes*. Marina was not part of their set but she knew most of them by sight from the various venues, which comprised black bohemia at the time. She naturally found perverse joy in the irony of going from nudity on Broadway to being corseted, mummified, and strapped into the long-flowing raiment of the Afro-Victorian's salon straitjackets.

It was at one of Dearborn's photo shoots that she met Bono Pruitt, another beautiful star/outsider Dearborn had brought in to break up the drawn-and-puckered monotony of the underage Afro-Victorian clique. It was through Pruitt that she'd become acquainted with the Chimurenga Twins (later known as the Robo Coptic Boy when they abandoned theater for music), who kept an Afro-Warholesque enterprise on Governor's Island. Thus it came to pass that while performing on the Chimurenga's catwalk our Marina made indelible eye contact with three massive ruffians who insisted they be addressed collectively and indiscriminately only as The Big Truck. (Never as just "Big Truck," either; even if they liked you they had no tolerance for people who got too familiar too fast and rushed past the preposition.)

It further came to pass that while hanging out and about with The Big Truck that Marina became introduced to their little brother, The Definitive, a solo act who would, naturally, allow himself to be addressed only as The Definitive. The Definitive would turn out to be, point-blank, the only man she would ever meet whose sex-with-guns desires rivaled, if not outstripped, her own. Their ballistic love affair began when The Big Truck, upon learning Marina was a gun freak, brought The Definitive to catch her on Broadway.

Having been informed by his brothers of her adoration for men who carried heat to bed, The Definitive flashed her from the fourth orchestra row with some of his most prized pieces. There was the transparent Glock with all synthetic moving parts he kept in a shoulder holster. There was the midget sawed-off he barely concealed bulging beneath the thigh of his tear-off cargo pants. There was the loaded and fully operational toy derringer locket that swung from a chain to the left of his heart. There was also, lest we forget, his pièce de résistance, a row of powder-packed gunshell-shaped fronts fenced across his front teeth.

Marina, who could barely contain her delight in this exhibition, raced through her first ovation bow, skipped the company bow, and barely said good-bye to anyone before running off into the night with The Definitive. That night, for the first time in the show's two-year run, her vaginally projected spume was seen arcing high enough to bounce when it splashed onto the catwalk.

The Definitive lived in a private building just across 110th Street. His bedroom turned out to be a gun-toting shrine. It was, indeed, a veritable firearm lover's temple; one that came replete with several seven-foot glass gun racks. These were wrapped around the room's cylindrical circumference and were stocked with every sort of rifle, pistol, gun mount, and ammo belt imaginable.

The bed itself was designed after the rounded recoil chamber of a Tommy gun. The curved walls and ceiling were pasted with several of The Definitive's personal-best target-shooting posters. Between two of the gun racks there was a polished ebony bureau, a special holding place, he told her, to memorialize all his one-time-only pieces—all the ones that had bodies on them, bodies that, in his humble opinion, "will never be found, least not in one piece." An altar sat atop this bureau laced and littered with dead-looking metallic flowers and an Ogun-like statuary figure carved from an alloy she couldn't place. There was also on the bureau's top a necklace composed of animal fangs and bronzed shell casings.

While Marina undressed and freshened up, The Definitive dumped the red silk sheets draping the Tommy-gun mattress with a treasure trove of weaponry from various nooks. He then sprinkled another sprawling selection of ordnance around the bed as if they were rosy romantic petals (his "petals of evil," he called them). When she embraced him he turned his body into hers in a manner assuring that the sawed-off on his thigh would lean in hard against the side of her buttocks. Then, as she wrote in her diary the next day, "He lavishly stroked my liquefied bushy meadow and lusciously lubricious pudenda with an unmistakably expert knowledge of tension and release."

Over breakfast the next morning The Definitive asked Marina to pass along a letter he'd written to her producer, the one and only Malcolm Jack Spratt. When she asked what was in the letter he told her it was confidential, a correspondence between gentlemen. He added somewhat ominously how he hoped she would honor his wishes and not break the seal because "discovering you possess any capacity for betrayal of my trust might one day prove fatal." She assumed he was joking and tittered. She further assumed that the letter contained warning of some ridiculous gift he was going to have delivered to the theater for her.

When she turned the letter over to Malcolm Jack, he opened it quizzically, read it with a look of incredulous consternation, and then guffawed bitterly in her face.

"I'd say you've really gone and done it this time, Miss Gunswoon. You really haven't read this, have you? Well, listen to this, my friend: Your pretty-boy gangster friend has been kind enough to let me know that since you're "his woman" now, it's no longer appropriate for you to continue in my—ha! Get this! 'My'!—show. I'm to sign my understanding of such, release you from your contract, then send you home to him this evening before curtain time, after having informed you that your understudy will be taking over your part. Where do you find these rubes, babycakes? I mean, really?"

Marina nearly fainted, less at the threat of violence implied than at the threat of actually becoming party to that dreadful state of interpersonal coupling known as A Relationship. As best she could remember she had been in only three of those "bejesusgawdawful thingees," as such, in her life.

The first had been shortly before she graduated from high school. That spring she had gotten very close to a once lovely Serbian boy, one possessed of a ripe and hungry mouth that had been malformed into a permanently twisted grin by a nasty car collision the previous winter. Their three-month tryst had been set in motion only by her desire to disgust her parents and her entire graduating class.

The second time had been her marriage to a hook-hanging sadomasochist who turned out to be battling a bout of abnormalcy before returning to brokerage, much to her disgust. The third had been an unrequited lesbian entreaty involving cowriter and best friend Duck, who formed her only true female infatuation to date.

Marina, she had to admit it to herself, had indeed thought about becoming The Definitive's steady woman for a brief but oh so brief time after their first satisfying night together but never, ever, had she considered becoming his longtime concubine. And she was certainly not the kind of woman who was to be traded between fellow patriarchs in some sort of pimpological auction-block scenario.

"So call me a drama queen," she declared to Duck, "but yes, girl, I nearly fainted right there in Jack's office. I mean this barely out of adolescence fool actually assumed Malcolm Jack owned my ass because I perform naked nightly in his house. Then he's furthermore got the nerve to think I'm Spratt's property that the man can just unload on the open market? Oh, no. Oh, hell, no. Just what kind of antebellum throwback is this young nigga? Okay, girl, yes, the kind who shoots people for a living, but still, this is the twenty-first century and certain forms of politically correct decorum need not be discarded.

"So while he is precisely my kind of throwback, you know I'm not one to deconstruct basic feminist principles, especially at risk of my career. So here's what I've decided: I'm going to send my understudy over to invite The Definitive to tonight's show. She'll request that I'd so love it if he could bring another copy of his letter over as I seem to have lost the original in the cab I took on the way over. Meanwhile I'm going to go find The Big Truck and see if they might be able to talk some sense into that boy's head before things really get out of hand."

As luck would have it, though, fate kindly intervened. Duty called, and The Definitive and The Big Truck had to suddenly leave town, therefore making Marina's subterfuge unnecessary. Just before curtain call Marina received a message from The Definitive saying he and his brothers had a business trip but "don't bother calling because we're traveling Incog-negro, way under the radar. I'll ding you when we get back, which should be in about two weeks."

With that mysterious, serendipitous adieu The Definitive was virtually gone, leaving only worrisome vapor trails and big, Roy Lichtenstein–sized thought balloons of anxiety to form over Marina's head.

"What the hell is this shit, Duck? Two weeks of him having the upper hand, the element of surprise? Oh, no. Oh, hell no, I'm not with that."

Marina now had no clear-cut way to outfox The Definitive and counter his insane demand for her retirement. The stress alone was enough to make her think about quitting the show and even show business.

"Call me a drama queen but I am ready to just quit this whole highfalutin' Broadway diva life. Just take all my savings and run off for a spell. Like go see some friends in Sicily or Sardinia or Dakar, or Bari or . . . hell, even Albania might be relaxing this time of year."

What she chose to do instead was to go into her own form of protective custody, a witness protection program of her own invention, as it were. One where'd she'd take the low roads, do a brief supper theater tour, and stay on the down low until she'd gotten word The Definitive and The Big Truck had definitively returned to Gotham. After that her plan was to come back and cross that bridge when she came to it.

Exactly how long to stay away was a question that got thrown into confusion by hearing from The Definitive via postcard that his disappearance from the city might now extend itself from two weeks to three to six months.

The depression and indecision that ensued from her desperation and anxiety over his unknown date of return had the desired effect of forcing Marina to resign from her own Broadway hit. Now she had only to extract herself from the Relationship as easily as she took to her bed of malady, and vapours, in the face of career-suicide.

Once again, however, the perpetual good fortune that came with being a show-biz gypsy gracefully intervened, showing up at her door with news of a touring production of an earlier Marina work called *Killer Dykes of the Ki-Kongo*. Marina had concocted this production nearly a decade ago. It was largely about an imaginary troupe of legendary African Amazons who became, in the mythical story, hooked up with Harriet Tubman during the Civil War.

After alerting the production's management of not only her approval but her availability for the cast, she set about relearning the piece. Joining the company automatically meant weeks of travel out of the limelight. The goal was to hit isolated, culture-starved, lesbian dinner theater spots around the country. What it would mean for Marina, though, was not sitting in New York fretting and sweating in a panic and waiting for The Definitive to show up again. All gun-toting 6'3" of him and his expectations for her to run away from the circus, come home to Poppa and wait on him, and only H.I.M., hand and, surely, *bound* foot.

On audition day, Marina sauntered in, idly basking in the glowing awe the young idolator of a director shined at her. She quickly plotted and executed usurpation of said director's authority, then took it upon herself to run an abridged version of the whole show, masterfully showing producers, directors, cast, and crew not only how she expected every role to be merely played, but how she expected the parts to be passionately surrendered to, mind, body, spirit, and Kirlian aura.

Her five fellow thespians, already cast, consisted of one hard-rock girl named Cookies who believed the term "thespian" meant "theatrical lesbians"; a transplanted South African and aspiring hip-hop singer named Ndebele who was toying with changing her MC handle to either MC In De Belly or MC Gutt; two around-the-way girls from Gary, Indiana, Pam Mella and Marzipan; and an unusually Zen, unusually sanguine she-male named Julia Robertson ("of the Poughkeepsie Robertsons") who refused to relent on the claim that Julia Robertson was her birth name even after all the surgery she'd obviously had to make her resemble the film star whose name she had, tackily and far from cleverly, grafted a "son" onto.

After a shaky week of rehearsals the troupe piled into a large passenger van, to be followed by an even larger props truck. They then hit the road for parts previously unknown to Marina in the wild Midwest.

In the show Ndebele played Harriet Tubman while the others, led by Marina, paraded around in faux spear-chucking Zulu warrior gear, kidnapped Miss Julia Robertson from the plantation, and, thanks to the magic of audiotape and slides, lynched various massas, rubber-necklaced hordes of informers, set trained backwoods dogs on dogged slave catchers, and kept on keeping on in their march for The Great White Way on a North Star–lit yellow brick road to freedom.

The "Killer Dyke" threat of the show's title drew the target demographic in but when it turned out to be more killing than loving going on, and killing of white women at that, complaints began to pour in from patrons who felt "eaten alive by the show's incomprehensible anger at progressive women of a fairer color."

Ndebele took up the Braveheart task of representing the cast and producers in asking Marina to consider toning down the anti–white female violence of this early work, and perhaps consider inserting a sympathetic white woman into the character line-up. Under other circumstances Marina might have ranted and raved until the poor girl regressed into a Jell-o–like state. But since this was one show she needed to go on and on, she chagrined everyone by, for the first time ever, revising an early, juvenile piece of writing that she too, in all honesty, actually found as insufferable as any of her critics did. Marina even gave the good white woman not only a speaking part but a love affair with her Amazon leader character. It had originally been her stance that she did not want sexual escapades overwhelming and obscuring the history lessons she hoped to impart about African Amazons and the precedent they set for Tubman.

"Now, however," she wrote to Duck, "there's a silly fertility dance scene where all us big buck women bare our breaststesses together, bay at the moon, shaketh our derrieres, basically just

shake that azz, and generally, show these cloistered huddled les-
bonic masses what we're working with."

This scene had the powerful effect of driving all the ladies in
the house wild and getting some of their crowds hopeful for
even more bawdy, integrated afterplay during the after party.
After their fourth rust-belt-town bacchanal, Marina came to con-
clude that the Midwest, and by default middle America, was actually more decadent than she had been led to believe. New
Yorkers might have been more overt and stylish, while in public
pursuit of getting their freak on but they were certainly no more
aggressive than their party-hearty Midwestern counterparts.

What she also realized, after sighting the frequent odd groups
of thugs in every house, was how many criminals, and especially
the pretty ones like her type of man, loved to hang out in girl
bars. The disastrous law of averages and rude coincidences being
what they were, she knew it was only a matter of time before
somewhere out there, in some under-the-exit-ramp roadhouse
establishment, way out here in no-man's land, she was going to
look up and find The Definitive and possibly even the whole
The Big Truck clique "fittin' to drag her offstage, toss her into the
trunk of their vehicle, and haul her ass back to be wall-chained
and chastity-belted in the efficiency-sized wardrobe closet of The
Definitive's Gotham boudoir."

Week four found the troupe just outside of Toronto in a
super-small suburb that had once served as the setting for an
X-Files episode. This claim to fame was extolled in the local
diner's star-worshiping menu, where "David Duchovny Spinach
Salad" held forth with "The Smoking Man Smoked Trout Salad."

The script for the episode in question had required building a life-scale model of an alien spaceship that came complete with surgical tables and an array of operating instruments of extraterrestial design. Many of the townsfolk who'd been recruited as extras had idly taken to returning to the abandoned site after the show aired. This soon turned into the longest wrap party in show-biz history before finally becoming a regularly scheduled local *X-Files*–themed rave/cult. The event and the tribal gathering it jumpstarted both went on to survive the cancellation of the program.

First-time initiates at the rave found themselves made to stand alone in a shaft of light before being hoisted by a crane into the bay of the faux mothership, which was itself suspended by yet another crane. Once inside, newcomers allowed themselves to be alien-probed, plucked, and massaged to the musical accompaniment of the burbs' resident gothic-triphop genius, DJ E = mc Spock, all while conveniently tripping on Spock's other homegrown invention—an ecstasy derivative that one needed only sniff mightily to get high on.

As Marina's lifepath would have it, this Spock fellow also happened to be the region's number one inspired amateur manufacturer of hallucinogens. As she and Spock's commingled pot of luck further insured, The Definitive and his brothers The Big Truck had been hired to make the young funk doctor Spock an offer he couldn't afford to refuse. Their employers, it seems, were a shadowy, quasi-revolutionary, and some thought pseudoscientific group known as the Quantum Black Movement. This group was bent on taking over the Midwest's lucrative white trash drug trade and using the illicitly gained loot in support of their own probing, prodding, and scraping Mengele-like genetic experiments on a political opposition they freely and liberally dubbed the "whitebodypolitic." Marina and young Spock's parallel trails would come to a crossroads the day of the troupe's closing party.

That small, intimate affair had been organized by Dame Robertson, who, after deciding she'd missed the company of good friends for too long, went online to www.chickswithdicks-andthewomenwholovethem.com and invited half the she-male population of the East Coast to the affair. It further occurred that when Dame Robertson went down to the local Greyhound station to pick up the meager party of seven who answered her E-vite, Marina came along to drive the second car. Thus our heroine came to see that when Robertson's colorful, caustic, estrogen-injected crew (somewhat stiff-necked from traveling 18 hours) debussed so did The Definitive and The Big Truck.

She also noted that the team of assassins had that world-weary look, which we all know so well from the movies, of slick killers who come to an absurdly hick town and find that their already high quotient of meanness has risen several notches due to the general shithole quality of the place their work has driven them to. Since The Big Truck didn't see her she figured she was off the hook, not knowing that The Definitive had made friends with the she-males on the bus and had promised to demonstrate his expertise in shiatsu message after the long trip from New York.

Imagine Marina's surprise when The Definitive and two of the guest she-males came ambling over to her vehicle. Her first thought was to jump the curb and run him down, but she wisely thought the better of it. When the group began piling in she made a point of looking out her window as long as she could, hoping he'd somehow wind up in the backseat. "With those long legs of his, Duck, ha, fat chance." And so they soon found themselves staring into each other's eyes again for the first time in weeks.

"Girl, I come back home to no note, no call, no news at all. I go down to that theater, you've blown the coop, nobody knows where you are. Some people had heard you had a nervous breakdown, and had wound up drugged back in some clinic somewhere. And you out here gallivanting. Damn, I thought we were soul mates."

In response to this earnest outpouring of love, Marina gave it her all and responded in kind.

"I love you, baby, I really do, and we are soul mates. But I can't stop being a hoofer in the name of love. That would just be a slow death. And I'd want to kill you. And everything just wouldn't really be that much fun anymore."

"But you understand my position, don't you, Marina? I mean, I can't have my woman flashing her pussy for pork chops to the world at large. People would talk. I might have to hurt a civilian or even a smart-mouthed relative or colleague or two. Or three."

"But, baby, this performing thing is what I love to do. I'd never ask you to stop popping strangers if that's what makes you happy."

"Woman, how you gonna go there? I mean, that's so different. You're mixing apples and kumquats now, 'cause I don't like what

I do. It's just something I'm really, really good at and the pay is nice, and I don't have to deal with a lot of bullshit interference and whatnot. But I don't make people pay for the privilege of watching me do it and I wouldn't get off on it if I did."

"So is it the money or the exposure that bothers you?"

"It's you telling me it was my pussy and then selling it to the world. And don't tell me that was just pillow talk."

"No, dear, I meant it in more than just a romantic sense, but what I do onstage is just a show. It's not my love for you I'm giving away. Baby, you're my last gunman. I only wish you had been my first."

The sexually ambiguous parties from New York in the backseat oohed and ahhed at every sick twist and turn of this unabashedly icky conversation. Given other circumstances, Marina and The Definitive might have soon found themselves in her motel room getting it on with lots of guns around. The winds of change, however, had other ideas as Marina, caught up in The Definitive's web of ill logic, found herself sideswiping an oncoming Chevy van, which piled into a parking meter backward and quickly spilled out of its busted innards DJ Spock, two Vestax turntables, four Bose monitors, and a few thousand chemically dipped sheets of his choice synthetic drug product.

In the ensuing bedlam the he-girls from New York snatched up every sheet of the stuff they could manage. DJ E = mc Spock, showing little concern for the fruits of his lab work, locked his fingers tight around the handles of the two aluminum roadcases that contained his rarest vintage vinyl (virgin pressings of Earth, Wind & Fire's score for *Sweet Sweetback's Baadasssss Song;*

producer, director, and writer Melvin Van Peebles' own score for his stage musical *Aint Supposed to Die a Natural Death;* several original, warped pressings of Sun Ra white label singles from the 60s and 70s; Kool and the Gang's *Live at the Sex Machine,* and the Lyman Woodard Organization's *Saturday Night Special*). Upon retrieving this case Spock then shot like a bat out of hell into a nearby strip mall that had seen better days, while The Definitive, immediately recognizing his prey, took off after him like a silver bullet.

Meanwhile Marina, having rethought the prospect of spending a lifetime with a man who shot other men down in the street like dogs, just kept driving until she found herself in Saskatchewan, where she took one look around at the tundra and rightfully believed herself in desperate need of a well-stocked fur trapper and a respectable black box theater.

TYEHIMBA JESS

Blackout

When the lights went out, where were you? On a freeway, in an elevator shaft, on a subway? What did you do when electricity fled the grid, when the TV switched off, the radio died, the clocks stopped, and the cell phones disconnected; when you slowly realized that the nation was stalled from Gotham to Detroit to D.C.? Did you panic at first, think the words *terrorist attack* or *riots* before you started to ponder the more mundane: *How the hell do I get home? How many candles do I have stashed away? How many batteries? How much water?*

When the city shut itself down and darkness overtook the avenues, winning the battle against streetlight and stoplight and neon for the first time in over 25 years, maybe you were lucky like me. Maybe you were in a Broadway office building, and the woman with you happened to be Karmen. Someone you weren't supposed to fuck around with, but whose budding lips and the swish of her so-tight skirts slowly converted you to a religion of X-rated daydreams, and made you a hider of unexpected hard-ons.

Couldn't see it coming, not at first. She gets the best of you one day at a dry-as-dust meeting about management structure. Catches your eyes lingering on that full moon of ass for just half a millisecond too long, just before your coworkers can spot the lust curling in your slightly arched eyebrow. Since she is new and works in another department, you hadn't really noticed her, and now here she is in policy development straight up in your face.

Later, you might ask yourself, *But why Karmen? Why all this risk for Karmen?* Not model fine. Not picture-postcard pretty. Not all toned and ready for a three-hour workout at the gym. Not sunglasses-and-designer-jean Afrofabulous. Instead, a somewhat bowlegged walk and a smallish scar over her left eye. A mocha complexion sprinkled with chocolate freckles. A Bert and Ernie laugh that might make you roll your eyes.

But you can't stop thinking about the way her dreads drape luxuriously across her face. The way her smooth tint of skin peeks through each rope of hair. You find your thoughts lingering on the curve of her lips. You try not to glance at calves thick enough to bring water to your mouth, shapely enough to invade your daydreams. You try not to think of the soft weight beneath her blouse—a glimpse of coffee brown cleavage that makes your brow furrow with worry until you drag your gaze away, seeking escape across the room. You try to remind yourself about the #1 Rule for Happy Bachelorhood: Don't Get Laid Where You Get Paid.

Yes, Lawd, plenty of women outside of this office to get with— ain't gotta pay this one no mind at all. No way, uh-uh. Who cares about those lips, luscious enough to make you rise every time she flies that pink bird of tongue across her smile? Who cares about the way those dreads look like the perfect kinda wild, and why even imagine their cotton-soft tangle between your fingers? And that neck—so what if it tempts you like a fruit that would make Adam shoulder Eve aside, reachin' for the devil's tree? So what if the husk in her voice leaves you wondering how she'd whimper in your ear drowsy with morning, unfurling from twisted-up sheets? This was business, pure and simple, and paychecks just don't mix with pussy. You're not thinking about that quarter-moon mound of ass at all. Not at work. Work is about the money, baby. Pure and simple.

But nothing is pure, and simple is something that don't come your way too often. At the quarterly report meeting the next week, you are assigned to work with Karmen on the Admunsen project. *Need some heavy hitters for this* is what the director said. *You work with Karmen on this one. She's got all the info. Start Tuesday.* Tomorrow.

Aiight. Cool. You can handle it. And you do handle it. She is serious, let's-get-this-thing-done-yesterday serious, and after an initial handshake greeting and a to-the-point-smile, everything goes smooth as butter. The fact that she's sharp as hell makes it easier than you expected. She even teaches you a few things that you hadn't known before. And when you show her a better way to phrase a sentence and format a paragraph, she actually listens to your ideas, a quality that most of the corporate honchos you've dealt with thus far seem incapable of grasping.

When 8 P.M. rolls around, you're both so wrapped up in your exchange of ideas that you don't even notice the deserted office, or that the maintenance crew has already been by, and you two are the only ones left. It's 8:30 by the time fatigue and hunger settle in. The hard talk about business starts to soften up over a pizza delivered from down the street. You manage to make her laugh with a story about your hometown neighborhood, and you notice the way her eyes crinkle and her mouth slowly smirks before she lets out a mischievous giggle. You can still see her smile as you walk to the subway alone. You remember the way there was laughter, then silence as you both looked at each other, and it must've lasted five whole heartbeats—no, an even dozen—before you both realized the danger in the quiet. Your gaze filled in where words were impossible, cautiously drifting down past the small apple of her throat to the fragile grace of her collarbone to the sling of her breasts, then slowly journeying back to her eyes. Karmen broke the silence with a slightly flustered look down at the desk. She busied her hands collecting papers into folders, then cleared her throat and let out the smallest of stammers: *W-well, guess we should wrap this up, huh?*

Yeah, sure. I'll file this away and, uh, we can start again tomorrow.

Okay. Sure. Well, it was nice working with you.

You're wishing you had more composure as you board the A train. *Damn. Lose control for a split second, and look what happens. Everything shuts down. See, that's what happens when you mix business with pleasure.* Nevertheless, you find yourself hardening as you lie in bed that night, thinking about the soft bend of her knees, the perfect O of her lips.

* * *

On Wednesday, with the project due on Thursday morning, you have to strain hard against the temptation of Karmen sitting across the table. You have to concentrate harder to keep things nice and professional, and when the hours stretch past lunch, into afternoon and evening, the numbers start to make more sense, meshing together with the paragraphs of policy and insurance code. But forgetting desire can be hard work, especially when all of your senses are being ravaged by the presence of Karmen's caramel-colored eyes.

Damn. Why'd she wear that blouse today? Why'd she choose to sport the high heels that accentuated the curve of those calves? The ripple of muscle was barely hidden by her skirt—how the hell are you gonna concentrate with the roar of all that fineness clouding up your head? How can you ignore the way her neck makes your mouth water, beckoning to you from across the conference table?

Her habit of sucking on the tip of her thumb when she's figuring out a problem makes you ache. And her perfume: subtle, but enough to catch your attention when you get close enough to breathe it in. The distance between you shrinks as the day wears on, no matter how hard you try to stay at least three safe hand lengths apart. When you look over her shoulder as she's typing on a computer, when you lean in close to point out a line in a graph, and when the sly brilliance of her smile and the shine in her skin draws you in like a hungry bee to a honeypot, you come close enough to wonder about that scent she's wearing. Maybe that's how the touching starts, anyway.

Maybe it's because you've both ordered sandwiches and stayed in the office talking for a half hour that stretches into sixty minutes that means it's now 8 P.M. and the office is empty. Maybe it's because she makes you laugh as hard as you ever have, and this time, when she laughs at one of your jokes, that little giggle of hers blossoms into a homegrown belly laugh. Maybe it's that uncomfortable silence that follows, your eyes meeting and telling the story of want that you couldn't find the right words for. When you try to fill that silence by asking what scent she's wearing, maybe it's the second unbearable pause before her answer, a pause that must've lasted four heartbeats and causes you both to fill the quiet with a kiss.

The kiss takes time and presses gently between your lips, melts with the heat between your mouths, wraps slowly around your tongues. Your tongues find each other tentatively at first, then spread their stories out to each other, leisurely, luxuriously, laden with the taste of hunger that is a long-awaited twist and twirl in the darkness of your mouths. Time becomes the stories your tongues dance upon each other in that night, that you create between your mouths; the taste of tastebud and lip, and the slight scraping capture of tongue between teeth. The kiss, an act of consumption that leaves nothing swallowed but the hunger of each other's mouths, leaves you hungering for more, tongues urging farther into each other's warmth and wetness.

When the kiss stops, time begins again, you realize where you are, what you are doing.

Look . . . you start to explain. *I'm sorry if* . . .

No you aren't. You better not be.

And she's back in your arms, a lip-to-lip and tongue-to-tongue once again, then your hands grasping her tender ropes of dreadlock, gently pulling until her neck is exposed. You discover that the scent of her perfume is almost as sweet as the vibration of sighs escaping through her throat as your tongue uncurls against her flesh.

Somewhere in the back of your consciousness, you realize where you are, that someone could come into the office. You know you should stop, be cool and business-like, but with this kiss the temperature between you two is rising to a zenith, and all of a sudden you aren't thinking anymore, you are simply doing. You are the action, not the person doing the action. You are the caress, not simply the owner of the hand that slips down between the buttons of her blouse and caresses her breast. You are the kiss; not the owner of lips and tongue and heat and pulse exploring her mouth, cheek, eyelids, brow, and the flesh behind her ear. You are thought becoming nerve, muscle, tendon, and flesh, becoming action all at once. The worry that you are in the office, where you could be found out by another late-night worker, the fear of breaking your #1 Rule for Happy Bachelorhood, disappears into the back of your consciousness, is subdued by the pressure growing between your legs, the slight touch of her hands on the back of your neck and on your chest. So it is only after a second pause from kissing leaves you breathless that you somehow find the air to whisper.

What are you thinking?

That we should stop.

Are we gonna stop?

I don't think so.

I just want you to know—I don't normally do this.

This is totally against my rules too.

I got a lot on the line, you know. I don't need people talking. I worked hard to get where I am, and I don't need to throw it away for some interoffice drama.

Hey, look—you ain't the only one with something to lose, Karmen. Ever hear of sexual harassment lawsuits? I need one of those like I need a hole in the head and an unemployment check.

She sits down and looks away, sucking on the end of her thumb again. Damn. You should just walk away right now, but something keeps you in the room, reaches your hand out to hers, and makes you draw words from a place you didn't know existed.

Look. I'm not trying to play you or anything like that. I got carried away, I know. It's a risk, I know. But I also know that I couldn't put your laugh out of my mind last night. I know that I spent the night thinking about the way your smile curves, wondering if a sister like yourself was attached, and pitying the fool who gave you up. I know that I really like the fact that you're intelligent and got it goin' on. I mean . . . I guess . . . Look, whatever happens, I wouldn't tell anything to anybody. This one is up to you. I know it'll be hard, but if you're scared or feel uncomfortable, I'll understand. Just let me say one thing—thank you. Thank you for what happened just now. If nothing else happens in the future, at least I'll have that moment to remember.

And the next thing you know, that smile is coming back, and you are lost again in the space between her lips.

*   *   *

The next day is Thursday, August 14, 2003. The morning presentation with Karmen goes well, and your workday is just about over when the power goes out around the city. You can feel the slow sense of panic gripping the city, the sudden realization that the entire populace had been thrown back a century to a pre-Edison existence. And the walk home? As New Yorkers say—*forgetaboutit.* Your place deep in the heart of Brooklyn was as far as Karmen's place deep in Queens. You decide to wait it out, certain that the glitch is only temporary, surely the power would be back on soon. *This is New York,* you think. *They can't just let the place go without power for too long.*

It isn't until 6 P.M., as the sky starts to darken, that the entire picture—the knocked-out grid from the East Coast to the Midwest—becomes clear. By that time, most of your coworkers have left for the day. That's when Karmen sidles up to you in the hall and asks you what your plans are.

Hell, I don't know. Don't really feel like hoofin' it to Bed-Stuy and walking up twenty stories.

Same here. Fifteen stories waiting for me after a hike in the dark all the way to Jamaica? Not fun. And the traffic? The radio says it's ridiculous out there.

Yeah, I heard.

You can't help but notice the smile that comes to her lips as she seems to suddenly think of something.

Look, most everybody's gone. Go get that tablecloth that we used during that last company picnic, bring any food you've got left in the office fridge, and meet me here in five minutes.

Hmmm. Okay. You nod, wondering what's up. *See you in five.*

When you meet again, Karmen has a yoga mat rolled up under her arm, along with a large bottle of water. You've got the tablecloth, a flashlight, some spare batteries, and another stroke of luck—the large container of homemade spaghetti that you hadn't eaten for lunch and you were planning on spreading out over several days.

So—what's the plan?

Follow me, she whispers.

Karmen heads toward the stairwell exit sign and opens the

door. But instead of going down the stairs, she heads up. She looks over her shoulder to explain as she climbs up.

We're on the top floor. I happen to know that some smokers here ain't into going all the way downstairs just to scratch their nic itch. They showed me how to open the door. We might have the whole roof to ourselves.

When you escape the confines of the building, you realize that she's right. The roof is your secret hideaway. You both tiptoe to the edge of the building and look down, see the map of lower Manhattan stretch out below you, the mass of people headed on their long trek home.

After a dinner of cold spaghetti and a toast to the city, you realize that darkness is surrounding you faster than you'd expected. You turn the flashlight on low, illuminating the space between you and Karmen.

The darkness falls, bringing the skyscrapers' shadows in relief against the setting sun. Stars take over the cloudless sky, letting you realize how small the city really is, and as you sit on the cushion of the yoga mat and lean with Karmen against the wall, you remember the warmth of her skin. As you turn toward her, your mind set on what you need right then and there, she asks you a simple and straightforward question.

What do you want? What do you really want?

She finds her answer in the palms of your hands, as they reach to caress her face and your lips meet hers.

This is what you want? This what you need?

Yes. That's what I need.

She smiles, then leans back, gently lifting the cotton skirt you've been jealous of all day, reveals that wet slice of bliss you realize you've wanted to taste since Tuesday. Her fingers slowly trace the outline of mound between her legs, index fingers slowly dipping inside her wetness, then tracing your lips before you take it deep inside your mouth. Your tongue wanders down to her palm, tracing the path of her long and thick life line, her luck line low and wisping, her love line twisting a way across a map of her future where you searched for yourself in her crease and grasp and touch. And when she moves her hand toward her breast, you follow it there. She burns a question into your ear, the words hissing out of her mouth as you hunch over her with her nipple nestled between your fingertips:

You want this pussy, baby?

Pussy. Tender-petaled flower of flesh. Well of fresh beginning where a man can end himself, lose himself, find himself made new. Lioness purring in the heat of a woman's thighs, where you're devoured under each waking morning, every sliver of starlight. Shrine of birth. Muscle of creation. *Nine months gettin' out of it, a lifetime tryin' to get back in.* She turns her back to you, then stands and leans against the wall with her ass up toward you and the moonlight. You rise to your feet behind her, lean over her back to savor her neck. The space between your mouth and the sweet spot in her nape grows smaller and hotter with every inch forward, till all else is blur, from her kinky soft tangle of nap in one hand, to the vibrato of groan trembling up from the place that has your other hand wet.

You like this pussy, baby?

You tell her the well-worn line that you didn't realize was truth until it came from your gut and squeezed through your lips in a whis-

per: *This the pussy I want, girl. Pussy.* Yes, yes. A rose petal–perfect ending to every hard-workin' day. Have you workin' from sunup to sun-
down just to make sure it's there when you get home, and then you
gladly work some more: back bent, shoulders arched, hips plunged,
Fuck that pussy, baby is what she'd say then, but since you and Karmen
have also learned that a little overtime never hurt nobody, y'all are
workin' off the clock and gettin' paid a wage that's worth more than
dollars. Right now you realize that she's saying the words you've been
waiting to hear for so long:

Eat that pussy, baby . . .

Pussy. Place where your hand has curled around thigh and entered slow and smooth to work a circle inside, and when you hear
that first low sigh you slide your lips down her dark shoulder blades,
leaving a scattered trail of kisses. Desire buckles you down to your
knees as your trail of soft bites and kisses arches down her curve of
ass. Tongue and fingertip trail down one cheek, then the other. Fingers spread, head arches, neck tilts, tongue stretches deep inside her
parted lips. *Suck that pussy, baby, suck it hard* and you answer with an
oh-so-gentle bite that nearly sends her knees buckling, but you keep
her steady to *Eat that pussy, baby. Eat that pussy up.*

Eating pussy is a job that's never complete; no matter how
much you swallow you always comin' back for more. And so
you are between her legs, your mouth an open gateway to moan,
a moan open like a virgin note falling fresh from heaven's grasp.
Open like the space between her legs that you memorize with
your tongue until you've learned the language that arches her
back and clenches her thighs. Vocabulary that parts your teeth
to graze vulva ever so gently, moves your tongue in orbit around

and around the slick rise of nerves soaked between her folds. A sacred circle of hum rises from beneath your gut and into your throat, snakes its way into your tongue and onto her clit, shudders its way past her sweet candy of salt.

She collapses on top of you, and your moan breaks loose to become hers. The moan is a wild mare in her thighs, galloping its way through the dark hills of her flesh, burning its way up the curving arch of her spine. The moan does a slow grind while rising through her throat, and works its way past her lips as they part and wrap around the tip of your cock that she has released from inside your pants, her tongue lingering along the shaft, and you sing this note together, giver and receiver, well and water, call and response, a closed circuit of redemption found in the filling of mouths.

They give this yin and yang of bodies a number, 69, but there is no number for your joined hands—they are their own alphabet, silent signals for a rapture deciphered in midnight hours of stroke and slide. In the dark, hands find their own way, past barriers of button and bra strap, zipper and buckle, toward the skin held captive beneath, toward the wet, the hard, the soft, the plunging, and the giving and taking. Four palms and twenty fingers coupled, rooted together in rutting, entwined fingers with their own ballet. The circular union of your moan from mouth to groin to mouth to groin.

There are the thumbs she slides into your waiting mouth, thumbs you suck harder and deeper than you could suck her clit. There are her fingers that you take into your mouth one at a time, savoring nail and knuckle, fingerprint and palms. Her fingers, with nails that dig into your backside with a solid sugar of pain, the kind you want to sacrifice your skin for, whispering

That's right, baby, hold on tight, knowing it'll take weeks for your back to heal, knowing she's staking her claim, cutting her mark into your skin to warn off women who might get as far as your naked back and say *Who you been fuckin' that scarred up your back like that?* And you know and you don't care when you're deep inside Karmen's sweat and sweet funk.

Your eyes shut in their own private darkness to let your hands discover the world of her body. Your fingers create their own language of stress and pull. Fingertips teach you the gentle, insistent Braille of her aureoles, the small brush of hair surrounding her sex, the garden of nerves in the small of her back that's sweet to the touch like a watermelon heart is summertime sweet. Your fingers there make her shoulders jump with anticipation, then your touch wanders down to trace the length of her slit from back to front and back again. They show you the circles she wants inside her, the exact amount of weight for a fingertip flick on her clit, and feed you her taste afterward. Your fingers, you will tell her later, sometimes got a mind of their own, but can explain to you the meaning and difference between *want* and *need*, and could tell from the get-go that she fulfilled both definitions.

Your palms gain a life of their own when spreading themselves over her skin. They get their own rapture when embracing her face as her lips touch yours. Your palms are holding her steady when she trembles in the midst of coming, burying your face in her mound, and they shift her weight to break the 69 as you stretch her out beneath you. Your palms become cushion for her ass held high and her legs wrapped solid around your back. And when she tells you just how hard she wants that ass slapped, those palms are the sound of flesh on flesh, a sharp tender claiming of territory.

Gimme that ass, girl.

A contract she co-signs with each sharp whimper, claiming your hands and their ownership as much as you claim her flesh.

Your palms are across her mouth holding in a scream when you fuck her from behind, her back bent, ass up, legs open, skirt lifted. Palms moistened in the heat of her breath, her tongue and muffled scream baptizing the pink of your flesh, and then you let your hands uncover the sound of her moan as you are lost in your shared moment of arrival. You are one in the depths of her pleasure that is your thrust and thirst and two pelvises locked and riding a rhythm eternal as darkness, the palpable absence of light and fullness of touch, taste, sound, and smell when you are coming. Your eyes close tight with the sharpness of release, your eyes close next to hers when sleep overtakes you both on the roof, under the sky, above the city, somewhere close to heaven.

In the unexpected darkness of failed power lines and overloaded grids, we are reminded of how human and how animal we are, how the darkness hurls us against each other and teaches us mercy or mayhem, and how we can find both bundled together in each other's arms. In the darkness, whether the city is imploding or re-joicing, hungering for morning or reveling in the night, you can find yourself buried in your lover's bosom caring only about the city of her skin, her forests of hair, the gravity of hunger between you. You can find yourselves wrapping a cloak of stars around your rhythm, discovering yourselves in each other's skin.

CONTRIBUTORS

Preston L. Allen is a recipient of a State of Florida Individual Artist Fellowship in Literature. His short works have been published in numerous literary journals, including the *Seattle Review, Crab Orchard Review, Gulfstream,* and *Drum Voices Review.* His collection, *Churchboys and Other Sinners,* is the winner of the Sonja H. Stone Prize in Literature (Carolina Wren Press, 2003). His novels *Bounce* (Writer's Club Press, 2003) and *Hoochie Mama* (Writer's Club Press, 2001) are available on Amazon.com. His erotic fiction has appeared in all the *Brown Sugar* books, the combined stories making up a novella, *Nadine's Husband.* He lives and teaches creative writing in Miami. He can be reached at pallenagogy@aol.com.

asha bandele is the author of three books: a collection of poems, *Absence in the Palms of My Hands* (Harlem River Press, 1996); an award-winning memoir, *The Prisoner's Wife* (Scribner, 1999); and most recently a novel, *Daughter* (Scribner, 2003). She is features editor and a contributing writer for *Essence* magazine, and lives in Brooklyn with her three-year-old daughter, Nisa.

Kalisha Buckhanon has been the recipient of awards and fellowships from the NAACP, Andrew Mellon Fund, Illinois Arts

Council and the Chicago Black Writer's Conference at Chicago State University. Her work has appeared in such publications as *Michigan Quarterly Review* and *Warpland: A Journal of Black Literature and Ideas*. She holds an M.F.A. in creative writing from New York City's New School University and a B.A. in English literature from the University of Chicago. She has taught literacy and writing to children on Chicago's South Side, in Harlem, Brooklyn, and the Bronx. Her first novel, *Upstate*, will be published by St. Martin's Press in 2005. She lives in New York City.

Angie Cruz, a New York–born Dominicana, is the author of *Soledad* (Simon & Schuster, 2001). She is currently at work on her second novel, due out in 2005, and lives in New York City. This story was written while in residence at La Napoule Art Foundation, France (2003).

Edwidge Danticat is the author of *Breath, Eyes, Memory* (Soho Press, 1994); *Krik? Krak!* (Soho Press, 1995); *The Farming of Bones* (Soho Press, 1998); and *The Dew Breaker* (Knopf, 2004).

Darrell Dawsey is the author of two books, *Living to Tell About It* (Anchor Books, 1996) and *I Ain't Scared of You* (Pocket Books, 2001), co-authored with comedian Bernie Mac. He is working on two books with adult-film star Mr. Marcus. Darrell's work has also appeared in *Essence, Vibe,* the New York *Daily News,* the *Los Angeles Times,* and *The Philadelphia Inquirer,* among others. He lives in Detroit with his girlfriend and their two children.

Trey Ellis is a novelist, screenwriter, and essayist. His acclaimed first novel, *Platitudes* (Vintage, 1988), was reissued by Northeastern University Press in 2003 along with his groundbreaking essay, "The New Black Aesthetic." He is also the author of *Home Repairs* (Simon & Schuster, 1993) and *Right Here, Right Now* (Simon & Schuster, 1999), which was a recipient of the American Book Award. His work for the screen includes the Emmy-nominated *Tuskegee Airmen* and *Good Fences,* starring Danny Glover and Whoopi Goldberg. He lives in Venice, California, and Paris.

Reginald Harris's *Ten Tongues: Poems* (Three Conditions Press, 2002) was a finalist for the 2003 Lambda Literary Award. He is Head of the Information Technology Support Department for the Enoch Pratt Free Library. His work has appeared in numerous venues, including *5AM, Poetry Midwest, Obsidian III, Sou'wester,* and the anthologies *Brown Sugar, Black Silk, Bum Rush the Page,* and *Role Call.* Born in Annapolis, Maryland, he lives with his partner in Baltimore.

Gar Anthony Haywood is the Shamus and Anthony Award–winning author of ten crime novels: six featuring African-American private investigator Aaron Gunner; two recounting the adventures of amateur crime solvers and Airstream trailer owners Joe and Dottie Loudermilk; and most recently, two stand-alone thrillers written under the pen name of Ray Shannon.

Kenji Jasper was born and raised in the nation's capital, and has been writing professionally since the age of 14. At 28, he is a regular contributor to National Public Radio's "Morning Edition" and has written articles for *Savoy, Essence, VIBE,* and *The Village Voice.* He is also the author of three novels, *Dark* (Broadway Books, 2001); *Dakota Grand* (Doubleday/Harlem Moon, 2002); and most recently, *Seeking Salamanca Mitchell* (Doubleday/Harlem Moon, 2004); as well as one nonfiction book, *The Lone Ranger and The Marlboro Man* (Doubleday, 2005), a double memoir about his grandfathers. He lives in Brooklyn, New York.

Tyehimba Jess, a Cave Canem Fellow, is a Detroit native who lives and writes in Brooklyn. He won the 2001 Gwendolyn Brooks Open Mic Poetry Award, an Illinois Arts Council Artist Fellowship in Poetry for 2000–2001, and the 2001 *Chicago Sun-Times* Poetry Award. He was on the 2000 and 2001 Chicago Green Mill Slam teams. Jess's fiction and poetry have appeared in *Soulfires: Young Black Men on Love and Violence* (Penguin Books, 1996); *Slam: The Competitive Art of Performance Poetry* (Manic D. Press, 2000); *Bum Rush the Page: A Def Poetry Jam* (Three Rivers Press, 2001); *Beyond the Frontier: African American Poetry for the Twenty-First Century* (Black Classic Press, 2002); *Role Call: A Generational Anthology of Social and Political Black Literature and Art* (Third World Press, 2002); and *Dark Matter 2: Reading the Bones* (Aspect Press, 2004). His first nonfiction book, *African American Pride: Celebrating Our Achievements, Contributions, and Legacy* (Citadel Press), was published in 2003.

Brandon Massey was born June 9, 1973, and grew up in Zion, Illinois. Originally self-published, *Thunderland,* his first novel, won the 2000 Gold Pen Award for Best Thriller; Kensington Publishing re-released the book in 2002. He is also the author of *Dark Corner* (Kensington, 2004), an epic vampire thriller; and editor of *Dark Dreams: A Collection of Horror and Suspense by Black Writers* (Kensington, 2004). He lives near Atlanta, where he is at work on his next thriller. For more information please visit www.brandonmassey.com.

jessica Care moore is an internationally acclaimed poet and playwright born in Detroit, artistically groomed in New York City. She is the author of the bestselling poetry collection *The Words Don't Fit in My Mouth* (Moore Black Press, 1997) and *The Alphabet Verses the Ghetto* (Moore Black Press, 2003). She is the CEO of Moore Black Press and has published noted poets Saul Williams and Sharrif Simmons. She is the author of the plays *The Revolutions in the Ladies' Room,* her celebrated solo drama, *There Are No Asylums for the Real Crazy Women,* and her latest work, ALPHAPHOBIA! Her work appears in numerous anthologies, including *Slam* (Grove Press 1998); *Listen Up!* (Random House, 1999); *Step Into a World* (Wiley/2000); *Abandon Automobile* (WSU Press, 2001); *Bum Rush the Page* (Three Rivers Press, 2001); and *Role Call* (Third World Press, 2002). When she grows up she wants to be the woman in red, black, and green. Support Moore Black Press! Visit www.jessicacaremoore.net.

Sandra Jackson-Opoku is the author of two novels: *The River Where Blood Is Born* (Ballantine/One World, 1997), winner of the Black Caucus of the American Library Association Literary Award for Best Fiction of 1998, and *Hot Johnny and the Women Who Loved Him* (Ballantine/One World, 2000), which ranked on several local and national bestseller lists. *Iguana Stew* is excerpted from her novel in progress, *God's Gift to the Natives*. Ms. Jackson-Opoku has earned such awards as a National Endowment for the Arts Fiction Fellowship, the CCLM-General Electric Award for Younger Writers, and Illinois Art Council grants. She is Assistant Professor and Fiction Coordinator in the Master of Fine Arts in Creative Writing Program at Chicago State University.

Mike Phillips was born in Guyana and has lived in London for most of his life. A novelist and historian, he has written *Blood Rights* (St. Martin's Press/Doubleday, 1989); *The Late Candidate* (St. Martin's Press/Doubleday, 1992); *Point of Darkness* (St. Martin's Press, 1995); *An Image to Die For* (St. Martin's Press, 1997); *The Dancing Face* (HarperCollins, 1998); and *A Shadow of Myself* (HarperCollins, 2000). He is also the author of several screenplays and nonfiction books. He is at work on *A Dark Corner of Heaven,* the second novel in a trilogy set in Eastern and Central Europe, of which *A Shadow of Myself* was the first.

Greg Tate has been a staff writer at *The Village Voice* since 1987. His books include *Flyboy in the Buttermilk* (Simon & Schuster/Fireside, 1992); *Everything But the Burden: What People Are Taking* *from Black Culture* (ed.) (Random House/Broadway Books, 2003); and *Midnight Lightning: Jimi Hendrix and The Black Experience* (Lawrence Hill, 2003). He is currently working on a collection of short fiction, *altered spades, fables of harlem,* and a book on black rock musicians, *There's a Specter Haunting Elvis: Invoking the Dark Gods of Rock and Roll.* He is also the conductor of *Burnt Sugar, The Arkestra Chamber,* whose most recent album is the two-CD set *Black Sex Y'all Liberation & Bloody Random Violets.*

Lisa Teasley's work appeared in the first *Brown Sugar* and in *Brown Sugar 3.* She is the author of *Glow in the Dark* (Cune, 2002), winner of the Gold Pen Award for Best Short Story Collection, and the Pacificus Foundation Award. *Dive* (Bloomsbury, 2004) is her debut novel. A graduate of UCLA, Ms. Teasley has received the May Merrill Miller Award for Fiction; the National Society of Arts & Letters Short Story Award, Los Angeles; and the Amaranth Review Award for Fiction. A painter as well, Teasley has exhibited widely throughout the United States.

Jervey Tervalon's latest novel, *Lita* (Atria Books, 2003), is the sequel to *Dead Above Ground* (Pocket Books, 2000). He teaches at the Bunche Center at UCLA and lives in Altadena with his wife and two daughters.

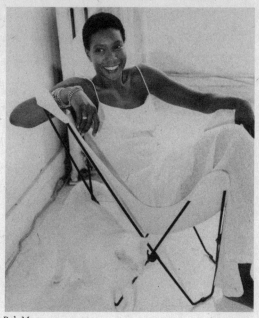

Bob Myers

ABOUT THE EDITOR

Carol Taylor, a former Random House book editor, has been in book publishing for over ten years and has worked with many of today's top black writers. She is a contributing writer to *Sacred Fire: The QBR 100 Essential Black Books*. She is also the editor of the *Brown Sugar* erotic series: *Brown Sugar, Brown Sugar 2: Great One Night Stands, Brown Sugar 3: When Opposites Attract* and *Brown Sugar 4: Secret Desires*. She has been featured in magazines and newspapers, and interviewed on TV and radio; and her fiction and nonfiction have appeared in many publications. Her online relationship column "Off the Hook: Advice on Love and Lust" is featured on Flirt.com. She lives in New York and is at work on an erotic travel anthology and a novel. She is the CEO of Brown Sugar Productions, LLC, and can be reached at Carol@BrownSugarBooks.com. For information on the *Brown Sugar* series visit: www.BrownSugarBooks.com.

"We are shaped and fashioned by what we love."
—Goethe